The
Little House
by the Sea

BOOKS BY TRACY REES

The Little Christmas House

Hidden Secrets at the Little Village Church

The House at Silvermoor

The Love Note

The Hourglass

Florence Grace

Amy Snow

TRACY REES

The Little House by the Sea

Bookouture

Published by Bookouture in 2022

An imprint of Storyfire Ltd.
Carmelite House
50 Victoria Embankment
London EC4Y 0DZ

www.bookouture.com

ISBN: 978-1-80314-150-3
eBook ISBN: 978-1-80314-149-7

This one, of course, is for Lucy Davies.
Thank God we never had to resort to plan Z!

PROLOGUE

FEBRUARY

'Kitty, it's time to go home now. Kitty? It's 6.30 – we're closing the office. Kitty!'

Finally, the voice filters through my reverie. Goodness, yes, it's dark outside and Rebecca the estate agent is turning off the office lights (it says a lot that we're on first-name terms, given that I'm neither buying nor selling a house – nor do I work here). As the fluorescent lights go out, one strip at a time, the display boards wink softly in the orange glow of the streetlights.

'I'm sorry,' I reply, flustered. 'Have I kept you late? I was in a world of my own.' A dreamworld. When some people need comforting, they pour a glass of wine, run a hot bubble bath or call a friend. My go-to uplift is visiting estate agencies and browsing the properties for sale. Immediately I'm transported away from rainy, dirty London and living my best life – a different variation depending on which house I'm looking at.

It doesn't have to be big or grand or lavish – I'm not totally unrealistic – but I want a nest: pretty and peaceful. Just two bedrooms would be fine – one for me and Mitch, and one for friends and family to come and stay. I'd like a garden with an apple tree, and muddy walks all around with pretty views. If

I'm really dreaming, I'd like to live near the sea and wake up each day to the cries of seagulls, but that's just pie in the sky. My big sister Cooper lives in the countryside in Surrey and we've always been close, so the 'real' dream – if there's such a thing – is to live near her. Then we could meet for coffees, mind each other's pets, cook each other dinner. It would be idyllic.

As well as the London properties for sale here at Mullins and Meade, they sell a good few houses in the Home Counties too and I've been staring at the listings for almost an hour. Where does the time go?

'It's fine.' Rebecca regards me indulgently as she buttons her coat. 'I was waiting for a survey to come in. But I do have to go home now.'

'Of course. Well, thanks again. Maybe one day...'

I hurry outside while Rebecca locks up and strides away into the dreary evening. It's mid-February, pitch-dark and drizzling. It's not a pleasant evening, but I'm *still* unable to tear myself away.

I now find myself gazing at the For Sale boards in the floodlit window display. Around me, London scurries and roars. An Oasis song drifts out of the bar across the road, floating on the damp, inky-blue air, making me feel nostalgic. A bus roars past, throwing up a tidal wave of dirty water that drenches my trouser legs. But what do I care? In my mind I'm in a charming two-bed end-terrace with views overlooking the Surrey/Sussex border. *Look at those pretty friezes in the dining room! And are those original tiles in the fireplace? How gorgeous.*

I'm hopeless. It's not as if Mitch shares my obsession with buying a place in the country. He's up for it, sure, but he's not a starry-eyed dreamer like me. He keeps telling me it'll happen when the time is right and that financially it won't be viable for at least two more years. Everyone's in the same boat, I know that – houses are silly money nowadays – yet whenever I have an early finish at work, I can't walk past Mullins and Meade without going in.

When it's quiet, I chat to the staff about the houses, and they joke that I should go and work there. Actually, I would love to, but I earn a higher salary in my current job and I'm all about saving up for a deposit. When they're busy, I tune out their phone calls and browse all the lovely houses for sale. They're very good to put up with me really. They've certainly figured out that I'm a timewaster, but they don't seem to mind me standing there in the corner, like a pot plant.

Oh, look at this one! Four bedrooms, a blue front door and whitewashed walls smothered by a climbing rose. Ample forecourt parking, double garage, large garden with mature orchard and a swing. *Window seats* in the lounge and master bedroom! An elegant conservatory...

Just like that, I'm there, curled up on a window seat with a hot mug of tea, gazing out of the window, watching the birds on the feeder... It's pure fantasy. Even after years of both of us working full-time and living in the cheapest (i.e. tiniest, most squalid) studio flat we could find in the dodgiest bit of London, we couldn't afford a place like that. Sometimes I wonder if we should pay more to live somewhere a bit nicer now. It would take us even longer to buy a place then, but maybe it wouldn't feel quite as urgent if life was a bit lovelier in the meantime. Mitch is happy to stay where we are though.

'It's *your* dream, babe, buying a house and all that,' he always says. 'I don't mind living here and saving like crazy so you can have what you want one day.'

It's sweet of him, but sometimes I wish it was his dream too. Then again, I'm the one who's been obsessed with houses ever since Mum and Dad got divorced. Cooper says I'm desperate to recreate the sense of security we had as children.

I sigh and eventually head for home.

Our block of flats is really horrible. Our upstairs neighbours are noisy and aggressive – they shout at us when we politely ask them to keep the music/shouting/stomping down – sleep is at a premium. There isn't a proper kitchen, only a little area in the corner of the living room with a hob, toaster and kettle, so we're limited as to what we can realistically cook. Our landlord won't let us make any improvements because he says we'll spoil the aesthetic. Who knew chipped, fake mahogany and dark green office carpet could be considered an aesthetic?

And this despite the fact that I'm an interior designer! Well, almost. I *work* for an interior designer as a project co-ordinator (which means I do admin). But next week I'll be starting work for my very own client – my first ever. Well, I'll be assisting – Leo will be the lead designer – but I'm still delighted. It'll be my first start-to-finish project and hopefully a stepping stone into interior design proper. The client, a wealthy banker in Wandsworth called Mrs Fortran, is demanding and chippy, but I don't care. It'll be the next best thing to decorating a home of my own.

It's a career choice based, of course, on my love of houses, but honestly, it's not what I'd imagined. My boss, Nigel, is tyrannical. The workload is insane, and the clients are often impossible to please. Between dull, stressful days at work and cramped evenings in the flat, eating pasta or takeaway like students, the only really great thing in my life is Mitch. I realise that's not actually a healthy dynamic, but what can I do? We've discussed it many times; these are the choices we're making to create a future together.

I take the lift – at least it's working tonight – to the third floor. I can't wait to tell Mitch about Mrs Fortran. If I do a good job, I'll get a pay rise and our deposit will grow faster. And for now, this is fine, isn't it? For all its faults, it's a place where Mitch and I can hold each other at the end of a busy day, where we can watch TV, curled up on the sofa, and laugh over a

Friday-night beer. It's the first place we've ever lived together, and that thought makes me smile...

Excited to share my news, I burst into the flat. And because there are no corners or nooks or tucked-away spaces in our tiny little home, I'm immediately confronted by the sight of Mitch entwined with a woman: arms, lips and, somehow, legs – *how are they not falling over?* They spring apart and stare at me, as I am staring at them. The woman is his work colleague Rachel and she has the grace to flush deep red.

'Oh God,' she mumbles. 'Kitty, I'm so sorry.' She doesn't look at me when she says it. Mitch looks horror-stricken.

Like an idiot, all I can think of to say is, 'Oh, hello, Rachel.' And we all stare a bit longer.

Eventually Mitch clears his throat. 'Christ, this is awful,' he says, stepping away from Rachel. 'Kitty, I'm really sorry. I didn't want you to find out like this. I was going to tell you on the weekend...'

And *that's* the moment when the world drops away from under my feet. Because that means there's something to tell, something he has to confess. It means that I haven't somehow misinterpreted the situation – as if that were even possible.

No, no, no, I can't deal with this! For what feels like a long while, I freeze. I can't move, can't speak, can't think. I'm rooted to the spot and the only sensation I can feel is one of cold – my hands, my feet. There's a sort of rushing in my ears. Mitch, as I was reflecting only moments ago, is my *everything*.

Eventually, the wheels of my brain start grinding. *I was going to tell you on the weekend*. His words play on repeat in my head. That means this has been going on a while and they've been wondering how to tell me, which means that Mitch is probably leaving me for her, or at the very least he's conflicted...

No, I can't go there. Life without Mitch would be... I don't even want to *think* about life without Mitch. My heart has been ripped out and flung across that scratchy forest-coloured nylon-blend carpet.

The worst of it is that they're both decent people. They wouldn't do this just for the hell of it. It means something. I resist the truth a moment more – numb, incoherent. Then it all comes crashing down on me.

Without Mitch, my boyfriend since university, my first love, my best friend, all I have left is a job I hate, a flat I loathe and the impossible dream of buying a house in the countryside – which I don't want to do without him anyway. *Oh God.*

CHAPTER 1

It's been six weeks since Black Thursday as I shall forever think of it and I can't sugar-coat it – I'm a mess. I've been through more boxes of tissues than a whole army with man flu, and I can't even console myself by haunting Mullins and Meade because there's no comfort to be found in looking at houses that I will never ever share with Mitch. That whole future has been snatched away from me now.

Now that I'm no longer plodding along towards that future, time has no meaning anymore. The six weeks have passed in a blur; new, unwelcome facts and developments have pelted me like hailstones.

Mitch moved out fast, beating a tactful retreat. In fact, he and Rachel have gone travelling. All his carefully saved pennies aren't going towards a deposit on a house in the country after all – they're paying for round-the-world airfare and hostels and bungee jumps. Meanwhile, in the rapidly unravelling nightmare that my own life has become, I'm unemployed. Leo and I had a meeting scheduled with Mrs Fortran for the day after Black Thursday. I shouldn't have gone, but I didn't know how to excuse myself without sounding flaky. I couldn't concentrate one bit and eventually burst into tears. She thought I was distracted (true), incompetent (untrue) and unprofessional (true, but only temporarily and not without good reason). She kicked me off the project. Nigel was furious and fired me.

I immediately ran away to my sister's in the country – previously my favourite place to be in the whole world. But this time, knowing I would never ever share somewhere like it with Mitch, it didn't feel like the refuge I needed. It was as if the huge log fire, the clucking chickens, the daffodils on the windowsills in jam jars were mocking me. So I spent seven days in the best guest room, working my way through one giant box of Maltesers after another, drinking red wine and crying. I couldn't even keep it together long enough to play with my two nephews, whom I adore, and they declared that 'Aunt Kitty's got *boring!*'

Then I came back to London and the realisation that the lease on the flat is up for renewal in a couple of weeks. I've ignored all the landlord's calls and emails. This is my chance for a fresh start, but I can't face flat-hunting in this state of mind. Also, who would take me on as a tenant now that I'm unemployed? The sensible thing would be to let the lease roll over – there's been enough change lately and I can't handle any more challenges right now. But I can't bear the thought of staying on here alone. Everything's happening too fast. I can't make sense of anything. I can't feel good about anything.

Cooper says I should quit the flat, pack up and stay with them for as long as I need. 'You've always wanted to live nearby,' she says in her daily phone calls, 'so come here. You don't need Mitch to live your dream. Come and do it without him. *Screw him!*'

But I can't do that either. It wouldn't count. It wouldn't be my dream – it would be a colourless copy of it. Being unemployed and single in my big sister's home, sad Aunty Kitty, would be just too depressing for words. *Can't go to Cooper's, can't stay here, can't look for somewhere new...* The weeks are vanishing without me doing anything constructive.

Friends and family remain sympathetic but they all agree it's time for me to move on. They say I should join a dating site, go on a blind date, get a job... I know I should at least sign up for temp work, but I'm paralysed. I'm crying so much that it's possible my face will be permanently altered into its redder, puffier version. Even so, everyone *insists* that it's time I pull myself together, face up to the unexpected turn life has taken, take some practical steps to better my situation.

So I decide to see a psychic. I doubt this is what anyone had in mind, but honestly, it's the best I can do.

Covent Garden New Age Centre is a maze-like building with corridors and doors all over the place. I've randomly chosen to have my palm read, rather than tarot or a crystal ball or any of the other options available to those in need of a destiny. The serene goth receptionist (two adjectives I'd never expected to combine) therefore directs me to a door on Rainbow Corridor. Outside, I take a deep breath. I've never done anything like this before. It's probably all a load of hooey and a big waste of time. Even so, I'm wearing my best red dress, as if by looking smart, I'll invite a better future. I knock.

I'm expecting someone middle-aged and matronly, wrapped in scarves and sequins with a Russian accent and possibly a turban. I'm briefly disappointed to see that the psychic is only half my age. Well, she's not literally fifteen, but she's considerably younger than me and far trendier: a tiny wisp of a thing with long platinum hair no stranger to GHDs, huge blue eyes lined in black and turquoise, and clothes that wouldn't look out of place on *TOWIE*. The receptionist looked more mystical! But she looks up at me with the biggest, brightest smile, which, in my fraught state, melts my heart, and I start crying. Again.

'Aw, come in, babes,' she coos, holding out her arms, and in a second I am in them, sobbing my heart out on her shoulder. *Oh boy*.

When I'm a little more composed, we get on with it. Her name is Angelique and even if I suspect her name is as natural as her hair, nothing could be more fitting. She is indeed angelic, and I already feel calmer than I have since Black Thursday.

She examines my left palm first and beams so brightly that I feel hopeful. Then she reaches for my right hand and grimaces. 'Oh dear,' she says. 'That's bad.'

Great.

I sit with my arm extended, palm upwards, while she squints over my hand for a while, then hmms and nods. 'Heartbreak,' she says.

I sigh. I don't want to be rude but that's not much of a deduction given my dramatic entrance.

'He's left you for someone else.'

Well, it's a likely scenario, isn't it?

'He's far away. I see palm trees and a waterfall.'

OK, that's a little more impressive but honestly, it's only making me feel worse! Never mind what Mitch is up to, what about *me*?

'He's taken something valuable from you,' she says and I frown. Mitch wouldn't steal from me.

'Your future,' she adds.

Well, now that's true. That's what my friends and family don't seem to get. They're very clear that he was in the wrong, therefore I deserve better, therefore I should move on, but they don't understand that in going, he's made that impossible. That losing my lovely, easy-going Mitch has broken something essential in me. Without it I can't move forward.

'You're floating in empty space,' she says, and I pay close attention because that's also completely true. 'The future is a blank page. But you've come to a crossroads. Don't stay where you are. It's time to move.'

I lean forward, avid now. 'Where to?'

She shakes her head. 'I can't see names. I see a small house, with a small garden, a five-minute walk to a small town.'

Is everything small in this scenario? Are there no regular-sized objects?

'Only there will you find the answers you need.'

No pressure then! If I don't find this miniature utopia, I'm screwed. What if I choose the wrong small house and the wrong small town? 'And will I be... OK?'

She closes her eyes and breathes deeply. 'You will be a great many things to a great many people. You will have choices – many choices. You must make them one at a time. And you will have a full and wonderful life.'

'As long as I move to this house that's a five-minute walk from the small town?'

She shakes her head. 'It's a five-minute walk *to* the town, not *from* it. It will take you far longer to get home.'

That sounds profound and metaphorical. Certainly it will be hard to recapture my sense of home without Mitch. If Cooper's right, I've been trying to find it ever since our parents split up.

'That's all I see,' Angelique concludes, closing up my hand and laying hers over it. 'You're going to be OK, babes – you're going to be just fine. Right now, there's a big mismatch between your left palm and your right one. But that's going to change.'

I've no idea what that means, but I have a more pressing question. 'But how will I know where to go? There are loads of small towns. How will I know the right one?'

'It's by the sea. You've been there before, but not for a long time. You'll know.'

And just like that, I do.

CHAPTER 2

Cooper's reaction when I tell her that I'm moving to Wales for six months – based on the advice of a palm reader – is near hysterical.

'You've lost it!' she screeches down the phone. 'That bastard's put you under so much emotional stress that you've lost your capacity for rational thought. I've a good mind to fly out to Bali or wherever the **** he is and hunt him down and *slay* him!'

'I appreciate that, Coop, but honestly this is the right thing for me.'

She can't hear me; she's too worried. I was eight when our parents divorced and always a sensitive little thing. I adored them both, and my favourite place in the world was home so the sudden rupture devastated me. Cooper, six years older, took me under her wing. Our other sister, Cassidy, halfway between us in age, didn't need that kind of care. She dealt with the changes in our family by disappearing into the woods, building dens, spending more time with her friends; she's always been free-spirited and lives in New York now. Back then, I don't know what I'd have done without Cooper. She's maternal, comforting, strong – a *little* bossy.

'I forbid it!' my big sister continues in outrage. 'This is not the choice of a right-minded person. Kits, *please* come and stay with us, even if it's just for a couple of weeks! I would spoil you rotten, I promise. Let that horrid flat go and come and be with family. You'll make far better choices from here.'

She makes good sense.

But it's too late. I've already rented a little house in South Wales. I've agreed a moving-in date and booked a rental car. Even after all these years of grown-up living, I don't need a removal van. Mitch and I didn't own furniture. Because I was saving hard, I didn't buy a lot of stuff – plus, of course, we had no space. As a result, my wardrobe fits into two medium-sized suitcases, and I have a couple of boxes of books, papers, photo albums and so on. A car will do fine. It's all done and dusted and even Cooper can't stop me now, though I can't quite bring myself to tell her that it's final just yet.

I came away from the New Age Centre that day astonished to say the least. For the first time since Mitch left, I took myself to a coffee shop where I sat pondering Angelique's words – which made a nice change from dark ruminations in the flat. For the first time in weeks, I had something to think about that wasn't Mitch, Rachel, their affair or their travels. I thought about Pennystrand.

Pennystrand is the small town to which I am somehow, temporarily, relocating. When Angelique said that it was by the sea and I'd already been there a long time ago, it all became clear. I still don't understand most of what she said, but she said there would be a crossroads, and to make my choices one at a time, so that's what I'm doing. She also said that I'd only find my way forward *there*, so I'm going! Somehow my longing for a life that is colourful and bright and beautiful has etched itself onto my palm.

We went there when I was small, six or seven: the last Roberts family holiday when we were all together. I've remembered it wistfully over the years – a quaint, characterful village with crooked lanes, friendly faces and terraced cottages painted in bright seaside colours. It was edged by a crescent of beaches where my sisters and I ran wild. The divorce happened soon afterwards, and it shines all the brighter in my memory for being the last really happy time we all had together.

I try to express some of this to Cooper now.

'Is that how you remember it?' she asks, sounding genuinely surprised, rather than argumentative. 'A really happy time?'

'Well, *yes*! We were all together, Coop. A proper family. Don't you remember that little café on the beach where we used to have those huge mugs of hot chocolate?'

'Yeeees...'

'And the miniature golf course where the last hole was the portcullis of the blue castle?'

'So you're moving to Wales to play miniature golf? That's your new life plan?'

'No! I don't have a life plan, I told you. I'm not ready to make long-term decisions yet so I need a bolthole. A stopgap.'

'I agree. And I keep telling you that it should be here. You'd be much happier here with us, Kits. You don't *know* anyone in Pennystrand. You'll be depressed!'

'I'm sure I won't. It'll be beautiful and interesting, and I need a clean slate, to clear my head. Besides, it's too late for you to talk me out of it. It's all arranged.'

'What? What do you mean?'

I take a deep breath and confess that I've already committed to a rental and a moving date. Then I hold the phone well away from my ear.

CHAPTER 3

It's the beginning of April when I say goodbye to London and drive to Wales. As I close the door on the flat for the last time, I feel no regret whatsoever at leaving this unlovely space. I do however feel the weight of closing the door on my whole life with Mitch. I remember us cuddled up on the two-seater sofa that we draped with a red velvet throw to cover up the brown Draylon. I remember us laughing like loons over *Frasier* reruns. I remember us whipping up ever more creative pasta toppings in a bid to overcome the limitations of our 'kitchenette'. I remember our excitement when one of us spoiled the other with a takeaway and an interesting microbrew. All over now. I try to remind myself that this is a fresh start.

The spring weather helps. The last thing I can remember is dreary February; somehow I've slept and cried the whole of March away. Crossing the Severn Bridge feels like a milestone, and when I come off the motorway at last, I drive parallel to the sea, catching glimpses of docks and an industrial-looking sweep of bay before I cut across country via the Burrows, an expanse of open countryside that stretches between me and Pennystrand.

I'm a bit more nervous driving here – the roads are narrow with corkscrew bends and locals belting along them apace. The satnav has also given up the ghost. The moorland is scattered with sheep and lambs who sometimes skitter alarmingly into the road. I also see a herd of hairy wild ponies sheltering under twisted thorn trees. There are tremble-legged foals whisking bottle-brush tails, and I feel a tiny smile tug at the corner of my mouth. It doesn't quite reach all the way, but it's early days yet.

And eventually, with only one wrong turn, I pull up outside a small house that I recognise from the online property listing. It's a two-bed end of terrace on a newish estate, not the characterful haven that would have been my dream house, but it was the right price in the right place, so I nabbed it. Even if it *were* a quaint fisherman's cottage or a mellow barn conversion, I couldn't fall in love with it because it's only temporary.

I climb out of the car, legs stiff, and feel suddenly daunted. It's been a long drive, and I just want to be home, but this isn't home – it's a strange place belonging to strangers.

It's also occurred to me, somewhere between England and Wales, that coming here without a job lined up means that I'll be eating into my carefully hoarded savings. I'll be living off my house deposit, when it's always meant everything to me. The thought of seeing that figure in my savings account dwindle instead of grow strikes a cold terror into my heart. *What if Cooper was right and this is a really bad idea?*

My landlady, Mrs Charlton, opens the door quickly to my tentative knock. She's a small, white-haired lady, immaculately dressed and accessorised with a pair of pink rubber gloves. Her hair is piled up in an attractive bundle and she's wearing blue eyeshadow and pink lipstick. By contrast I feel decidedly scruffy.

'Welcome to Rockspell Close. I'm just doing some last-minute cleaning. Oh, I've deep-cleaned it twice already, but you can never have too much sparkle and shine, can you? Come in, come in.'

Goodness, I hope my housekeeping will be up to her standards.

I step into a little vestibule that opens into an open-plan kitchen-lounge-dining arrangement, but they're three distinct areas, not a featureless mess like the flat, and there's room to swing a cat. There's also a proper oven, I see at once. A large, lidded pot sits on the hob and a delicious smell of herbs fills the air, reminding me that I haven't eaten since a service station sandwich some hours ago.

I look around, transfixed, trying to absorb the fact that this is mine for the next six months. Meanwhile Mrs Charlton inspects me closely.

'Pretty girl,' she judges. 'Nice dark hair, lovely dark eyes. Could be from around here, you could, with colouring like that. And it's nice to see some proper curls. I get tired of all the straighteners going on with everyone. God made us all different for a reason, for goodness' sake!'

'Um, thank you.' I'm not used to such personal comments from strangers, but compliments are always nice. I won't mention that my ancient straighteners finally died yesterday and this untamed riot isn't my usual look. I'd planned to buy some new ones when I got here; maybe I won't bother.

A movement outside catches my eye. A strange man, broad-shouldered, who looks to be in his sixties, is removing my suitcases from the boot of my hire car. My inner Londoner starts with alarm. 'Oh! My cases! Hello there!' I call.

But he's not stealing them – he brings them inside. He goes back for my boxes and lastly my laptop bag. 'Evan Charlton,' he greets me, shaking my hand. 'I'll leave you to it.'

'Uh, th... thank you?'

'Very good boy,' says Mrs Charlton to his retreating back. 'That's my son,' she explains. 'Man of few words, not like me.

Lives around the corner. My other boy lives in Cardiff. I've five grandchildren, all grown up now. Only one's stayed local, more's the pity, though the others are all very fancy, mind, with good jobs and no divorces.'

'Oh! Good.'

'Aye. Now let me show you around, then I'll leave you to your privacy and get back to my telly. At my time of life, I reckon I deserve a bit of telly.'

Upstairs there's a bathroom and the two bedrooms. The second one is a box room, really, but there's only me, and compared with the flat, the whole thing is a luxury of space.

Mrs Charlton shows me where the spare bedding and towels are, gives me the Wi-Fi code and explains how to work the thermostat. Dusk is gathering so we take only a cursory glance at the outside space, a handkerchief-sized courtyard with pots around the edge and trees from next door reaching in and making themselves at home. There's a weatherproof table with two chairs and I wonder if April in Wales is warm enough to sit out.

We return to the kitchen and she points at the pot. '*Cawl.*'

I squint at the unfamiliar word. It sounded like cowl, but isn't that a type of neckline?

'Soup,' she clarifies. 'I thought you'd like something home-cooked to greet you. Properly speaking it should be made with lamb, but I didn't know if you were one of those vegetarians – they're everywhere now. We even have a café for them in the village! Are you a vegetarian?'

I shake my head and she looks disappointed. 'I could have done you a nice lamb cawl then. I should have asked you. Never mind.'

'Oh no, veggie soup is perfect! Thank you so much – it was really kind of you to make me anything.'

'There's bread in the cupboard, and tea and biscuits, milk and cheese in the fridge, fruit in the bowl, just to get you started. You can shop tomorrow. You said you know Pennys-trand? You've been before?'

'Yes, but over twenty years ago and I can't really remember it. Is it easy to find the village from here?'

'Out of the close, turn left, then second left down the steep hill and you'll find yourself in the village. There's a supermarket on the right, the local shops down on the front. I'll be off then.'

'Have you got far to go home now?'

She smiles mischievously. 'Me? No, I'm in the next street! But don't worry, I'm not one of those nosy sorts – won't be popping round every five minutes. You know where I am if you need me. My number's on the corkboard, and there's a map of the area and some tourist leaflets on the table.'

'You've thought of everything! Thank you.' I mean it – this is better service than many hotels I've visited.

She pulls on a navy coat, remembers her rubber gloves and stuffs them into a pocket then disappears.

Left alone in my new environment, I sigh and lean against the kitchen counter. Really, it couldn't be nicer. The furniture is unfashionable – but comfy and attractive. The decor is a little worn – but everything's spotlessly clean. Gleaming! The log burner is lit; it's not particularly cold but the crackling flames and the smell of home cooking proclaim sanctuary. I've been very, very lucky, I realise, remembering how hastily I found and rented this place, how little real thought I put into it.

Despite all my blessing-counting, I suddenly feel desper-ately homesick. The weirdest thing is that I don't know where I feel homesick *for*. Definitely not the London flat. Not even Cooper's house – I love it, but it was never mine. Probably for Mitch, unfortunately. I shake myself and lug one suitcase, then the other, up the stairs to the bedroom.

I promised Cooper I'd phone her to let her know I'd arrived, so I do that now, sitting on the edge of the bed, staring into the gathering purple of the oncoming evening.

'Kitty! Are you alright?' I can hear the worry in her voice. 'Was the journey OK?'

'I'm fine; the journey was fine. I'm here safely.'

'Oh, Kits, I wish I could've taken you, settled you in, but I couldn't leave the boys.'

'Cooper, I'm not twelve!'

'No, but it's always nice to have company for something like that. Are you settled then? Is the house decent?'

'It's *really* decent.'

I tell her about Mrs Charlton and the soup and the fire, and she sounds mollified. 'I do miss you though,' I say, and my voice thickens despite myself. 'I feel quite... lonely. And... unsettled.'

'Well of course you do, you've barely arrived. But, Kitty – you know I didn't want you to go, but now you're there, you have to give it a try. Give it a week or two. Who knows, you might love it, but if not, come home. You know you're always welcome here. Don't stick it out through pride, if you're not happy. You've been through enough, OK?'

I feel tears threatening; I need to get off the phone. 'Gotcha, chief! Thanks, Coop. I'm going to have something to eat now.'

I hang up and waft around the house for a while, unable to settle to anything, the reality of knowing absolutely no one for hundreds of miles around settling over me like fog. My new anxiety about using up my money doesn't help.

I unpack my clothes and lay my PJs on the bed. I have a good hunt through the cupboards in case Mrs Charlton also left a bottle of wine but no such luck. I make a cup of tea instead and leaf through a history of the area that I find in the bookcase, but I can't take anything in. I put the TV on, but the programmes are too garish and loud. I turn it off again. At last, I ladle out a bowlful of soup and sit at the counter to eat it with some bread and butter. The hot savoury broth with chunks of tender vegetables floating in it is quite delicious. Then I go to bed and fall quickly into blessed sleep.

. . .

In the middle of the night, I start awake. Everything is silent, the type of silence you never, ever experience in London. Peace and quiet have always been a big part of my living-in-the-country dream, but the reality is intense and I finally understand the city folk who claim to dislike it. There's no indication whatsoever of human life – no laughter, no scuffling, no taps running, no coughing, no sirens – I could be the last person on the planet.

I glance at my clock in the light of a moonbeam. Of course – it's 3 a.m. The scariest time in any given twenty-four hours. I stare into the darkness with a pounding heart.

Running away to find myself in a beautiful new place was a romantic-sounding idea. But this is real. I'm hurt, scared and alone, my dreams in smithereens, and I've displaced myself further by coming here. Raw panic flares up, propelling me upright, gasping for air. I fumble for the bedside lamp, eventually finding the switch, which throws a golden glow over things. The room, of course, is entirely new to me.

The panic builds. How did I think this was going to help? The only thing that would help me now is if Mitch came back. Having taken a few masochistic glances at his Instagram page over the last few weeks, I don't think *that's* likely – he's having the time of his life. Even so, my mind turns to him for comfort out of habit. For a decade now, he's been my person. With a shock I realise that *if* he came back to the UK now and wanted to see me, he wouldn't know where I was! In my dazed, startled state, this feels appalling.

I spring out of bed, grab my laptop and connect to the internet. Then I email Mitch.

Dear Mitch,

I hope you're well and that you're happy – I want you to be happy. I want you to know that I forgive you – it can't have been easy realising you had feelings for Rachel – not wanting to hurt me. If she's what's best for you, I hope it all works out. But I still love you, Mitch, and I miss you. I'm in Wales, in Pennystrand. I couldn't stay in the flat without you, and I needed somewhere temporary to get my head together. I've rented a place for six months with an option to extend, but I won't extend. It's just a stopgap.

I pause and consider adding another sentence: *If you change your mind about us, you know where I'll be.* But no, that sounds too desperate. At least I've re-established that bridge between us that has always made me feel safe in the world. I type my address and sign off with two kisses.

Then I press send and snuggle back down under the covers, but I leave the lamp on.

CHAPTER 4

When I wake, my fear has vanished with the starlight. I lie in bed, enjoying the sense of well-being and the warmth. Sounds start up outside – a car door slamming, an engine starting up, a puppy's excited yapping, robin song. Peaceful Sunday-morning sounds, intermittent – not the wall of noise I was used to in London.

I get up and look out of the window to see my first morning in Pennystrand. The front of the house looks over the street, which is a little cul-de-sac, tucked away off another street. The houses are all eighties builds, of a style that Cooper, with her great love of traditional architecture, would probably wrinkle her nose at, though I think they're rather pretty. They're all quite similar, with white walls, black roofs and leaded windows. Although it's a housing estate, it's very quiet and spacious. Tulips bloom in neat planters. I see a small boy muffled in a blue parka running across the close into the open arms of a woman I assume is his grandmother, and I smile. It's that kind of neighbourhood.

I crack the window open an inch and smell the sea, though I can't see it. A fresh, sweet breeze drifts in. It's the sky that seals the deal for me – pale blue, like old, ironed sheets, stretched across a faintly glowing lemon sun, with scuds of cloud and gleams of light. I've never seen so much sky.

I jump in the shower, dress, and breakfast on bread and home-made blackcurrant jam, whilst squinting at Google Maps to acquaint myself with the area. Some bits look familiar from that long-ago holiday – I only need to figure out how to join them up to where I am now.

I see a text from Cooper: *How was the first night? Hope you're OK this morning xx*

I reply: *All good! About to explore. Call you later xx*

It's really easy to find my way to the village proper. Pennys-trand is down a hill so steep I can hardly keep from running and, true enough, it only takes me five minutes to get there. It instantly brings back memories of that long-ago holiday. There's a flat stretch with shops, offices, bars and cafés before the road plunges steeply again to the sea. Everything is closed and I don't see a soul; in my enthusiasm to explore, I forgot that it's not London and it's only 10 a.m. on a Sunday. So I keep walking, taking great lungfuls of briny air. That same sweeping expanse of sky stretches over the village, over the winking sea, on and on, blue and white.

At the foot of the next hill is a long pedestrian path running along the length of the bay. I remember we Robertses enjoyed many a walk and ice cream sundae here. It's unchanged, and this is where I see people: people out running or cycling; people walking their dogs; grandparents coaxing small children on trikes, fishermen wrapped up against the cold, perched on the sea wall. Couples wander hand in hand, and I feel a wave of sadness about Mitch, but I shake myself. I'm not here to wallow – I'm here to take stock and think of what I want to do next.

Bicycle bells ring, boat moorings tinkle in the wind, soaring gulls cry as they sweep low, cruising for food, then glide away again out to sea. It's exhilarating, but I seem to be the only solitary person in Pennystrand; even the fishermen and the joggers are in pairs.

I spot an open café, a greasy spoon with a waft of bacon shimmying out, making me regret that I've already eaten. I go in anyway, for hot chocolate and a sea view.

In here too, everyone is with families, friends or lovers. One young couple of about twenty are so far down each other's throats they're in danger of falling in. A few curious glances come my way and although they're not unfriendly I'm surprised to feel a little uncomfortable. Being alone in London is nothing remarkable. There, since it's impossible to guess at everyone's business, no one bothers to try. Here, being alone makes me stand out.

My old longing for family, for home, wells up and makes me want to cry. I don't remember this café specifically from our family holiday, but I remember countless hot chocolates that fortnight, with Mum and Dad and Cassidy and Cooper, all of us chattering excitedly, planning what to do next. Just like the families around me now.

It's only day one, I tell myself. Obviously I don't feel a sense of belonging yet! But is that the goal? To belong? Because if this is only temporary, what's the point? Who's going to want to invest in a friendship with someone who's leaving in six months? And do I really want to become attached to people and a place I'll be leaving? But if I don't, it'll be a very lonely few months. Perhaps Cooper was right and this wasn't my best-thought-out plan.

I look around and try to smile at people, but after those first interested glances my way, everyone seems once again absorbed with their own lives. Perhaps I've been influenced by books and films where moving to a quaint, beautiful place is easy and people make friends overnight, usually meeting a handsomely rugged local while they're at it. Every man I've seen so far has been accompanied by a pretty wife/girlfriend or a couple of kids. Starting over here may be more challenging than I thought. Still, I'm up to the challenge! *I'm not some pathetic, lovelorn— Oh no!*

With a lurch of horror, I remember emailing Mitch last night in the dark despair of 3 a.m. *Oh God, what did I say?*

I pull my phone out and reread it. It is *awful*. I sound pitiful. Yes, I'm shaken to the core by losing him, but I refuse to sound that sappy and needy. Mitch hasn't replied, and I don't know whether to be hurt or relieved. I dash off a hasty one-liner:

> *Please ignore previous email. First-night jitters. All fine today,*
> *sun is shining and I love it here! Cheers, K.*

He'll sense the bravado, no doubt, but that's still better than letting him imagine me wistfully checking my phone every five seconds, longing to hear from him. Right. Time to get on with my day.

I put money on the table and start to walk up the hill. After five minutes I'm blowing like a carriage horse. This hill is perpendicular! I spot a small supermarket and pause. Yes, why not stock up on food while I'm passing? I can take it all home and put it away before going out again, then I'll be well supplied. I'm a great believer, when times are tough, in spoiling yourself with small treats. I indulge in a really nice bottle of wine, an almighty tub of peanut butter and three large bars of chocolate. I get proper food too, all my favourites, and when I come to pay, I find myself with three bulging carrier bags.

OK, well, it's only a five-minute walk. I do this in London all the time – whizz in to do a food shop on the way home.

But London doesn't have hills like this. Oh my word – I thought the lower section of the hill was steep! But this stretch reminds me of the Maxi Climber at the gym – and there was a reason I only ever used it once.

Other people stride effortlessly past me. I didn't think I was especially unfit, but halfway up I want to die.

I stop, making a great show of admiring the view, unable to hide the fact that I'm gasping for breath. My legs are wobbling. My arms are being wrenched from their sockets and I seriously consider leaving a couple of the heavier items on the roadside. It may be a five-minute walk *down* the hill, but it's considerably more going back up. Now I understand why Angelique emphasised that the house was five minutes *to* the village, not from it. I thought it was a strange distinction to make at the time, but now I get it. A metaphorical hill would have been so much easier on the thighs!

CHAPTER 5

My first few days in Pennystrand pass uneventfully. I eventually made it home with the shopping, arms thankfully still attached. I collapsed for a good long while, then I set out again to continue exploring and that's pretty much what I've been doing ever since.

I've explored the village thoroughly. There's a chocolate shop, which is good news for me and my addiction, a wonderful gallery/gift shop where I could spend a fortune if only I had one to spend, and a cute dress shop with some gorgeous clothes I likewise can't afford unless I decide to wipe out my house deposit altogether. There are also two estate agencies, more or less opposite each other on either side of the main road through the village; they look as if they're facing off for a duel. I haven't stopped to look. Of all the things most likely to trigger my grief over losing Mitch, I'm afraid houses for sale might be it. I keep my distance from them, though I can feel their lure, tugging at me as I hurry past.

Of less interest are the surf shops – I've counted five so far. I've never been much of a water-sports person – unlike Mitch. I wonder if that's part of what led him into Rachel's arms? I

suppose, thinking about it, we were very different people, though I never thought you had to be a clone of the person you loved for it to work. Despite my fascination with houses, and my dream of buying one, I'm not a complete homebody. I love the outdoors and I'm really sociable – often out for a night with friends in London – which is why I find being here alone difficult.

But Mitch was on another level. He's one of those people who just can't sit still unless they've tired themselves out. Once he took me waterskiing in Chertsey with his friend Liam and Joanna, his partner. Joanna sat on the deck reading a magazine while the boys skied and dragged me in with them. I'm glad I tried it, and I don't mind giving things a go, but honestly, I'd far rather have been chatting in the sun with Joanna than being dragged repeatedly by my ankles through a lake. Now, when I torture myself by checking Mitch's Instagram account, there are countless pictures of him and Rachel dangling off bungee cords and brandishing paddles whilst white-water rafting. If he'd asked me to do this trip with him, I would have gone. But I prob-ably wouldn't have *loved* it.

Well, if Mitch were here now, he could take his pick of surf-ing, windsurfing, kayaking, paddle-boarding, jet-skiing, wake-boarding... I've seen them all. *Anyway, I must stop thinking about Mitch.* The point is that I love living by the sea. I've now walked the entire curve of coast that cups Pennystrand – four beaches in all.

First there's Pennystrand Bay, the big stretch of water that edges the long footpath and the touristy shops and cafés. People don't swim there, but it's busy with boats, and on the seaweed-strewn sand you see walkers plodding, dogs sniffing and metal detectorists with bowed heads and eagle eyes.

Next is Clogwyn Du, which is hardly a beach at all; it's the size of a postage stamp. It lies at the foot of tall, dark cliffs and I wouldn't have realised it *was* a beach except that it's sign-

posted. Sure enough, when I looked, I saw a thread-narrow
path, seemingly designed for mountain goats, winding down
the cliffs. I've seen anglers perched on the jagged rocks at the
bottom with their rods and lines, while the surf hisses and
leaps around them like a collection of bad-tempered white
cats.

A mile or so along there's Brightman Bay, a big golden
beach that seems to be everybody's favourite. It's gentle and
welcoming, with a sensibly paved road to reach it and rocks
washed smooth by the waves; children with nets and salty hair
clamber over them to the rock pools. Brightman Bay boasts two
classy restaurants, all extensive wine lists and glass frontage.

Again, I feel my solitude. They're places to celebrate special
occasions with loved ones, or linger over a glass of wine with a
friend. In limbo as I am, I can't justify the expense on my own.
It seems unlikely now that I'll ever buy somewhere of my own,
but the habit of living frugally in the hope of a dream coming
true is hard to break.

There's also a café right down on the rocks, as if washed up
by the tide. It's called Tymorau, which according to the English
menu means 'Seasons'. It's dog-friendly, kid-friendly and does
the best selection of hot chocolate. There are rafters and a log
burner and brightly coloured cushions on the chairs. I've been
twice already, clutching a book, but I can't seem to concentrate
to read; I get too distracted by the chatter around me. Everyone
seems to know everyone, and it pains me to be so very much on
the outside.

The fourth and final beach is my favourite: Lemon Cove.
Bigger than Clogwyn Du but much smaller than the others, it's
quiet and peaceful. There are no cafés, no beach huts selling
buckets and spades, nothing at all except for yellow sand in a
perfect curve and frilled waves.

'Yes, yes, I remember and it's all very delightful,' says
Cooper when I rave about the beaches to her, 'but what are you

going to *do* there? You can't just spend six months walking on beaches. Make some friends! Join a group!'

'I know – give me time. It's only been three days!'

I don't tell her that I've no idea how I'll ever get to know anyone in this vibrant but obviously close-knit community. It doesn't do to admit weakness to Cooper, or she'll wade in and take over completely.

'I suppose,' she admits grudgingly. 'And you're really OK? Not crying yourself to sleep at night or anything?'

'No, I'm fine. I do still feel a bit lonely – and sad about Mitch...'

At this, Cooper gives a guttural yowl, similar to a cat warning an encroaching cat off its territory.

'Well, we were together a long time, Coop. I'm a little subdued, but really I'm fine. I'll give it a couple of weeks, as you suggested. And it is lovely to be back.'

'It *is*?'

'*Yes!* Why do you find this surprising? You've been here – you know how beautiful it is.'

'Beautiful yes, but we went there and five minutes later, Mum and Dad got divorced! It doesn't seem auspicious for a new start.'

'But that's just random! It's not Pennystrand's *fault* they split up.'

'Look, I don't know what went down. I mean, I've got my theories, but I don't want to impose them on you. It's all ancient history now, isn't it? Mum and Dad are aces. We're lucky really, when you think of the hassle some parents give their kids.'

'Cooper, what are you talking about?'

'You really don't remember anything less-than-great about that holiday? I guess you were that much younger than me... Look, I don't want to spoil your happy impressions – you're there now.'

'You won't spoil my happy impressions. I want to know

what you remember that I don't! Spit it out – you keep hinting, and it's bugging me.'

'Sorry. It's just that it was sort of the beginning of the end, wasn't it?'

'I remember it more as the last great time *before* the end. I know the divorce came quickly after that, but wasn't that just timing?'

'I don't think so. See, I remember Dad being absent a lot. I remember rows too, him and Mum, after we'd gone to bed. I guess you and Cass were asleep, but I heard them.'

'Cooper! I never knew. I'm sorry.'

'It's OK. I guess if anything it meant I was that tiny little bit more prepared than you two when they split up.'

'Poor you. Poor all of us.'

'Yes. But no point harking back to all that – we're big girls now.'

She pauses. 'Kits, I did get out of bed one night, because I was getting really upset, and I went to listen from the landing— Crap, Nathan's hollering – got to go. I'm glad you're alright anyway, Kitty. Remember I'm here if you need me.'

She hangs up midway through me thanking her and I wonder what she overheard that night. When she's had time to settle Nathan, I call her back, but her phone rings out and she doesn't pick up.

CHAPTER 6

The next day I have a mission. Mission Meet People. Cooper's right: I can't roam the beaches indefinitely.

I go to the newsagent, which has notices in the window, and I scan them hopefully. There are adverts for cleaners and people to do the ironing – definitely luxuries I can't afford. There are a couple of motorbikes and a campervan for sale. But one faded index card catches my eye. In fact, it seems so serendipitous I can hardly believe my luck. There's an art group in the community hall every Wednesday at 2 p.m. Today is Wednesday!

I'm going to do it! I haven't spotted an art-supply shop in the village, but in the newsagent's, which is cavernous, I find a sketchpad, pencils and a putty rubber. No paint, but it's better than turning up with nothing at all. Then I kill time in a café before turning up ten minutes early. The only person there is an extremely elderly lady, creeping around flicking on lights and heaters.

'Hello,' I say. 'I'm here for the art class. Are you the teacher?'

'The what, dear?'

'The art class. I saw a card in the newsagent's. It said there's an art class at two?'

'Oh, we're not a class, love – we're a group.'

'Oh! Um, right?'

I'm not sure what the difference is, but she doesn't seem keen to elaborate and continues readying the hall. I bite my lip. She seems very nice, but I'm not sure she's the start of a social life. I'd imagined bohemian types in berets and chignons, arranging field trips to galleries and meeting up to drink red wine. Still, one shouldn't make snap judgements.

'So, um, can anyone come to the group? I'm new to the area and I'd love to have a go.'

'Well, yes, if you'd like to.' She looks uncertain.

Two more ladies come in, heads together, talking and nodding in hushed voices. They're younger than the first, in their seventies or thereabouts; they both wear quilted jackets and have purplish tinges to their hair.

'Oh! Hello, Betty,' says one to the first woman. 'How are you? We were just talking about Veronica's divorce, you know.'

'Terrible business,' replies Betty. 'How are you holding up, Diana?'

'Oh *I'm* fine,' huffs the other, looking affronted. 'There's no shame in divorce nowadays you know, Betty. It's Veronica I'm concerned about. The grief that man is giving her is nobody's business.'

But apparently it is *everybody's* business because she proceeds to list all his misdeeds loudly, even as more people arrive and pull chairs for themselves from the pile in the corner. She continues as people put the kettle on, produce a cash box, show each other photos of grandchildren on mobile phones. No one seems to be in charge. No one takes any notice of me. I'm the youngest person here by a good three decades and I'm standing around like a spare part. There are three or four conversations going on around me and I don't know how to

break into any of them. There's just no entry point – they're all about people I don't know.

'Valerie's gone completely doolally, if you ask me...'

'Neville's had another hippy. They done his right hip last year – well now they done his left one...'

'Megan's hysterectomy was no joke, I can tell you! But that doctor of hers was very handsome...'

I keep a polite, attentive smile plastered on my face, wishing someone would at least ask me my name. It's bound to get better when they start drawing – or painting. Perhaps the custom is to have a cuppa first then get stuck in. But with the exception of the one elderly gentleman among them, sitting on the edge of the group with a drawing board and a box of pencils, there isn't an art utensil to be seen.

I get up to make myself a cup of tea, hoping this will attract some attention. It doesn't.

I sit down again, and a box of biscuits gets passed around. The woman to my left – Eileen, I think – hands it to me without a glance. I take a biscuit and pass it to the lady on my right.

'Thank you, dear,' she says then does a double take. 'Oh hello,' she says. 'Are you from the council?'

'No, I'm a new member of the group. I'm Kitty.'

I stick my hand out and she shakes it. I resist the urge to hang on to it in an attempt to keep her attention.

She smiles vaguely, then looks back at her friend – Vera, I think.

Sod this.

'I'm Kitty,' I repeat loudly, leaning across and holding out my hand again. Damn it, *someone's* got to take some notice of me!

'Vera Poxley. How do you do?'

'I'm well, thanks. And you are?' I ask the lady next to me.

'Oh! Oh, I'm Catherine!' She seems flustered, as if it's a

trick question she might get wrong. Perhaps she still suspects I'm from the council.

'Nice to meet you, Catherine. And what kind of art do you do?'

'Art? Me? Oh, I... I...' She looks helplessly at Vera.

'I used to do the watercolour pencils,' says Vera. 'They *are* proper art, no matter what my Drew says.'

'Of course. And now?'

'Well, I don't really do anything anymore.'

'But I thought this was an art group?'

'Well, it used to be. But now, apart from Dafydd over there, we just come for the social.'

'For the...?'

But I've lost her. She and Catherine are deep in conversation again, and I learn that Graham Bowen has been knocking off Sharlene Howden...

It's hopeless! I pick up my chair and go over to Dafydd, who's covering his page in loose, flowing lines.

'Hello. I'm Kitty.' I seem to be stuck on repeat.

'Dafydd. Don't mind us. Terrible manners, I know, but we're not used to new people, see. We've all been coming here for... ooh, twenty years or thereabouts now.' He says all this without glancing up from the page.

'Really? Wow! So I'm not really sure what to do... and I don't like to interrupt people...'

He lays down his pencil and looks at me. He's shy – I can see it in his eyes. And his drawing is wonderful.

'Oh, it's driftwood!' I exclaim. 'And out of your imagination too. I could never do that. It's brilliant.'

He sets it to one side. 'The thing is, Kitty, they all stopped the art a few years ago now. They've all got kids and grandkids and even great-grands. This is just a chance for them to have a little hour to themselves and catch up with their friends. Even if some of them are... what do you call it now? You have that word these days... Frenemies, that's it.' His eyes twinkle at me. 'They'll take no notice of you – hell, they take no notice of *me*! We used to have a tutor, Brian, who was excellent, but he's long gone.'

'Oh, I'm sorry.' I assume he means that Brian has passed away.

He nods glumly. 'Spain. It takes all the good ones. They go for the sun and that's the last we see of them. Having the time of his life is Brian. We had the hall booking so we just kept coming.'

'And why do you come if they... ignore you?'

'Oh, I've the opposite situation to them. I'm on my own. It's nice to hear voices once a week. Well, sometimes I think so anyway. Other times I'm not sure.' He picks up his board and starts shading the edge of the driftwood.

'Could you teach me to draw?' I ask impulsively. 'You're very good and I haven't a clue!'

'You're very kind,' he says, turning scarlet. 'But I'm no good as a teacher, Kitty. Others have asked me the same thing, but I can't explain what I do. You're new to the village? Well, here's the thing – we're not the social circle you need. You need a younger, more vibrant art class with proper instruction, dear.'

I can't argue with him there. 'Is there one?'

He frowns. 'Not that I know of, no.'

I head off soon after that and start my way home. I can't face wandering lonely as a cloud today – my spirit is broken. When I first moved to London, it was easy to make friends. I went to a pottery class and a French class, I went to bars a couple of times a week, and before I knew it, I had a bunch of great friends from all over the world – they all needed a community too. It's much harder here, where the community's already established and apparently completely impenetrable. Really, *how* am I going to find any friends in this place?

CHAPTER 7

That night I can't settle to Netflix or my book. The solitude's making me edgy, so I pull on trainers and a coat and set out walking again. Loneliness is doing wonders for my cardiovascular health.

The place has a different character at night. Every house and garden seems to hold secrets. I walk through the darkness, gazing at cliffside houses and converted flats, wondering about the people who live in them.

Some of the curtains remain undrawn, and in the squares of bright light, I see glimpses into people's lives. In one very modern-looking flat, a dark-skinned woman around my own age sits at a workstation before a computer screen. Her hair is piled up in a loose curly bun and she's wearing a stripy top very similar to mine. I wonder what her job is, or if she's merely shopping online.

In a terraced house with bay window, a mother with long blond hair watches her son practise the piano. They both look like people I'd enjoy meeting – but how?

I miss my London friends. A week never passed in my old life without Mitch and I going to another couple's flat for dinner, without me meeting the girls for drinks. But even though they text me occasionally now, it's uncomfortable. After all those years together, my friends are Mitch's friends and vice versa. They feel awkward, I feel awkward... so it's really just Cooper who's my lifeline. And anyway, none of them are *here*.

In another street I see a woman in her fifties sitting alone at a kitchen table with a half-empty bottle of red wine and a glass. Her shoulders are slumped and her whole aura is one of despair. I pause for a minute, wishing I could offer some comfort, but really, you can't just knock on someone's door and say, 'Hello, you look sad. Can I make you a cup of tea?'

Soon I find myself at Brightman Bay, standing by railings above the beach, listening to the steady wash and plunge of the waves. A bobbing light down on the beach distracts me – dancing then settling to a steady beam. A man shines a large torch over the shoreline pebbles and out to sea. In the path of light, a woman in a bathing suit picks her way over the glistening stones to the water. I shiver. Is she seriously going in? It may be spring, but I tried paddling the other day and my feet nearly fell off.

She wears a rubber hat with a frilly flower on the side. Reaching the lacy water's edge, she dips a toe, high steps in, dances around a bit and retreats. Then she squares her shoulders and walks back in. When she's waist-deep in the ocean, she plunges underwater and surfaces with a hysterical-sounding shriek. Then she races out of the sea, back to the man, who throws a towel around her and rubs vigorously.

I feel tears spring to my eyes. If that's not the very image of love, I don't know what is. That's what your partner should be: someone who shines a steady beam of light ahead of you no matter what crazy thing you want to do. Is that what Mitch and I did for each other? I'm not sure that we did; there didn't seem to be space in our life for either of us to have mad whims – we just worked and saved and survived. Perhaps it was all my fault.

Perhaps my obsession with achieving that lovelier life I imagined robbed us of the chance to enjoy the one we had. But if he wanted something different, he never *said*. And he loved his work, far more than I did mine. Either way, Mitch is gone.

I wish I could go and talk to that man and woman, who are now walking slowly up the beach, leaning together, the torch beam bobbing again. But what would I say? 'Hi, you seem like cool people and I have no friends here...' *No*. I sigh and plod back towards home.

How many days have I been here now? Four? I don't think I've ever gone this long with so little human contact and I'm not sure how much longer I can endure it. I love it here, but it's *hard*. I promised myself I'd give it two weeks. Only ten days to go.

CHAPTER 8

The next day I stay away from the village. I've had enough of being surrounded by people who are enjoying other people's company and oblivious to me. I discovered a thermos in one of the cupboards in the little house; I fill it with coffee and go down to Lemon Cove with my new sketchpad and pencils. I settle myself on a rock and try to capture the shape of the coast-line, the pattern of the waves... I don't think my efforts are any good, but it's fun and absorbing. I don't stay long because the rocks are cutting into my bum and the sand is wet – plus, it's cold. Signs of spring are everywhere around Pennystrand, in the playful breezes and bright yellow daffodils dancing on the verges, in the washes of primrose and crocus and the darting birds with beaks full of moss and twigs. But nature has yet to turn up the thermostat.

I turn and march up the road, rather wearily foreseeing another afternoon curled up alone with Netflix, when there is literally a bolt from the blue. Or rather, a branch from the blue. It drops out of the sky and crashes to the ground at my feet, missing me so narrowly that I feel the draught of air brush my face. I stumble over it and can't help giving a little shriek.

'Oh God!' cries a horrified voice above me. 'Did it hit you? Are you injured?'

I look up. Behind a stone wall, up a tree, brandishing a chainsaw, is a young woman with a red-and-white-spotted scarf wound around her head with a knot at the front, forties-style. Her pixie-like face is as white as snow.

'I'm so sorry,' she goes on, clinging to a branch like a monkey. 'I didn't know it was going to fall that way. Please say something!'

I regain my wits; I think she's more alarmed than I am. 'I'm fine! Just a bit of a fright.'

I see her wilt with relief. 'Thank God. That's the most important thing. Now the second-most important thing is this: are you going to sue?'

I laugh. 'Of course not. It was an accident. No harm done.'

'Thank God again. And the third thing: will you come in for a cup of tea and a biscuit?'

As I come to my senses even more, I notice a red roof and the top of a cream-coloured house behind her. The wall is obviously the wall of her garden.

'Oh, there's no need...'

What am I saying? Politeness really has a lot to answer for. This is the first invitation I've had since I got to Wales, even if she *is* only asking because she's afraid she might have brain-damaged me.

'No, there is – wait there!'

Her head ducks back into the tree and I see her shimmying down. Then she appears through a gate onto the road before me. She's wearing denim dungarees over a white T-shirt and big clumpy boots.

'Cherry Morris,' she says, holding out her hand.

I shake it.

'Please, please come in. You might be in shock, and if so, you could do with something hot and some sugar. I'd feel much better if you do.'

'OK then, thank you,' I say, delighted. 'That's very kind. I'm Kitty.'

'Nice to meet you, Kitty. Nice to not have killed you, in fact.'

She bends to lift the offending branch, which has a certain heft to it.

'God, this could have done some serious damage. I knew I should have waited for Mike, but you know what men are like – talk about doing things for months without ever actually doing them. Sometimes I just have to have a go myself. But I've learned my lesson. Arboriculture is not my skillset. Come on.'

She goes back into the garden, dragging the branch, which she tosses to one side on the grass. There are apple trees and long grass and spring shoots of green clustered along the stone wall and a rusting bench on a slight rise. It's ramshackle but enticing, like a garden in a storybook.

We head up a flagged path, then five steps, to the front door of a compact, double-fronted house painted cream, with a burgundy front door.

I follow Cherry into a wide hall tiled in terracotta and white and filled with boxes. It looks as if she's just moved in. I wonder if she's new to the area too. If so, she might need a friend just as much as I do. She has the local accent though, so I don't hold out much hope.

A door off the hall leads into a big square kitchen with a coffee table instead of a kitchen table and packing crates for seats.

She fills a kettle then turns to face me. 'Take a seat. As you can see, it's a bit makeshift; we haven't been here long – well, eight months but it's all relative, isn't it? But at least you're safe. Tea? Coffee? Gin?'

I smile, tempted by the gin. 'Tea would be lovely.'

She brews a pot and grabs two packets of biscuits – choc chip and papaya and coconut. 'Have loads,' she orders, plonking them on the coffee table in front of me. 'Make sure you're not going to faint or anything.'

She comes to perch on a packing crate, setting two steaming mugs before us.

'Are you new to the area?' I ask hopefully.

'No, we've only moved round the corner.' She laughs. 'Well, a couple of miles, but you know what I mean – it's not a big life change, is it?'

'Why did you move?'

'Upsizing. We were in a poxy little flat – well, not poxy, cute, but way too small for us now that our daughter's out of a cot.'

'Oh, you have a little girl! What's her name?'

'Margaret-Lily, named after her two grandmothers, both still very much alive and kicking by the way. Somehow she gets called Magpie by absolutely everyone. If I'm honest, it suits her, she's so lively and naughty.'

I smile. 'It's adorable.'

'She's at school now. Well, nursery. How are you feeling?' She looks at me anxiously as if I might topple off the crate at any moment.

'I'm fine – really. Please don't worry.'

'OK then. I'll stop fussing. But tell me if you feel wobbly, right? What about you, Kitty? Are you local?'

'No, I've just moved from London. I've been here less than a week.'

'Wow, and what brought you to Pennystrand? Work?'

Briefly I fill her in on my recent unedifying life events.

Cherry tilts her head sympathetically. 'Oh no! Poor you. That's no fun. Well, I may be biased but I think you made a great choice. This is the perfect place to heal and start again, I should say. Ooh, what's that face? Are you not keen?'

'It's not that. I love it here – it's beautiful. It's just that I'm finding it really hard to meet people.' I tell her about the cafés full of smiling families and the art group – which makes her crack up.

'I can't seem to find a way in,' I conclude. 'I always thought I had pretty good social skills, but everyone here seems completely absorbed with their own lives. I feel... surplus to requirements.'

She considers. 'I think you're probably right. Loads of people do move here from elsewhere, you're not the only one, but there's a lot of locals and we all go way back... we probably seem a bit impenetrable from the outside. But look, you didn't need to find a way in – *it* found *you*, in the form of a huge branch almost dropping on your head.'

'I wouldn't want to intrude. You must have loads of friends already.' *Shut* up, *Kitty. I do want to intrude!*

'Well, yes, but that doesn't mean I can't have another one. And honestly, having a little one can be kind of curtailing – the friends who aren't into kids are staying well away, and fair play. So there's a vacancy!' She grins. 'I don't know if you like kids or not, but you're desperate, so that has to work in my favour.'

I feel excited. 'Then thank you. You're welcome to visit any time – I could make you lunch – and I'd love to come here again and see how the house is coming on. This place is beautiful by the way – you're lucky.'

'It's probably too big for us if I'm honest, but we fell in love with it and we'll grow into it. That's settled then. And I'll do a coffee morning or something for you to meet some of my other friends... Oh, listen to me – coffee morning! How yummy mummy do I sound? Only four years ago it would have been cocktails or a night in the pub. That's motherhood for you.' She pulls a face.

I shrug. 'Right now a coffee morning sounds pretty exciting to me. If there are other human beings there, I'm in!'

We chat for ages – three mugs of tea are poured and drunk – and I learn that she grew up around here and has lived here always apart from three years at university in Bristol. Her husband, Mike, has a desk job at the local council. 'Hence his excuse for nothing getting done around the house!' she complains, rolling her eyes. 'Eight months on and we haven't even finished unpacking yet. He's always like, *I don't have time, I work!* What does he think *I* do then?'

'What *do* you do?'

'Good question. My entire sense of identity has been called into question by motherhood, but I trained as a solicitor, had a career change before I got pregnant and now I work part-time from home designing greetings cards, plus looking after Magpie when she's not at nursery, plus doing the majority of what needs doing to get us settled in properly.'

'Hence the tree surgery.'

'Hence the tree surgery,' she agrees ruefully and stretches. 'It's been great talking to you, Kitty, but I've got to fetch Maggie-Magpie now.'

I scramble to my feet; I don't want to overstay my welcome. 'Thanks for the lovely afternoon – it's been really good meeting you.'

'Don't be a stranger. Come back any time – really. And I'll come to yours one day too. It'll be nice to get out of the house for once.'

She fishes a business card out of a bowl on the counter and hands it to me. 'All my details are on there. Text me so I have your number.'

I pocket it and feel a warmth in my heart that had been thoroughly chilled by cool sea air and solitude. Meeting Cherry has entirely dispelled the cold fog of the art group's indifference.

'I could help you with the house, if you like?' I offer. 'I'm basically obsessed with houses. I can do a lick of paint for you or whatever.'

'Are you serious? Don't say it if you don't mean it because I *will* take you up on it.'

'Be my guest.'

We walk to the top of the road together then I go left and she goes right.

As we part, she hesitates. 'I've just had a genius idea. Did you want a job while you're here, or was the idea to take six months off completely?'

I shrug. 'I wasn't going to force myself to get a job, but honestly I'm just using up my savings to be here, which isn't ideal. If I found something, that would be great.'

'Then allow me to kill several birds with one stone,' she declares. 'There's a job going at Rowlands, the estate agent. Have you seen it?'

I nod, a feeling of fate in action stealing over me.

'Well, you love houses, and you know interiors, so there's that. You'd meet a *ton* of people *and* it's only part-time, which means you'd still have time to help me paint!'

I stare at her. 'Oh my God, that *is* genius!'

'I know. I'm brilliant really. Right, gotta go. Bloody motherhood!'

She disappears off down the hill, waving as she goes.

I dither on the corner for long moments. Part of me wants to run straight to Rowlands in case the job goes in the next couple of hours. The other part would far rather go and see about it when I've washed my hair.

CHAPTER 9

The next day I wake feeling transformed. I have a friend... and a job interview! I phoned Rowlands when I got home yesterday and arranged a meeting for ten this morning. I hastily updated my CV and emailed it over. I was up early today, washing my hair and ironing a nice dress, digging out the smart brown boots I was starting to think I'd never have occasion to wear.

It's a fine day so I walk down the hill and take a deep breath as I stand outside for a moment – out of sight of the office so they don't think I'm weird. I've kept my distance from the estate agents since I've been here, but last night I had a good long browse of the Rowlands website so I could sound knowledge-able today and my obsession is back in full force. It was an endless parade of mouth-watering yellow-stone rural cottages, farmhouses, barn conversions, fisherman's cottages and ordinary enough semis made inspirational by huge gardens, or sea views, or both. Nostalgia for Mitch didn't sweep over me quite as dramatically as I'd expected; meeting Cherry has really buoyed my spirits.

I really want this job. Cherry's right – I'd meet loads of people, and I'd have the chance to try out a job I've *always* wanted to do. Imagine spending my days looking at houses, exploring houses and talking about houses! Also, hopefully, selling some houses.

I take another moment to contemplate the gleaming navy-and-gold shopfront and logo of Rowlands. Wilton-Granger, across the road, is kitted out in ivy green and white. The breeze lifts my hair into banners and wraps them round my face. I tuck them behind my ears and go inside.

There are three desks inside. At the front sits a large man – broad shoulders, a foodie's belly – resting hefty arms on his desk. He stares into space with a visionary air, as if seeing profound truths in the shape of the clouds. He wears an immaculate navy suit which wraps him fairly tightly but looks beautifully made. A lilac silk square rests in his jacket pocket.

At one of the desks behind sits a woman of around my own age – hooray! She looks up and smiles.

'Hi, can I help you?' she asks, twirling her chair to face me.

The third desk is empty. I desperately want it to be mine. I want to twirl my chair and greet customers. I want to be an estate agent.

'Hello, I'm Kitty Roberts,' I announce. 'We spoke on the phone yesterday.'

At this, the man at the front rouses himself and rises to his feet. He must be six foot two at least, in his fifties, both solidly built and well fed.

He grins at me, extending his hand. 'Roly Rowlands – pleased to meet you. Thanks for coming in.'

I can't help grinning back because his *joie de vivre* is infectious. 'Thank you for seeing me. I'm really excited about the position.'

'Nerys, stick the kettle on,' he says, glancing over his shoulder. 'Oh, she's already gone.'

From out the back of the office comes the sound of a tap running.

A moment later, Nerys, all blond curls and magenta lipstick, returns and leans against the door frame. 'Coffee or tea?'

'Just water please.' I've drunk so much coffee this week it'll be a miracle if I don't develop a heart condition. I mustn't be lulled by the sociability of the welcome; I want to impress Mr Rowlands. I want to concentrate and be calm.

'Tea for me thanks,' says Mr Rowlands, waving me to a chair. 'And a slice of the walnut cake.'

'Roly, it's not elevenses yet.'

'Never mind – it's a special occasion. Cake?' he offers.

My resolve wavers but we're now sitting on two chairs in the window – I don't want to be balancing a plate and dropping crumbs and wielding a fork whilst trying to look professional. 'No thank you.'

'Now then, I had a look at your CV and it's first class. Well done.'

'Oh! Thank you!' I hadn't thought it was that special but that's a good start. 'I'm happy to discuss any parts of it that you want to know more about.'

He beams. 'Wonderful!'

Nerys appears with a mug for her boss, which he places on the floor, and a modest piece of cake on a plate, which he eyes askance.

'Damn, woman, that's not a slice!'

'It's a sliver,' she counters. 'Compromise. There you go,' she adds, handing me the water.

I thank her, he rolls his eyes and the interview recommences.

'So what brought you here?' he asks companionably, wolfing the cake in two bites.

I try to explain succinctly. Of course the story sets the scene for the inevitable question: why did I leave my last job? I take a sip of water and set the glass on the floor. I have to be totally honest.

'I was let go. I went to an important meeting the day after my partner and I broke up. It was a horrible ending – I won't bore you with the details – and I was in a terrible state. I realised afterwards that I shouldn't have gone, but I wasn't thinking straight. The client was unimpressed and that was that. I want you to know, though, that I'm usually extremely professional and it was completely a one-off.'

'I see. Thank you for explaining,' says Mr Rowlands, and I'm not sure what he makes of it all. 'So I suppose there's no reference from your latest employer to be had?'

Over his shoulder I notice that Nerys is listening avidly, her mouth slightly open, her expression sympathetic. I try not to be distracted.

'There is, yes.' Nigel's a tyrant but he's not evil. 'He said he was happy to provide one in view of the years of good work I'd put in there. He's still on my CV along with my employer before that and a character reference. It's a shame it ended that way, but I had come to realise it wasn't my dream job so I have to see it as an opportunity instead of a disaster.'

'Is this your dream job?'

'Honestly, yes.' I tell him about my strange passion for houses, my fascination with floor plans and architecture and, of course, design. I tell him about haunting the office of Mullins and Meade in London and how they used to joke about employing me.

He smiles.

'But it's more than that,' I go on, encouraged. 'I love meeting people, and I have excellent social skills. I've wanted to buy a house of my own for the longest time and I'd love to help others make it happen. I'm utterly obsessed with what makes a place the right home for someone. I always think of it a bit like falling in love,' I conclude. 'What makes a good match? Will it be love at first sight or a slow burn over time?'

Mr Rowlands smiles. 'That's an excellent way of putting it. We see that exact phenomenon here every week. Some people walk in, their faces light up and boom, true love. Others go back for viewing after viewing – they dither and weigh up pros and cons till the cows come home.'

I nod. 'I can imagine. I think it's... wonderful.'

'Wonderful, eh?' He has a lovely Welsh accent, rich and refined, and a lovely voice too, deep and full of music. 'I happen to think so too. Do you have any questions about the job, Kitty?'

I ask him the usual keen-girl questions about hours and days and duties, and he outlines it thoroughly. The job is for four days a week. They're open seven days, though with shorter hours on a Sunday. I'd be working weekends, but not every one; Roly rotates the weekend cover to make it fair. I tell him it all sounds ideal and ask if he has any more questions for me.

'Just the one, Kitty.' He glances behind him at Nerys, who nods. 'When can you start?'

In the background, Nerys squeals and claps her hands, which gives me a wonderful feeling.

I stare at Mr Rowlands in disbelief. 'Are you serious? I've got the job? Just like that?'

'Why, certainly. I think you're the perfect fit. I'll follow up your references of course, just to be sure you're not a closet lunatic.' He grins. 'But if you're interested, it's yours. Can take that damn notice out of the window then.'

'Oh my God. Amazing. Thank you so much, Mr Rowlands. I'm... thrilled.'

'You'd better call me Roly. Everyone else does. We're very professional here but we're not formal, see?'

'I see. Well, thank you, Roly.' I can't deny it suits him.

'Can you start this Sunday, by any chance?' he asks. 'Nerys and I will both be in to explain matters to you, and we've got

some interesting viewings lined up. It would be a good time for you to start – in at the deep end.'

'I can, yes, absolutely I can.'

'Fantastic. What do you say, Nerys?'

'I say bloody brilliant.' She comes to shake my hand and I thank her too, both of us grinning like idiots. 'Piece of cake now?' she asks.

CHAPTER 10

The two days before Sunday fly by. I call in to see Cherry after the interview, to tell her the outcome. Today she's wearing another Land-Girl-style headscarf, this one lemon yellow with burnt-orange spots.

'Oh my God!' she squawks, pushing an escaped lock of paint-spattered hair back under the bright fabric. 'That means you'll definitely stay the whole six months now. And you'll meet loads of people and be really happy and you might stay for good! Imagine, you get to go into everyone's houses, getting glimpses into their lives. I've always wanted to do that, haven't you? It cries out to my inner nosy-parker.'

I can't help laughing.

I end up staying all afternoon to help her paint – it's a wonderfully companionable thing to do. With music playing, we acquaint each other with all the facts of our lives that we didn't cover yesterday, and when we get hungry we scoff French bread and cheese and olives and chocolate laid out on the coffee table in the kitchen, sitting on the crates. In fact, I'm not sure the last time I can remember having quite as much fun.

I walk to the school with Cherry to meet Magpie, who has

her mother's dark shiny hair and bright blue eyes from, Cherry says, her father's gene pool. Back at the house, we paint for another hour, finishing the dining room, to Cherry's delight, while Magpie perches on a box, eating Wagon Wheels, and tells us a long story about a talking sheep. Then I go home and make ratatouille, smiling to myself. Then I call my big sister.

Sure enough, Cooper is less effusive. I think part of her hoped it wouldn't work out for me here, that I'd go to her and she could take me under her wing again. But she did grudgingly concede that it was a good way to meet people, and a good thing to be earning some money while I'm finding myself.

'And if it doesn't match up to your expectations, you can always give notice. I'm always here for you,' she says.

And for the first time I feel a flicker of irritation, rather than gratitude. I love my sisters, God knows. Cooper especially has always been my rock, something I'll never forget; our friendship runs as deep as an underground stream. But she *does* mother me, and I *am* thirty, and I wish she could just be excited for me without sounding any note of caution that it might not work out. Of course it might not – that's true of anything, for anyone. But I want to *enjoy* this bubble of excitement I feel. Cherry and the job seem *wonderful*, but it's early days yet – too soon for me to trust that things will really all work out. The loss of Mitch, the sense of being an outsider in a strange place, these things still hover at the edges of my mind and it would be all too easy to fall back into low spirits. I don't need my own sister nudging me into them.

When Sunday comes, I don't let any thoughts of failure stand in my way. I wear my favourite brown boots again and a smart skirt and blouse, and I drive down the hill because it's raining and I don't want to arrive on day one looking like a drowned rat. I'm at the office ten minutes early and Roly turns up five minutes after me – by which time I look a bit like a drowned rat. Good intentions and all that.

By the time we've hung up our coats and exclaimed over the weather, Nerys is there. She shows me where the toilet is and the kettle, then starts talking me through the admin systems and the process of selling a house, with Rory interjecting occasionally from his seat at the front of the office. Otherwise he's resumed his oracle-like staring into space. Clearly my new boss is a deep thinker.

'Likes to mull things over,' murmurs Nerys, seeing me look. 'Right, first thing we do every morning is check the diary, get our heads around the day, right?' She flips open a large black hardback diary on her desk. 'We just have one copy obviously, or we'd end up all over the shop, and we keep it on this desk.'

I nod. 'Do you have an online diary too?' That's what we used in my firm in London. They're pretty much par for the course nowadays, though of course when it crashed, it was a disaster.

Nerys wrinkles her nose. 'Roly's old school, prefers paper,' she says, then mouths at me, 'Dinosaur!'

I smile.

'Nothing like seeing it all laid out in front of you,' says Roly serenely. 'Good for the brain.'

Glancing at the page, I see that four appointments have been written in four different handwritings for today, and the first one is in an hour.

'Now, normally, we'd each do different ones, depending on who's in and what else is going on, who's needed where and so on. But today, we'll all go to all of them for you to get the benefit of our combined expertise.' She grins.

'What happens to the office when we're all out?'

'Normally we'd avoid that happening, arrange it so there's always someone here. But sometimes it's not possible, and then we just lock up and put a notice on the door.'

'Sunday tends to be our quietest day for people dropping in,' adds Roly. 'I doubt we'll miss the deal of the century.'

I then carry out my first official duty as an estate agent – making tea for us all.

Back at my desk, Nerys shows me the listings system, how to enter the details of a new property, how to look up a property when someone enquires about it, how the paper filing system works, where everything is duplicated for Roly's benefit.

'Not just mine,' he points out. 'It's also for customers who like to have a paper brochure to take away with them. Houses look more real on paper.'

He stands up and opens the top drawer of the filing cabinet, taking out as many files as he can fit in one meaty hand. He drops them on my desk in front of me.

'Have a read through – you'll get the idea. You'd better familiarise yourself with our stock.'

'What about today's?' I ask. 'Shouldn't I get my head around those first?'

He shakes his head. 'No need. Nerys and I will tell you all you need to know on the way, and you won't have to do any talking while we're there, unless you want to.'

I apply myself to the files. It's surreal. I'm being paid to read about houses!

You might think it would get boring, reading about house after house. It's not even lush descriptions, just the bare facts – bedroom one: 11'3" x 9'8", south-facing aspect, recessed window, plaster ceiling rose, etc, etc. – but for me, it's house porn. In my job in London, I'd dream all day of the moment when I could scarper home via Mullins and Meade to do just this. Now I'm being paid, and I can drink coffee while I do it. This job is too good to be true!

For a moment I hear Cooper's voice – *If something seems too good to be true, it probably is* – but I ignore it. For now, at least, I'm content.

The office falls quiet, Nerys and I busy with our tasks, Roly contemplating life. Occasionally I glance out of the window, but the street is Sunday-morning quiet.

The door opens once, and I sit up to attention to see a man as blade-thin as Roly is large, in a gangster-like pinstripe suit. 'Hullo, Rowlands. Business roaring I see.'

'Hello, Matthew. Sunday morning,' says Roly, unperturbed.

Matthew half-laughs, half-snarls, looking around like a wolf scenting prey. His glinting grey eyes fall on me. 'Ah, new blood,' he observes.

'New member of staff, Matthew, this not being *The Jungle Book*. Kitty Roberts, meet Matthew Granger of Wilton-Granger.' He gestures to the estate agent across the road.

'Nice to meet you,' I say, wondering if I should go and shake hands. But I'm reluctant to go anywhere near his lupine paws.

'Charmed, Kitty, if I may. Bad luck we're fully staffed across the road and you've had to resort to this. If anyone moves on, I'll let you know there's a chance to join the winning team.' He laughs heartily, doing that thing where you mean what you say but you don't want to own it so you pretend it's a joke.

'And there probably will be a vacancy soon,' says Roly, getting up to shake out his coat. 'Staff don't seem to stay very long, do they, Matthew? Well, must be going. Four viewings today. So long now.'

Matthew Granger skulks out and I look at Nerys. 'What was *that*?'

She shrugs. 'Werewolf? Dementor? Evil in human form? No one really knows. I'm kidding. Just a bit of local colour. An occasional feature of the job. He pops in, baits Roly then slinks out again. Thinks he's in the Mafia. Keeps banging on about how Wilton-Granger are way more successful than we are, makes out he's going to sabotage us all the time by poaching our staff or stealing our clients, but it's all hot air.'

'*Are* they more successful?'

'They're bigger. More bells and whistles. But when it comes down to brass tacks – number of clients and turnover and so forth – it's level pegging. Which is downright impressive when you consider they're three times the size of us. People prefer doing business with us, don't they, Roly?'

Roly turns with his serene smile. 'They won't actually let Matthew go to houses. Paula Wilton or one of the others always go. They keep him in the office to do the negotiating because people don't like dealing with him. Here at Rowlands, we find it best not to terrify our clients.'

I laugh. 'He is a bit sinister,' I agree. An estate agent who's not allowed to visit houses – whatever next?

'Come on then, ladies,' says Roly. 'Time to see some houses.'

CHAPTER 11

The first two viewings are within walking distance. Such is the joy of working in a small village. The rain has eased to sparkling spring showers; we march briskly round a few corners and start off at number three, Helena Row.

'The vendor will be there,' Roly explains on the way, 'but she's elderly, and she doesn't like to do the viewings herself. That works better for us. The elderly have a little tendency to moan a bit and point out all the house's flaws, which isn't necessarily the approach we take.' He laughs richly.

'We don't lie,' he goes on hastily. 'We never lie. And if asked a direct question, we answer it. We're not Wilton-Granger. We're all about facilitating the sales that fate wants to happen, not forcing sales that were never meant to be. But we don't consider complaining at length about every disappointment the house has, is, or may ever offer to be an effective sales pitch. Not that Mrs Vincent is a moaner, mind you – she's a lovely woman. I'm just saying, in general it's easier if the vendor lets us do our thing.'

'Facilitating the sales fate wants to happen,' I muse. 'I like that. That's not the reputation estate agents have a lot of the time.'

'No, but that's how I do business. If you want to do the killer-shark thing, Wilton-Granger's the place. If you want to help people through a stressful time, Rowlands it is.'

'The Holmes–Rahe Scale of life stressors lists buying a house as the third-most stressful life event after the death of a loved one or divorce,' Nerys chirps, opening the gate of a mid-terrace house of modest size.

'Nerys is training to be a psychologist,' Roly explains. 'Now keep your eyes open, Kitty. This is a very typical Pennystrand house. You'll find plenty around here just like this.' He rings the doorbell.

The door is answered by a small woman with neatly waved salt-and-pepper hair and glasses. She's wearing a heather-coloured suit and a cream blouse, tights and smart lace-up shoes. 'Hello, Mr Rowlands,' she says cheerily. 'Oh my goodness, you've brought the cavalry! Do come in.'

'Sorry we're rather a horde, Doris. This is Kitty. It's her first day today – we wanted to show her the ropes. And you know Nerys of course.'

'Of course. Hello, Nerys. And hello, Kitty. How are they treating you?'

'Very well thanks, Mrs Vincent. I'm excited about the job.'

'Wonderful! Now, you're not from around here, are you?'

'No I'm not. I've just moved here from London.'

'Oh, I love London. Lived there for many years myself.'

'You did? Whereabouts?'

But before she has time to answer, the doorbell rings again, and she scowls.

'Pesky buyers. I'll be in the sitting room listening to music, Mr Rowlands, and leave you to do your magic.'

'Right ho, Doris!'

The prospective buyers are a young couple – younger than

me. I feel a pang. *How can they afford to be on the housing
ladder already? How did Mitch and I never make it this far?*
Though perhaps it's just as well we didn't, all things considered.
I briefly wonder if Rachel would have happened if we'd moved
to the country, then shake off the gloomy thoughts and follow
the others into the first room off the hall, a small sitting room.
Mrs Vincent is there listening to Brahms on a pastel-pink
Roberts radio.

'Hello there,' she says politely when Roly makes a brief
introduction, but then she averts her head, jaw set.

I narrow my eyes. It must be excruciating having strangers
roaming through your home, debating whether or not it'll suit
their needs. But a sudden intuition tells me it's a little more than
that with Mrs Vincent. I think she doesn't want to sell at all. In
which case, I wonder why she is. She looks perfectly healthy
and didn't have any trouble walking, so it can't be that she can't
manage the stairs or anything like that. I hope she doesn't have
know-it-all children badgering her to sell. I know a thing or two
about bossy relatives who think they know what's best for you.

We don't linger long in that room. We all file out into the
hall and, the last in the line, I close the door behind me. Mrs
Vincent catches my eye and smiles.

The young couple are full of beans, delighted with everything they see, from the bay window in the large lounge, to the
startlingly fashionable wallpaper in the halls, to the dining room
that looks out into the garden, where a birdfeeder positively
bustles with chaffinches, blue tits and a thrush. The kitchen is
immense, and beyond it is a downstairs loo and a utility room.
Goodness, this place is like the TARDIS! It looked so compact
from the street. Roly explains that most of the houses along here
have been extended into the long gardens; they go on and on.

A break in the showers gives us the chance to inspect the
garden, which draws forth more squeals of delight from young Mrs

Samson, then we go back inside. I listen carefully to everything Roly and Nerys say about the age of the house, the window latches and which rooms catch the sun, so that I'll be able to answer the same questions one day. I try not to be distracted by the framed photographs on the piano, of a much younger Doris Vincent with a jaw-droppingly handsome man, or by the collage of beach photos on one wall: draggle-haired kids eating ice cream; Mrs Vincent in a swimsuit brandishing a spade; the gorgeous man buried up to his neck in sand. This was a family home. Is she all alone in it now?

Upstairs are three bedrooms and a giant bathroom. And upstairs again is a loft conversion, with a sizeable hall cupboard as well.

'There's *tons* of space!' shrieks the young woman.

Her husband, trying and failing to play it cool, nods quietly. I can see the gleam in his eyes as he gazes around the attic room, imagining a man cave or a gaming room or a recording studio, depending on his inclinations.

After a decent length of time peering out of the windows, one at either end of the loft, and exclaiming over the views of the sea and the town, Roly asks if they want to look around again.

They don't. They've seen enough, they tell us. 'And we're not likely to forget a single detail,' gushes Mrs Samson. 'We love it – really. We've just got to sell our house now.'

'Of course,' says Roly smoothly. 'And is it on the market yet?'

'Yes, we put it on last week with Wilton-Granger,' says the young man.

'Excellent, then I wish you luck with your sale, and do get in touch if you'd like to arrange another viewing.'

I watch him closely. Not a trace of chagrin on his face that they've appointed his ghastly rivals, not a whisker of exasperation that it could be months or years before they'll be in a position to buy. He's certainly different from the London estate agents I've met.

We all troop downstairs, see the Samsons out, then let Mrs Vincent know that we're off. Immediately she's sociable and friendly. 'And how was that?' she wants to know.

'They absolutely loved it, but they've got a house to sell. Not proceedable at the moment, I'm afraid, Doris.'

'Well, there's a shame,' she says, sounding anything but disappointed.

Again I catch her eye as if in some sort of understanding. I wait a beat before following Roly and Nerys outside. 'They only put their house on the market last week,' I whisper.

Mrs Vincent smiles broadly. 'Good girl,' she says. 'That's good.'

CHAPTER 12

The next house is seven houses further down the same road. Its exterior and layout are identical to number three, but it feels completely different. It's empty, the owners long gone, thick dust everywhere. There's an atmosphere of neglect, and the air smells damp.

'The owners died and left it to their only son,' Roly explains. 'He's in Dubai and did nothing with it, thinking he might want to move back here one day. Years later he's decided to sell.'

'His parents didn't really look after it before that,' adds Nerys, 'so it's not looking lovely. It was on the market with the other lot for two years and the vendor swapped it over to us last month. We have to sell it so we can laugh at them.'

'And so the poor house can be loved again,' I muse.

Nerys pats me on the shoulder. 'You are an old softie, aren't you?'

The viewer is quickly shown around. 'Too much work. Bloody depressing,' he mutters as he hurries off. We lock it up with a fatalistic air.

Because we have a few minutes to spare, Nerys decides now

is a good time to explain the car system to me. 'We have two company cars, Scarlett and Saffron,' she begins, as if the cars are receptionists or typists. 'We always park them on one of four streets, space allowing, and the idea is that we always leave a note in the office saying where they are. In practice it doesn't always happen and we end up wandering round quite a bit looking for them – you need to factor that into your timing when you go out on viewings. Of course we all have each other's numbers – I'll give them to you before we go home – but people can't always text back right away. So you need to know the places they're likely to be. Shall I show her now, Roly? We don't need to go just yet.'

'I'll make a phone call. I'll wait here.'

Nerys tows me around the backstreets, explaining the pitfalls of residents-only parking and time restrictions.

'Ah! There's Scarlett!' she exclaims delightedly, as if the tiny red Suzuki is an old friend. 'I *forgot* where I left her yesterday – my bad. Now I remember. Now, we sometimes park here, or here...'

I hope I remember all this.

'We have two sets of keys to each car too, in case someone takes the keys home by accident... That's usually me too,' she confesses. 'You'll find the hardest part of this job is finding the cars. And here's Saffron.'

Saffron is a mustard-yellow Nissan estate wearing more than a smattering of mud.

'We'll take Saffron today because Scarlett's a bit small for Roly.'

We hop in, Nerys adjusts her seat and mirrors then we drive back to where we left Roly. I'm about to get out to let Roly sit in the front, but he waves me back and clambers into the rear.

'If you could just pull your seat forward a little bit, Kitty? Grand, thank you.'

We head out to the countryside, Nerys whizzing along the narrow, winding road across the Burrows as only someone who does this drive many times a week could. I should probably be full of questions, but I'm stunned by the views. With every hill and bend of the road a new vista unfolds: a field of sleek chestnut horses, pretty woodland copses, old stone walls, white-washed and weather-worn. I want to file them in some sort of mental art gallery.

The next house is called The Chantry. It's an old chapel on a lonely stretch of moorland, and I'm enraptured. Originally a medieval chapel, it was dedicated to the memory of the Horton family, the local aristocrats back in the day. The original chapel was destroyed somewhere along a timeline of battles and skirmishes for land rights, but in the sixteenth century, a new chapel was built on the same spot, in memory of the original chantry. I'm fascinated by this chain of memory, stretching back into the past and still here today.

Roly tells me that the chapel hasn't been used for worship since the nineteenth century. It's been converted and extended to within an inch of its life, but the bell tower remains (*sans* bell) as do a trio of arched windows and a gallery landing. The stained-glass in the landing window is definitely not original but it's beautiful, depicting a fox's head against a sunset. It looks out over miles of bracken and sepia countryside, dotted with grazing sheep. In the far distance you can see the sea, a silver rim along the horizon.

I'm besotted. This is it – The One – the house I would live in if all the money in the world was mine.

'You'll think that about at least twenty others,' says Nerys. 'I was like that at first – falling in love with every which one – but there are so many gorgeous onès, and they're all completely different. You become a bit of a house whore.'

'Can we not talk about whores in front of the clients please?' Roly suggests mildly, but the viewers, a highly groomed pair of Londoners, are out of earshot, debating whether it would be possible to tear down the country-style kitchen with its flags and Aga and build 'a proper one' and whether there's scope to add a sun lounge... I want to cover my eyes with horror.

The garden is astonishing, full of secret corners, glossy shrubs and rambling climbers not yet bearing their blooms. It's just as well Roly doesn't expect my input today – I'm slack-jawed and stupid with awe.

'This is the best bit!' exclaims Nerys, leading us to some mossy stones in a circle, with a small stone pillar on one side that leads nowhere.

'What is it?' I breathe, enraptured.

'What is it?' demands the man-viewer in an entirely different tone.

'It's the only remaining bit of the original medieval chapel,' says Roly. 'It was a holy well. There used to be a stream leading into the grounds, and the well was built to collect the water, which was considered sacred – a belief that was a throwback to an even earlier Pagan community who worshipped up on the hill there. Archaeologists came to verify it in the early 1920s. So whoever buys The Chantry will become the custodian of a living piece of history. It's thought the stream still flows deep, deep underground, bringing good fortune to anyone who visits it. Some say it can even grant wishes.'

He smiles genially to suggest that he's a sensible, professional man who doesn't necessarily believe in magic waters, but Nerys and I stand bug-eyed and spellbound.

Mr Porter peers into the mossy dip and frowns. 'Isn't it a bit of a hazard? You could stumble in there and break an ankle.'

'Perhaps you'd walk around it,' suggests Roly in the same even tone.

My eyes widen and I suppress a smile. Roly's very calm and easy, but he's no pushover.

Mr Porter frowns. 'But if you were drunk? If you had a party.'

I close my eyes at the thought of a bunch of drunken Hooray Henrys trampling all over this special garden.

'It's a shame the other pillar's gone,' complains Mrs Porter. 'It looks very... broken.'

That would be the ancient-history thing. No one says it, but I know all three of us are thinking it. Roly's face maintains an expression of polite interest, which I try to emulate.

'Perhaps we could build another pillar on the other side and add a roof,' she goes on. 'Pop a garden gnome on the wall – that might be cute.'

'Do you think?' Mr Porter looks doubtful. 'It might brighten it up a bit. Damned inconvenience if you ask me. Wouldn't mind filling it in – and a bit of AstroTurf wouldn't go amiss – but I suppose there's a preservation order on it or something like that?'

Roly agrees that there is while I clutch Nerys's arm in terror.

'I don't like not being able to do as I like with my own property. Then again, it's light and airy and there's plenty of space. It's a remote position, we could have a glass wall or two...'

'But is it *too* lonely?' frets his wife. 'It's very isolated, Gavin.'

'I'm sorry to hurry you,' says Roly. 'But we've had to book two appointments very close together this afternoon and we need to be on our way. Obviously we're delighted to arrange another viewing for you if you want a second look.'

Nerys opens her mouth with a frown then closes it again. I'm sure they told me the next viewing was an hour after this one.

Soon, we're all climbing back into Saffron, while the Porters roar off in their silver Mercedes.

As Nerys turns the key in the ignition, she looks back at Roly questioningly.

'I wouldn't sell it to them if they offered,' says Roly.

Nerys nods and drives off.

On we go to the coast, to a little village that's clearly geared up for the tourist season, with a concrete seafront, a little band-stand, mock-Victorian lamp posts, a car park and two beach kiosks. Only one is open since it's not high season.

We park in the car park and clamber out, stretching, grin-ning and breathing the sea air deeply, as if it had been a much longer drive.

'Would you really not sell it to them if they wanted it?' I ask, still preoccupied by The Chantry. 'Wouldn't you sort of have to, if the owner wanted to?'

'Technically yes, but I'd strongly advise him against it. The owner's an artist. Moved to Colombia now – tired of the climate – but I'm sure his artist's soul wouldn't allow that wonderful place to fall into the hands of someone who wants to cover the medieval well above the sacred stream with AstroTurf, for God's sake! Some people have no sense of soul.'

'I actually want to hug you now,' I say, then clap my hand over my mouth. 'God, sorry, I just meant, I'm glad it's not just me... that place is so special.'

Roly turns his considering gaze on me. 'It is. I know for most in our industry it's just about making the sale and getting the commission and on to the next, but as I said, that's a living piece of history passing through our hands. How can I not feel a sense of responsibility towards it?'

'Hence beating a hasty retreat,' Nerys adds. 'You know we're here half an hour early now?'

'Yes. Get your coats, ladies. It's brisk out.'

We follow Roly to a bench on the front, facing the sea. He wipes off the rain spatters with a scarf then heads to the open kiosk, reappearing two minutes later with three ice-cream cones and three cans of Coke.

'Sugar hit to see us through the afternoon,' he says, handing them round.

I haven't drunk Coke for about ten years but here, with the cold April winds nipping at us wickedly, the briny air and the waves churning and hissing – the sound of infinity – nothing could taste better.

'And this is why we love him,' declares Nerys, 'and why we will never ever leave to go and work across the road.'

CHAPTER 13

I'm working the next day too and I'm there bright and early. 'Keeny McKeeny,' as Roly observes approvingly. He's in before me today. Truth to tell, I couldn't wait to get here.

I finished my first day so full to the brim with new impressions I didn't even visit Cherry to tell her about it. I didn't phone Cooper or email Mum until much later in the evening. I just wanted to sit quietly and let it all settle. I sat on the sofa with my hands wrapped around a large mug of herbal tea and stared into space for a while, just feeling my feelings, which, for the first time in a really long time were... *happy*. Not just OK but actually happy. Even sort of... euphoric. What a day! Work was never like this in London.

The last property of the day was an Enid Blyton-esque house with a long lawn sloping towards the sea. I immediately thought of tea on the lawn – struck by a vivid mental image of a table laid with china, wildflowers in a glass jar and a pile of golden scones. I could imagine children romping about wearing short trousers and striped pullovers, shouting things like, 'I say, Jimmy, come and see this spiffing toadstool!' Sadly, it's only a holiday home, empty much of the time; what a waste. I immediately fell in love and started to understand what Nerys meant about becoming a house whore.

Today Nerys isn't working, but Bella is, a larger lady in her late fifties with a brisk manner and cool purple-rimmed glasses that make her look like a secretary from an old sixties movie. She knows her beans, Roly tells me.

Roly's in and out most of the day with a steady succession of viewings and valuations. Bella and I stay in the office, where she teaches me the process of taking on a house, of seeing a sale through, of handling people who pull out just minutes before they're due to exchange contracts. I listen to her when she's on the phone and learn as much by observing as I do from her explanations. I also realise how much I already know from my hours hanging out in Mullins and Meade.

Several times the phone rings when Bella's on another call and she nods at me to pick up. I'm a bit nervous and fully prepared to admit to being a newbie and put them on hold until Bella's free. I do say it once or twice, but I'm surprised how many queries I can already deal with.

When I'm asked something like the price of the house in Drover's Lane, I simply look it up on the system and answer. When someone says they'd like to view the house in Hampton Walk, I look up the viewing arrangements, grab the diary and sort it out. When someone wants to know the last time we spoke to their solicitor, I can either find a note on the file telling me, or I say that I'm not dealing with that sale and that I'll ask my colleague to call them back. Bella doesn't say much when I pass on messages to her, but I like to imagine that she's quietly impressed.

What does hold me back is my lack of local knowledge. It's amazing to me how often people identify a house by surrounding landmarks rather than by the actual address. 'The

white house on the beach,' they say. Which beach? If we
manage to establish that, I'm still flummoxed; houses are filed
alphabetically by house name or street name, not by nearby-
beach name. Or I hear, 'You know, the flat over the shop that
used to be Carlton's before Bob died!' I have to confess that I
have no idea where Carlton's was or who Bob was and then
they sound very irritated. Or else, 'That lane. You know, the one
off that other one. With the bend. And the big tree.'

'Don't worry – it'll come,' says Roly on one of his pit stops
for tea and biscuits and to catch up on developments. He
rummages in his desk and hands me a paper map. I shall spend
every spare moment scrutinising it. 'If local knowledge was the
most important thing, I wouldn't have hired you; I'd have hired
Debbie Demerara.'

Bella snorts into her coffee. 'She's a local busybody,' she
explains. 'Knows all the gossip, true or completely made-up.
She's lived here all her life, never even been to Spain on holiday,
but thinks she knows *everything*, her erudite source being Face-
book. I nearly died when she applied for the job.'

'Demerara?' I wonder. 'Is that really her surname?'

Roly laughs. 'No. Davies it is. But she'll only eat demerara
sugar. Won't have any other type. Makes a huge fuss if she's
eating out and there's no demerara. The cafés round here keep a
stash now, just in case she comes in.'

'Good grief.' This is a level of idiosyncrasy I've never
encountered before.

'So you see, dear Kitty, you could be worse!' cries Roly,
downing his tea, blowing us a kiss and hurrying out.

We don't see him again until just before 5.30 p.m., which is
when we close. He blows in with a red shiny face and an air of
great excitement.

'Didn't expect to see you again today,' says Bella, gathering her things together. 'Is everything alright?'

'*Very* alright. Ladies, listen to this! I've just taken on a new house in *Fortescue Crescent*!'

Bella drops her notebook. '*No!*'

The name, of course, means nothing to me.

'And guess whose house it is?'

There's no point me even trying to answer that, but Bella mulls it over. 'Dan Taylor's?'

'No.'

'Wait, don't tell me. Oh, I know, that barrister, Whatsis-name? Who had the affair with that acupuncturist and then turned out to be gay?'

'Nope!'

'Not the big blue one with that family with the dogs?'

'No.'

I'm getting a little frustrated now. Seeing as I don't know anyone anyway, I'm unlikely to be wowed by the news, though Bella is fizzing. Clearly Fortescue Crescent is the big cheese of property around here.

'Lisa Parnell!' announces Roly triumphantly. He actually flourishes his hands, like a showman.

Bella's jaw drops. 'No.'

'Yes.'

'*No.*'

I have a feeling they could go on like this for a while. 'Who's Lisa Parnell?'

'Only the richest woman in Pennystrand,' says Bella. 'The richest and the proudest. Who would *never* sell a house in Fortescue Crescent.'

'Yet who is, nevertheless,' insists Roly. 'The Parnells are a huge local family, Kitty. I'm surprised you haven't heard of them already seeing as you've been in town more than, oh, three minutes! They go back a long way – I think the first Parnells were here in the 1700s.'

'You *know* they were,' Bella puts in, 'seeing as one of them will bring it up every five minutes.'

'Well, yes. That's true. They're very wealthy – even the younger generations, who don't seem to do much if I'm honest, don't really have to worry about money because they know they'll inherit.'

'Oh to be a Parnell,' sighs Bella.

'Bella's thinking about retirement.' Roly cocks his head at her. 'I pay her a pittance so she can't afford to. Don't want to lose her. Anyway, the Parnells have fingers in all the pies, and Lisa is the matriarch, I suppose you could say. In her sixties, but doesn't look it. Terribly glamorous and a bit scary, if I'm being totally honest. She's married but she's kept her maiden name of course. Fortescue Crescent is the absolute gold nugget of real estate around here. It's up on the cliff overlooking Brightman Bay. We call it Fortune Crescent in the biz. Houses literally never come up for sale.'

'Wow,' I say.

'Indeed. I'll take you there tomorrow. I need to finish measuring up, and we all need to be able to talk about it knowledgeably. This is serious business.'

'Why didn't you say anything?' asks Bella. 'I didn't even know you had an appointment there.'

'Didn't think it would come to anything, did I? Lisa called my mobile and asked me to pop up this afternoon. I never dreamed... I thought maybe she'd be thinking of selling one of her other houses.'

How many has she got? I wonder.

'But her mind was made up. She *said* it's too much work keeping it up and she'd like to downsize now she's getting older.' He frowns. 'Which is a bit strange because she looks about forty and she's got the energy of a tornado! She could beat me in the gym any day.'

Bella rolls her eyes. 'Roly, *I* could beat you in the gym.'

'Well, there it is. I'm just thanking God that she wanted to list it with us, not the other lot. It's going on the market at the end of the week.'

CHAPTER 14

The next morning at nine, I meet Roly at the house on Fortescue Crescent. It's number nineteen, an enormous white mansion with a fairly normal-looking – if huge – front aspect but with soaring wings beyond, dotted with balconies and skylights and that's just what I can see from the street! I feel as if I'm about to meet a member of the royal family.

We don't say much besides the usual good-morning greetings, but as we wait on the doorstep, Roly smiles at me. 'The Parnells can be a bit much sometimes,' he warns me. 'Just be calm, and be your lovely self.'

'Thanks, Roly.'

In the event, I only meet one Parnell today – Lisa – but she is plenty. She's absolutely gorgeous, with gleaming shoulder-length conker-brown hair glinting with expensive honeyed highlights. She has wide grey eyes and elegant bone structure, the sort of timeless beauty you might see on the cover of *Vogue* or in an old Grace Kelly film.

She regards me with dismay.

'Roly, good morning. Who's this?'

'Good morning, Lisa, lovely to see you again. This is Kitty

Roberts, the newest member of our team. She's getting to know all our properties, and I wanted her to see this one with me.'

'I'm not sure about that,' she says crisply, her slender, gym-toned figure actually barring our entry. 'I want you to handle it, Roly, not some neophyte. Is there really any need...?'

I can't help but bristle, but I endeavour to smile that polite, remote smile that Roly favours, as if it's all the same to me either way.

'I'm happy to handle all the viewings myself, Lisa, if that's what you prefer, barring acts of God of course. But this is a lot of property and we absolutely cannot undersell it. Every single member of my team needs to be able to speak about it knowledgeably and with passion on the phone, which means they all need to see it. If I'm out of town or laid up for some unspeakable reason, we can't put the whole thing on hold. You said you want to sell quickly. I don't see a problem there – to be honest I think it will be snapped up – but that does mean it has to be a team effort. That's how I do business.'

She curls her lip. 'I see. Well, I suppose you'd better come in. And with... the *whole team*' – she pronounces it gingerly as if it's a venereal disease – 'being involved, can we rely on... discretion?'

Roly pats her arm – brave man. 'Lisa, you know as well as I do that when this goes on the market, everyone in town will be talking about it. Ravening wolves will fall upon it, my dear, and the discretion of my team will be the least of your worries. But you have my absolute assurance regarding Kitty and the others. Each of them works with as much integrity and confidentiality as I do. I wouldn't have employed them otherwise.'

She sighs and favours me with a slight nod. 'Very well.'

I decide this is a good moment to say something. 'Morning, Ms Parnell. It's lovely to meet you.'

She twitches slightly, as if a fly has landed on her.

'Lisa, I must ask, are you sure you want to sell?' asks Roly. 'I know this is your family home and it's always meant a lot to you. Come Friday you won't have a moment's peace in the village. Do you want to reconsider or at least take more time to think about it?'

'Thank you, Roly, it's kind of you to offer, given the money this sale will make you. No, I don't need more time. Let's make a start.'

She stalks ahead of us, though I'm unsure if stalk is the right word; it sounds a little stiff. Lisa has a sinuous quality to her movements, like a panther. Panthers stalk, right? Well then, she stalks like a panther. I'm struck fairly dumb by the opulence of this magnificent home – and I saw a fair few wealthy homes in London, working for Nigel.

The hall is a sweeping expanse that takes my breath away. I try not to gawp too openly, but it's hard not to feast my eyes on the colonnaded gallery landing above, the sections of ceiling made of glass, the flagstone floor peppered with paprika-coloured rugs. I can tell just from how they feel under my shoes that they're silky and fine and expensive. Ornamental pedestals bear huge spillages of red geraniums in sparkling bowls, and the mirror on the wall is the size of a small swimming pool. Whatever I may think of Lisa, I can't deny that her taste is exquisite. Oh, and that chandelier... I drink in the sparkling crystals, the graceful swoop of chains from arm to arm. It's a good thing that Roly's keeping Lisa busy with questions and comments. He has his clipboard and his bleepy thing that he uses to measure the rooms, and he's all business.

'When you're speaking to people about this house, Kitty, you might want to mention the hall. Some people might be put off by such a large expanse that's not actually used as a living space. Tell them that when they see it, they'll think it's a highlight but that it merely sets the scene for the rest of the house.'

I nod in what I hope is an intelligent fashion.

We go on to see three different living rooms, which Lisa

calls the lounge, the formal lounge and the snug. Each is more impossibly beautiful than the last. It's possible of course that Lisa Parnell hired a designer to kit out her fabulous home, but instinct tells me she did it herself. Its lavishness does nothing to detract from the obvious love with which it's been furnished. Why on earth is she selling it? Of course, it must cost an absolute fortune to maintain, but from what I've heard, that's unlikely to be the reason.

We move into the kitchen and I can't stop myself from exclaiming. It's almost as big as the hall, with floor-to-ceiling glass in the back wall which means that all you can see beyond the garden is the Atlantic Ocean and the sky. In the centre of the floor stands a granite island the size of a... well, island. One corner hosts an informal seating area with three comfy-looking armchairs around a coffee table. In contrast to this cosy, inviting nook, on the opposite wall is a breakfast bar with chic chrome stools and a variety of scary-looking coffee machines and juicers. There's also an *actual* bar, complete with optics. I note at least a dozen spirits, cocktail shakers and a mass of glinting cut crystal. A luxury hotel in Mayfair would not come better equipped.

Lisa looks at me when I squawk. 'Pardon me. It's just so beautiful. Unbelievably beautiful. Such a wonderful home, Ms Parnell. Could I ask, did you design it yourself?'

She frowns as if I might have an ulterior motive for asking. 'Yes. Why?'

'I thought so. It's immaculate yet homely. It looks as if it's been decorated with love as well as professionalism. I used to work for an interior designer in London, so I notice these things.'

She looks at me for a long time, her face inscrutable. I find it hard to believe what Roly said – that she's in her sixties – but then again there's always Botox. Or maybe yoga and clean living.

Lisa looks longingly at the bar. 'I suppose 9.15 is too early for a gin?' *Maybe not clean living.*

'None for me thanks, Lisa,' says Roly in a jovial tone that works whether or not she was joking.

She walks off. I glance anxiously at Roly, who shrugs and follows.

She glides up the sweeping staircase, and we trail after her along a landing with Italianate frescos, into one bedroom after another; I lose count but Roly's still scribbling away. There are sea views and balconies and rocking chairs and window seats and places where traditional Edwardian architecture yields seamlessly to cutting-edge modern design. Most houses look like a mash-up when they're altered too radically, but here, it's perfect. The newer wing of the house looks like a ship's sail, white and sharp and beautiful in a completely different way. I don't hazard any more comments or questions. I can't figure out Lisa Parnell, and I don't want to get it wrong.

I never thought I would have my fill of gawping at other people's houses, but by the time I've seen the whole place, I'm chock-full of sensory impressions and quite relieved to be going. This must be the ultimate house in the world.

We bid Lisa goodbye on the doorstep, and Roly checks again that she wants it to go on the market on Friday.

'Yes,' she says, sounding bitter. 'And may the hordes descend.'

'Descend they will,' he says, sounding concerned. 'I know it's a difficult time but please be reassured that we at Rowlands will do all we can to make the process as painless as possible for you. You said you don't want to do the viewings yourself?' he recaps.

She shudders. 'Definitely not!'

'So I'll do them myself – but if there *is* an emergency that prevents me, please remember I have complete faith in my team. Do you want to be here when the viewings take place or would you like us to try to schedule them for times that you're out?'

'I hadn't thought of that. My schedule is very... ad hoc. I'd rather not be here, to be honest. Could you let me know so that I can just take myself out at those times?'

'Absolutely. Nothing easier.' He makes another note.

'And you will... keep a close eye on the viewers, won't you, Mr Rowlands? I don't mean to sound like a paranoid rich bitch...' She glares at me as if I might be thinking just that. 'But people are... what they are, and there's a lot of temptation here.'

'I totally understand, and yes, of course we will. Usually, after showing someone around, we ask if they'd like to look around on their own, to form their own impressions with a bit of privacy. But we won't do that here – we'll stick to them like glue. There'd be no point anyway – it's pretty obvious what everyone's impressions will be. Right, Kitty?'

'Absolutely. No one could fail to fall in love with it. And please don't worry, Ms Parnell – as Roly says, the whole team will handle this sale with the utmost respect.'

'I'll be hearing from you then.' And she closes the door behind us.

Roly and I walk to his car at the end of the road before we say anything.

'I'm glad you were there,' he says, 'so you could see for yourself why we'll need to handle every call with kid gloves. You can tell the others, back me up. I'm sorry if you felt she was a little... prickly with you.'

'I didn't take it personally. It's obvious she'd have been like that with anyone who wasn't you.'

'Yes, that's it. When people are doing something really difficult, it makes them feel reassured to have the boss on the case.'

The wind whips my scarf up out of the collar of my coat

and plasters it across my face. I pick it off and stuff it back into place. 'I feel a bit sorry for her actually. I know it's none of our business why she's selling, but I can't help but wonder. I feel like we're forcing a young girl to give her baby up for adoption.'

Roly nods, gazing over my head in that characteristic way he has.

'That's a brilliant way of putting it,' he says at last. 'I have the same feeling. Poor Lisa. But she *is* a difficult woman, Kitty – don't forget that. We'll all have to do our utmost not to give her any grounds for complaint.'

He gives himself a little shake. 'Rather takes the gloss off such an exciting sale, doesn't it, knowing she's unhappy to sell? Lift?'

'Yes please.'

We climb into the car and I look back at the house. I don't think Lisa's *only* unhappy about the house. I think she's an unhappy woman in general. I wonder why.

CHAPTER 15

When we get back to the office, Roly fills in Nerys and Bella on everything they need to know and decides to take the next day off work. 'May as well take the chance before the Parnell house goes live,' he says. 'I doubt I'll have a day off for a while after that. I'll leave the details for you to type up, Kitty.' Then he spends most of the day writing up his notes.

And I spend most of the next day typing them up – not an easy task since Roly's handwriting is a cross between slug trails and Viking runes. Several times I pause in confusion before realising that the door does not have an orchestra, as it appears, but an architrave, that the kitchen is south-facing, rather than somnolent.

Today I'm working with the last member of the team, Derrick, who's full-time but has been on holiday. He's twenty-five but looks much younger, despite his stiffly gelled hair, sharp suit and expensive aftershave. He's skinny, rambunctious and jokey. Roly asked me to pass on the information about the Parnell house and I feel anxious that Derrick may laugh at me for explaining so earnestly. But he listens and nods, adjusting his silky purple tie. 'Loud and clear, Kitty, loud and clear,' he says.

As the day goes on and I hear how he handles the calls that come in, I start to see why he's part of Roly's team. His humour is relentless with me, and with his friends, who call in to see how he enjoyed Ibiza. But with customers, he pulls it out only when it's needed, to defuse an awkward moment or charm a huffy vendor.

I'm glad of it when the vendor of a house I haven't seen yet stomps in and demands to know why we haven't had any viewings for a month. Derrick's on the phone and I explain that I don't know, I'm new. 'If you wait for my colleague to finish his call, I'm sure he'll know more,' I suggest winningly. 'Take a seat. Would you like a cup of tea?'

'No, I haven't got all day! I just want a straight answer to a straight question. And was it one of you lot who's knocked over the pots in the shed? And why did Roland Rowlands put it on at this price if it's not going to attract any interest? And what's the new strategy seeing as this one's clearly not working?'

I start to feel flustered and again say that Derrick will be with him in a moment.

'I don't want to take advice from a twelve-year-old,' he says, looking dismissively in Derrick's direction. 'This is useless. I've a mind to take my business to that Wilton-Granger lot. That Matthew seems a sound fellow.'

But just then Derrick comes off the phone.

'Derrick Mitchell – pleased to meet you,' he says, smoothly shaking hands and waving the disgruntled vendor to a seat. 'We won't keep you a moment, but I overheard a bit of what you were saying. We need to get you some viewings, don't we? This market, eh? But don't worry, we're already looking at plan B. We can look at pricing, put it back in the window, offer free beer to anyone who goes to see it...'

He goes on in this vein, not letting the vendor get a word in edgeways until he's mollified, then waves him off with a joke about rugby that goes completely over my head.

'Bye now,' calls Derrick with a gleaming smile, shutting the door carefully behind him. 'Tosser,' he adds, going back to his seat.

'Impressive!' I say. 'Thank you, I was completely thrown.'

'It's my skill. You were fine – he's just a tosser, like I said. You'll always get a few.'

Towards the end of the day someone phones wanting to see number three, Helena Row. The last few days have been so full that for a moment I can't think which one that is but quickly remember. It's Mrs Vincent's house, the first I visited.

The prospective viewer is in a hurry. 'What about today?'

I glance at my screen. It's four o'clock. 'It's short notice – the vendor's at home – but I'll certainly ask. Are you alright to hold for a moment?'

I turn to Derrick, who's one step ahead of me, reaching for the phone. I'm touched by how lovely he is with Mrs Vincent, enquiring after her cat – I hadn't noticed a cat – and whether the lilacs are out yet in the garden.

'Mrs V, we've got someone on the other line who wants to view the property today. If it's too short notice, just say so and we'll put him off till another day. Yes? Kitty? Yes, she's very nice. Well, I've only worked with her for one day – I've yet to discover if she has any dark ways. Hang on, Mrs V, I'll ask her.'

He puts her on hold. 'She says today's OK and would you be willing to do it?'

'Me? But I'm not a proper estate agent!'

'Yes you are. You work here, you know the drill, you've seen the house. She's asked for you. We could say five o'clock and you could go home from there.'

'Erm, OK.'

I go back to the man on the phone, Derrick confirms it with Mrs Vincent and we're all set.

. . .

At ten to five I walk round the corner so I can say hello to Mrs Vincent before the viewer arrives. The viewing is quickly conducted; after all his impatience, the viewer, Ken, doesn't seem to take a great deal of interest. I'm practically sprinting as I follow him from room to room.

He leaves ten minutes later saying he found it 'a bit underwhelming'.

'I completely understand,' I say. 'Do keep an eye on our listings – we have new properties coming on all the time.' As much as I'd have liked good news for Roly, I'm thrilled on behalf of Mrs Vincent.

When I go to tell her we're all finished and that he wasn't interested, she beams. 'That's good, dear. Now, do you have to hurry or can you stay for a cup of tea?'

'Oh!' What's the etiquette here? I know that people in offices aren't supposed to accept gifts that could be seen as backhanders, but I don't think a cup of tea is the language of bribery. 'Yes, if you're quite sure it's no trouble.'

'None at all! It's why I asked for you. I wanted to have a little chat.'

CHAPTER 16

Number three, Helena Row has a beautiful sitting room. French windows stand ajar, looking out over the garden. The foot of the lilac tree is awash with crocuses in the colours of Cadbury's Creme Egg wrappers. Above their confectionary brightness, lilacs form a white haze like summer clouds.

'What a lovely home you have, Mrs Vincent,' I tell her as she reappears, carrying a tray laden the old-fashioned way: a teapot wearing a brown-and-yellow knitted cosy, clinking cups and saucers, gleaming silver spoons, a sugar basin and a plate piled high with biscuits. 'Are you... are you quite happy about selling it?'

She smiles and sets the tray down. 'Thank you. I've had a lovely life in fact. And the answer to your question is yes...'

She hesitates and I decide I can't push her, even though that's not the impression I've had.

'Of course it's sad to leave somewhere one's been happy, but I'm at a choice point in my life. They come every so often and you have to rise to the challenge.'

'They certainly do,' I say with feeling. 'And... excuse me if this sounds intrusive... it is *your* choice?'

'Oh certainly, yes. I'm not being forced into this by well-meaning children if that's what you're wondering. It's just the timing, you see, that's tricky. I need a little more time.'

'For what?'

'I need to find some lost treasure.'

I have a record-scratch moment. *What?* Is this elegant, intelligent woman in the early stages of dementia? Is that why she's selling? But she looks at me shrewdly and chuckles into her teacup.

'There, that got your attention. I can't resist a dramatic opening. You probably think I've lost my marbles now, but it's true, and I need your help, Kitty.'

She takes a silver-framed black-and-white photo from the dresser and hands it to me before sitting down.

It's a wedding photograph. I can immediately see that she is the pretty blond bride in the picture and the groom is the dark-haired heart-throb I've seen in other pictures.

'It's beautiful. You look radiant. And your husband is very handsome.'

'He was a dish. He should have been a rogue, with a face like that, but he was one of the good ones.'

She sighs again and we contemplate the glamorous, smiling couple in the photo in silence for a moment. I can't help glancing at her and comparing the two. Obviously, fifty years on, she looks very different, but it's the similarities that interest me. Her bright eyes, gracious bearing and enviable bone structure are still there. And she still has a sense of style. Her wedding dress is timeless – a fitted lace bodice with a collar that's high at the back and low at the front, like a fairy-tale queen. Adorning her décolletage is a beautiful necklace: a double rope of pearls with an embellishment front and centre in what could be crystal or glass.

I squint at it. 'Is that a Claddagh?' I ask. It looks elaborate, like the Irish symbol for love and loyalty.

She shakes her head. 'It's a Celtic love knot. Those are diamonds.'

'Wow. And are the pearls real too?'

'Yes. It was my wedding day gift from Lawrence. It cost a ridiculous fortune. He wasn't given to lavish gestures and expensive presents, thank goodness, but on this one special occasion he said he wanted to take my breath away. He said that we didn't know what was ahead of us on life's road, that we might be rich or poor, most likely a bit of both at different times, but that he wanted me to have one tangible object that represented the magnitude of the step we were taking that day, and the unchanging fortune that was our love.'

'Wow,' I breathe again. 'What a treasure to have.'

'Quite. And now it's lost.'

'Oh no!'

'To be precise, it's not lost, it's hidden. And I want you to help me find it before I move. Biscuit?'

I reach for one in something of a daze. *I wasn't expecting a mission like this.*

'Let me explain properly. I've known for a long time where I want to go when I leave here. There's a retirement village where my two best friends live and it has everything – beautiful gardens, lovely rooms, a great community. We'd be like *The Thursday Murder Club*, the three of us. But places don't come up very often. One became available last month and I jumped at it. It was three years since the last one, and who knows what havoc three years can wreak at my age? I didn't want to miss my chance and end up in some godawful place away from Minnie and Laura. It's a bit sooner than I'd expected, but that's alright except for this one thing: my necklace.'

'How did it go missing in the first place?'

She sighs. 'It's a bit of a tale, Kitty. As I said, I've had a lovely life. Lawrence and I had a wonderful marriage. He died five years ago and you can imagine how I've grieved. But to have lived the life that we've had, the love we shared... well, that was a blessing.'

I nod to show that I'm listening and reach for another biscuit. Outside, a blackbird trills a song.

'We had two sons, Rory and Dudley – the loveliest boys, full of life, always coming home sunburned from the beaches, showering sand all over the house. They grew up as boys do and married. In all our years, we only really had one dreadful, dark time and that was twenty-five years ago, when Siwan came along.'

'*Shew*...?'

'It's a name, dear. Welsh.'

'Right.' I've come across a few Welsh names that are unfamiliar. Owain. Myfanwy. Gruffydd... I'm trying to learn them. 'So who was Shew-un? Is that right?'

She smiles. 'Very good, yes. She was Rory's first wife. One of *those* women. What's that word all the psychologists use now? Toxic. I'm not always a fan of the modern jargon, but it really is the perfect word for her.'

I pull a face in sympathy.

'She'd never finished school, never kept a job for longer than six months, she'd always been deeply unhappy, but it was all her parents' fault, according to her. Abusive, alcoholics, you name it. She played a wonderful victim role in life. She was very beautiful though, and Rory fell for her hook, line and sinker. For a while she had us all sucked in, trying to make her happy. I found out later that much of what she told us was out-and-out lies. But never mind that. Well, she couldn't have found a man to love her more than Rory did. But, Kitty, she treated my boy appallingly. She drank, she cheated on him, she rubbished him at parties in front of other people, she gossiped about me and Lawrence and Dudley. To this day, I don't know what her story was. A personality disorder maybe? Never mind all that – she's long gone thankfully.

'At one point she and Rory lived here with us because she'd spent all his savings without telling him and they lost their house. She spun some sob story and we all forgave her. They were here for eight months, Rory worked his socks off then they moved into a flat and started again. Shortly after that, I found that my necklace was missing. I knew she'd taken it. By then she and I were not getting on. The scales had fallen from my eyes, if not from Rory's. I challenged her, but of course she denied it. I'm not vindictive or paranoid; I knew what I knew. I told the police, but there was no proof and nothing they could do, other than list it as missing and tell all the pawnbrokers and jewellers in Wales about it. If she had planned to sell it, that scuppered her. If it had turned up anywhere, it would have been recognised.

'A year or so later, she and Rory split up. And that was the end of that horrible chapter, thank goodness. Rory found a new love, Belinda, who's a poppet, so all's well that ends well, except for the necklace. I wrote it off mentally then. The main thing was that Rory was happy again and Siwan was gone from our lives. Some things are more important.'

'That's true,' I say, though I'm boiling with indignation on her behalf. 'So she still has it, you think?' I'm not sure how I can help her if that's the case.

'I've always thought so, yes. But last year I saw her at a party. I hadn't seen her in years. I stayed out of her way and left as soon as I politely could, but as I left, she came after me. Came right up to me on the street and stuck her face in mine – I remember seeing her red-wine lips and her red-wine tongue. I was quite scared. At my age you start to worry about brittle bones and how you'll manage if you hurt yourself. I was afraid she'd push me over or something. Anyway, I stayed very composed and greeted her and wished her goodnight.'

'Good for you!'

'Thank you. Well, she laughed like a maniac, then

simmered down just as quickly and said, *I took your necklace.* I told her I'd never doubted it. *Where is it?* I asked her, not really hoping she'd tell me. And she said, *It's hidden. Hidden in the house.*

'Well, what good does it do you there? I asked. And she said, *None, except for knowing you can't have it.* Then she turned around and staggered back into the party. Kitty, I wondered about going after her, about trying to trap her into some sort of public confession in front of other people. But I'm old. I wasn't about to start up the old nonsense with her, and I thought she was probably just – what do you say? – messing with my head. I went home intending to forget all about it. But the flat in Summerdale came up, and I jumped at it and then realised that I'll be leaving here soon and what if the necklace *is* still here? She sowed a seed, and I've been looking for it, on and off, ever since. I don't want to abandon it, like something forgotten. With Lawrence gone, it would mean so much to have that tangible reminder that we talked about on our wedding day.'

'Well of course it would! Do you really think it's here though? Maybe she *was* just messing with you that night, as you said?'

'It's entirely possible, and I'll never know, I suppose. She's left the area at last. Gone to live with a sister, apparently, in Tenerife. We never knew she had one.'

'And what do you want me to do? I'll help of course, if I can, but you know this house a million times better than me. I can't go around pulling up floorboards and bashing holes in walls. I'd lose my job!'

'I'd never put you in that position, dear. All I need is an afternoon or two, if you can spare the time to come and do some grunt work for me. I've searched the whole house except for two areas: the built-in cupboard in the loft – it goes back a long way and I can't crawl – and the shed, which is full of old shelf-racks and boxes. There could be a dozen hidey-holes in there, but it's full of junk and treacherous. I'd better not attempt it alone.'

'Of course I can spare the time, and yes, I'll help. But why me? Not that I'm not very flattered.'

'Thank you, dear. Well, you see, Dudley's in New Zealand. I don't want to bring it up with Rory because he hates any reminder of her – understandably. I don't want to drag the grandchildren into it because it's the one family skeleton in the closet and I don't want to upset them. And my friends are all my sort of age or older – they're no better equipped to poke around in small spaces than I am. I suppose there's also the fear that people will think I'm barmy.

'Then you walked in last week and I knew you were my girl. I could tell at once that you're a good person. And there's something familiar about your face somehow – it makes me feel reassured. Yes, you're my girl, if you're willing. I know it's only a material possession, but my Lawrence gave it to me, then that horrible banshee took it from me and I've been without it a long time. Now I want it back.'

CHAPTER 17

The following day is my day off, and I'm ready for it. I've loved every minute of my first week, but my brain's suffering from information overload and I'm keen for a change of pace: a luxurious lie-in, a long beach walk, maybe a coffee with Cherry. I'm preoccupied too by the people I've met and the mysteries I've glimpsed. *Why* is Lisa Parnell selling her beloved house? Where on earth is Doris Vincent's necklace? The pair of them haunt me, completely different in their situations, their personalities, their attitude to me, yet both vulnerable in different ways.

After a blissful day of rest, I'm back in the fray!

The Parnell house goes on the market, and Roly wasn't exaggerating – the office explodes with interest. Slimy Matthew from across the road comes in more than once to bait us, saying we're too small to do justice to such a prestigious property and generally undermine us. He's obviously furious that we got the instruction. Roly responds with serene indifference and carries on doing things his own way, and we take our cue from him. Because he's wholly occupied at Fortescue Crescent, the rest of us are busier than usual with the other listings, and I'm thrown in at the deep end.

During my first weeks at Rowlands, I live in an almost perpetual state of confusion. I spend my days searching for cars and keys. I'd be entirely useless without the map that now lives on my desk – when I'm not toting it about the countryside; around here, satnav can only take me so far. I must have spent hours poring over the streets and lanes of the surrounding area, trying to memorise that Larkspur Lane is a right turn off Blue Pool Road, and that Carpenter's Corner leads into Southlands Way. I've worn such creases in the folds that I've had to reinforce them with Sellotape.

I still can't remember all the properties, prices and vendors – considering it's meant to be a difficult market, there seem to be one hell of a lot of houses! I've caused offence countless times, suggesting, for example, that Mrs Paul Jones lives on the west side of the village when in fact she lives on the far more rarefied south side and actually it is Mrs *Owen* Jones (Alcoholic, you know! Second wife!) who lives in Aspen Grove to the west. Will I ever get all these people and places straight in my head? On the plus side, I know my way around the kettle a treat!

And I'm learning. Roly seems pleased with me, and if my progress is OK by him, I suppose it should be OK by me. I'm not only learning the tasks of the job. I've learned that the woods bordering Hasterly Avenue hold a different secret every week – deep pools of black shadow or hazy glades of bluebells or white wild garlic, looking like stars and smelling like a bistro dinner. I've learned exactly how quickly lambs grow; when I first arrived they were everywhere, wobbling across roads, causing massive hold-ups, tottering over the Burrows, snoozing on village greens, but now they are large and adolescent and sheep-shaped. I've learned a little about the surf conditions that lure the locals into the waves, where they bob on their boards, waiting for the perfect ecstatic swell. These are the things that make me glad of Roly's praise and hope that I can learn and improve and come to feel I know the business as well as Bella or

Nerys or Derrick, because these are the things that make me want to stay.

'What do you mean *stay*?' demands Cooper when I voice some of this to her on the phone one evening. 'You're not thinking of settling there for good, are you?'

'I guess... no... But would it be so bad if I was?' It's still very early days and I'm trying not to rule out any possibilities yet.

'No, not *bad* exactly. Just, you belong in London. Your whole life is there.'

'And how well did that turn out?' I muse wryly, watching a peacock butterfly travel from branch to branch in my little courtyard garden. Most evenings are warm enough now to sit outside after work for a while. 'Besides, I spent the whole time wanting to move to the country.'

'Yes, but *this* country, near me! Of course, you're not *obliged* to live near your big sister, but I always thought that was the plan. With Cass in the Big Apple, I always longed to have *one* of you in walking distance. But that's just me being selfish.'

I always thought that was the plan too. And all I know about my new venture at this point is that I'm happy *now*. And I'm grateful for that. Considering how this year started out, the weeks I spent crying into my pillow, I think it's pretty spectacular progress.

I change the subject. 'I've been thinking about the holiday we had here – what you said about Dad being absent a lot. Tell me more, Coop, because I was either completely oblivious or I've repressed the memories, and it's weirding me out. You never told me your theory.'

A heavy sigh drifts down the line to me. 'I've never known for sure,' she says, 'but I have ideas. I'm not sure you'll want to hear it though.'

'No, tell me, Cooper, really. I'm not a little girl anymore.'

'No, you're not. Well, if you're sure... I always wondered if he had an affair that summer.'

'What? No way, Coop! You're crazy! Dad would *never*...'

I stretch out my legs, propping my feet on the stone wall for reassurance. I wouldn't say I was a daddy's girl, because I've always been equally close to Mum. Even now that I'm grown-up and they're no longer together, I have a great relationship with them both. Mum's in Bath, working as an archivist, soaking up the history and eating scones in the pump rooms every week like it's some kind of sacred ritual. Dad's further afield, in Edinburgh, running a restaurant. I visit them both regularly, and they've always come to London to spoil me too.

But Dad has always been *easier* than Mum, in some ways. Sunnier, more straightforward. The type of dad every little girl should be so lucky to have, free with bear hugs and laughs, happy to take me roller skating, buy me tampons in an emergency. It wasn't that Mum was less affectionate, and we did loads of fun things with her – from cinema trips to pantomimes to a local swing-dance troupe. But there's something a little more guarded about Mum. I wouldn't go so far as to say secretive, but she's always had very strong boundaries and would sometimes be utterly lost in thought, miles and miles away, which has always seemed a little at odds with her otherwise neat and practical persona. The point is that I can't even *begin* to think that my hearty, smiling, life-embracing dad would have done anything to hurt Mum or jeopardise our family.

'That's what you thought about Mitch,' says Cooper, breaking into my thoughts. 'Sorry, that was harsh. I wasn't trying to do a low blow – I just mean that you can never really tell with anyone, can you?'

'True... but what makes you think it?'

'Item one,' says Cooper. I can imagine her serious expression and the way she'll be marking the points off on her fingers. 'We were there for two weeks and I can remember at least six times that we kids did something with only Mum, so what was that about?'

I shrug. 'I dunno. I can't remember.' I watch a huge puff of a bumblebee buzzing dreamily from one side of the garden to the other, its song summery and sleepy.

'Yes you can. Remember that day we were going to walk the cliff path? Dad had bought a book of local walks in that café with the swings, and there was a walk to a place called Pixie something. Pixie Bend or Pixie Hill, I don't know. And you were desperate to go there even though we told you it was just a name and that three miles was a long way.'

'Ummm, vaguely.'

'You talked us all into it and Dad packed us girls little rucksacks in the morning for us to carry our own drinks and snacks, and bigger ones for him and Mum too, but then he didn't go.'

'Why?'

'I can't remember.'

'Maybe he was ill?'

'I don't think so. I remember Mum being really put out. Which she wouldn't have been if he was ill, would she? Then another time we were in a café, overlooking the sea, and we had lunch, then cake, then ice cream... we were there *ages*! And Dad wasn't there then either. I'm pretty sure we were waiting for him though. I remember Cassidy getting really fractious and bored because she wanted to go swimming. Stuff like that.'

The butterfly is back. To my delight, it settles for a moment on my ankle. The simple beauty of the present helps me negotiate the murky questions about the past. 'I do have vague recollections now... But maybe Dad had something going on. Maybe he had a health issue, or maybe they were in debt and he was trying to sort it out...'

'But why when we were on holiday, rather than in the place where we lived?'

'I don't know. Maybe they were trying to carry on as normal to protect us from anything worrying. Maybe he had to juggle sorting things out with showing up for our holiday.'

'Perhaps,' Cooper concedes, 'but remember I told you I heard arguments too? Why would Mum be cross if it was one of those things you said?'

Suddenly I remember her saying she heard a row one night and got up to listen from the landing. I always meant to ask her about it again, but in all the rush and colour of my new job, I completely forgot. 'You started telling me about that then one of the boys needed you. Tell me now. You said you listened in one night?'

'Yes. I didn't understand it and I don't remember much, but at one point, she definitely said, *I don't want you to see her again.* Then Dad said something I couldn't hear and she said, *You've betrayed me and I'm not sure I can forgive you.*'

I lapse into a stunned silence. Our mother's pain echoes down the years to us now, two of her girls in two different places, connected by the phones in our hands and our love for each other.

'Kitty? Kits, are you there?'

'Yes, yes I'm here. I'm just trying to figure out what I make of it all, that's all. It's... weird, Cooper. It's... fairly damning!'

'I know. And I'm sorry. I don't want to change how you feel about Dad. After all, people do *have* affairs; it doesn't necessarily make them completely evil – except for Mitch. I've made my peace with it by thinking, *a)* I don't actually *know* – as you said, there may be some completely innocent explanation – and *b)* even if I'm right, well, he's still a great dad to all of us and he's a good man in general. Maybe he was having a breakdown, or Mum wasn't the love of his life. We can't judge. No one's perfect, right?'

'Right.'

'Anyway, I have to go again. Jerry's threatening Nathan with the teapot. It's not your typical battleground weapon but I'm glad to see he can improvise. Are you OK?'

'Yes. Go and save Nathan, Coop. We can talk again.'

But I'm not sure I am OK.

After she's gone, I sit frowning as the air cools around me, my good mood gone. That's what you get for asking. I don't want to know any of this, and I especially don't want to associate it with *here*, this place that is my fresh start. I can't bear to think that Dad could have run around with some woman while his kids were in the same town, on holiday, waiting for him to show up to go swimming. In fact, no. He just wouldn't have done that. Whatever was going on for him and Mum, he wouldn't have behaved like that with the three of us girls on holiday with them. And despite what Cooper said, I always thought Mum *was* the love of his life. After the divorce, he was heartbroken.

I don't want you to see her again... You've betrayed me and I'm not sure I can forgive you.

It's hard to imagine another explanation for that, but perhaps Cooper remembered it wrong? Because seriously, have a steamy liaison, then go back to play snap with his kids? No. He's just not that guy.

CHAPTER 18

The next morning, I make my first sale and it's the most exciting moment of my new job so far. Me, Kitty Roberts, who used to loiter in estate agents' offices and dream of buying the houses, has made that dream come true for someone else. It's thrillingly rewarding.

I'm on my own in the office when a young woman around my own age comes in to ask about a cottage in the village that I haven't seen yet. Number six, Sunset Terrace. From the information, it looks cute.

'When can I see it?' she asks, visibly jittering with excitement. 'I'm free all the next couple of days, if that's not too soon. I'd love to see it as soon as possible. I'm Stacey, by the way.'

Bless, I love when people know how lucky they are to be viewing houses. A disappointing number are blasé, as if they've never known the angst of the home-lover denied a home.

I check the viewing arrangements. 'It's empty,' I tell her. Then I look in the diary. 'I can take you now if you want. My colleague should be back any minute. If you're not in a hurry, you could take a seat until he gets here.'

'Are you serious?' she squeaks. 'Ohmigod! That would be amazing!'

I call Derrick to get an ETA. He answers, out of breath.

'Walking up the bloody hill,' he pants. 'Two minutes.'

I scribble the appointment in the diary, knowing how important it is to have a full record of every viewing conducted. Every Monday, one of us goes through the previous week's appointments so we can follow up any loose ends.

Derrick bursts in, red-faced and puffing, and throws the car keys at me.

'Oh, could we not just walk?' I ask. I looked on the map and it's not far.

'Hill. You'll thank me,' he explains briefly.

As Scarlett crawls up to Sunset Terrace, I see what he means. There are some hills around here that, whilst you *could* walk up them, it's just kinder to yourself not to. As Scarlett slows alarmingly, engine whining, I'm actually concerned we might start rolling backward! Perhaps I should have taken Saffron, but, whilst Scarlett is puny, Saffron is elderly. It strikes me that Roly could do with investing in some more robust cars.

But we make it up there and I park on an earthy track.

'Well, you won't have to worry about security – no sane burglar would ever bother with that hill,' I say, laughing, as we climb out.

'Oh *wow!*' cries Stacey with stars in her eyes. Her dream has always been to live by the sea, she told me on the way here.

I click the car locked and look around. We're right at the top of the village, with only a narrow crest of cliff, like a pie crust, above us. Number six is the middle house in a long terrace tucked away in this inaccessible corner and it looks out over the entire sweep of Pennystrand Bay. The rooftops and crooked lanes of Pennystrand drop away below us, and the sea is a blue dazzle, dotted with white sails, a tanker on the horizon. It would be glorious to wake to this view every day.

I give Stacey a satisfying moment to take it all in, then I unlock the door. 'Shall we?'

I step into a dark hallway. I've noticed that a lot of the cottages around here struggle for light. They were built for fishermen or oystercatchers and were built low and compact, although people have extended them now in all kinds of imaginative ways. There are stairs going up, a door on the right, and I step through that into a lounge/dining room that used to be two separate rooms but has been knocked through.

'Oh wow!' Now it's my turn. It's traditional cottage style, with a Welsh dresser, wooden beams on the ceiling and an open fireplace. The decor is all cosy armchairs and wicker storage baskets and fluffy throws. And through the bay window, the view of the village and the bay is as clear here as it was outside. It's beautiful.

I turn to look at Stacey and then I see it: the moment she falls in love.

'Oh,' she says softly. And I know she's imagining herself here, sitting in an armchair, gazing out to sea. 'I could sit on the doorstep in the sun when I come home from work, couldn't I? Have a little glass of Prosecco sometimes.'

I nod, smiling at the thought.

'I'll take it!' she says, only half in jest. She has the rest of the house to see, but it's unlikely anything will change her feelings about it now.

Together we discover a decent-sized kitchen, obviously a later addition, and a steep garden climbing up the cliff and arranged in three tiers. Upstairs we find two bedrooms and a bathroom, all cosy and fit for purpose. We look around once more and we're done.

She looks at me with a determined face. 'Right then, I want it. How do we do this? I'll offer the full asking price.'

'The full...?' I echo weakly, remembering the tales the others have told me of weeks of haggling and the hours of persuasion needed to talk people up to anything resembling a sensible offer.

'No point messing around. I want it. I've been saving. I'm not going to change my mind, so can we do it, like, now?'

'Er, yes! We can. I'll go straight back to the office, put a call in to the owners to tell them and I'm sure they'll say yes because why wouldn't they? It's the perfect offer and you're in a great position as a first-time buyer. You'll need to appoint a solicitor. Shall I give you a call as soon as I have the owner's go-ahead?'

'Yes please! I'll go straight home and sort it out. Don't let anyone else buy it, Kitty. This is my house.'

I smile wistfully, happy for her but wondering if I'll ever have my own moment like this.

CHAPTER 19

It's amazing to have a social life again. I've been out twice for drinks after work with Nerys and Derrick, and I had a blast both times. One was a quick pint in the pub at the bottom of the hill, a nice way to unwind after a crazy afternoon. The second time was a more serious session, starting with a bottle of wine in a nice bar over the road from the office. The crew from Wilton-Granger occupied a large table in the window, and a number of sniffy looks and frosty comments were batted around when we walked in. We tucked ourselves into a corner at the back and Nerys and Derrick proceeded to gossip about them ferociously. Then everyone got hungry so we tottered to a nearby pizzeria and I got home late, despite work the next day. It was glorious.

On my last day off I spent the afternoon with Mrs Vincent, helping her scour the last remaining places her necklace might be hidden. Disappointingly, we found nothing. As I withdrew from the last cobwebby corner of the shed, shaking my head, her face fell. 'I'll have to leave it here,' she said with a little sob in her voice. 'My beautiful gift from Lawrence!'

It's desperately sad, but I'm inclined to think that Siwan only said what she did to unsettle her. Probably it's hidden somewhere entirely different or else it's been sold in some dodgy way that might have escaped police attention.

Tonight, I've been invited to dinner with Cherry, Mike and Magpie. I go straight from work, stopping in the deli on the way to buy a good bottle of red, some green olives stuffed with things I didn't even know you could stuff olives with and some cocoa-dusted almonds. Then I pop into the newsagent's and buy some ridiculous jelly snakes for Magpie before pottering contentedly to their place, thinking how nice it is to live somewhere you can go everywhere on foot.

'Ooh! Posh! Lovely!' cries Cherry when she opens the gifts.

'Ooh, posh!' Magpie grins her gap-toothed grin when she sees the lurid red and green sugary snakes, a wild light in her eyes.

Cherry smirks. 'Maybe not the word I'd have used, but yummy, right, Magpie? You may have one before dinner. ONE! Save the rest for tomorrow please.'

Since I was last here, they've taken delivery of a dining-room table and chairs, and the table's been decorated with a white tablecloth and garden flowers.

'It looks lovely!' I exclaim, looking around with pleasure. The curtains are open and I look out at a side garden where roses are blooming in profusion. It's somehow mid-June already and definitely summer rather than spring.

'Better than crates,' admits Cherry. 'Though we've still got those in the kitchen. Hang on, I can hear something boiling over. Back in a sec.'

As I wait for her, it occurs to me that I'm surrounded by people doing what I've always longed to do: making a nest of their own. I'm fond of my little house up the hill. As rentals go it couldn't be better. And compared with the London flat... well, there *is* no comparison. But it's still not *mine*. I chose it in a rush, I can't decorate it or buy furniture or get a pet, and I'll be leaving in four months. Or maybe more, but it's not permanent.

I tell myself that all the home-buying vibrations will affect me and make beautiful changes in my life – I hope so – but sometimes it just feels as if everyone but me is settling down.

Dinner is a wonderful Moroccan chicken dish made by Mike, followed by a gooseberry tart baked by Cherry. Mike is lanky and funny, and Magpie is precocious and adorable, though how she manages to eat anything I don't know. She's more gap than teeth!

Mike takes a great interest in my job. 'I mean, it must be fascinating,' he says. 'It's people watching on a grand scale, isn't it?'

'Sort of,' I agree.

'I mean, all those glimpses into other lives,' he goes on. 'The big houses, the small ones, the houseproud people, the slovenly ones, the secrets and scandals, the joy, the heartbreak!'

'You need to write a soap opera,' observes Cherry.

He's summed up my feelings about it perfectly though. It's exactly that, and to me it feels like a privilege. I always used to envy people who had a vocation, like nursing or teaching – well, maybe this is mine. They pepper me with questions about people and houses, but I'm careful what I say, not wanting to be horrendously indiscreet.

Conversation inevitably turns to the Parnell house.

'I don't think a house on that road has gone up for sale in my whole lifetime,' said Cherry. 'My friends and I used to go for walks up there when we were kids, and we used to stare in disbelief at the sheer *size* of those houses! Once, some guy came out and threatened to call the police.'

Mike beams. 'My wife the reprobate.'

She snorts. 'What about you? Tell Kitty about Halloween, Michael Morris.'

'When I was twelve,' Mike relates, 'a bunch of us boys went trick or treating at Lisa's place. Obviously, the door never opened so we sat on their front lawn to drink cider.'

'Cheeky gits,' says Cherry.

'Horribly cheeky. I think we were hoping they'd come out to tell us off – we just wanted to get a glimpse of them.'

'And did they?' I ask.

'Nope. But our parents appeared as if by magic and hauled us out of there sharpish. I guess the Parnells phoned people who knew people who knew people...'

'So what's the deal?' I frown. 'Were they recluses or something? Were the children home-school kids?'

'Not recluses,' says Cherry. 'Just incredibly choosy about who they hung out with, and who they let into their inner sanctum. The kids went to school, just not the local one. They went to this posh private school over in Lowbridge. Pretty much all their friends came from there and we never saw them. That all changed once they hit sixteen and started sneaking out to pubs and clubs locally of course – Parnells are as fond of misbehaving as the rest of us – but we hardly glimpsed them before that.'

'They're this really old family,' Mike continues. 'You see the name in churchyards going back centuries. That house is the mothership – it's where Lisa and her siblings grew up; it's where her parents and grandparents lived. They were influential back in the day – donated money to schools and theatres, political causes – all sorts. There's a couple of alcoholics, a supermodel, an opera singer, a rugby player... they're a colourful bunch.'

'And tell her about Agatha,' Cherry interjects.

'Oh God, yes! There's an elderly aunt, Agatha, who claims to have been kidnapped by mermaids as a child.'

'Wow,' I say. 'This sure is an interesting place.'

'Then you should stay, shouldn't you?' pleads Cherry, who hates it whenever I talk about going back to London.

By now, Magpie has grown bored with the conversation and is swirling some mashed-up butternut squash over the table-cloth, making a henna-coloured pattern against the white.

'I think it's bedtime for monkeys.' Mike gets up and lifts his daughter out of her chair. 'Say goodnight, Mags.'

'I'm serious, you know,' says Cherry when Magpie's in bed and Mike has excused himself to fix his racing bike in the garage. We're lounging in beanbags now, sipping Baileys from big brandy goblets. '*Do* you think you might stay in Pennystrand after your six months? I know it's early days but...'

I bite my lip. 'I do think about it,' I admit. 'So much of my old life is just *gone*. If I go back to London, I'll be starting over just as much as I am here really. But my family's closer there – well, Cooper is. And David and the boys. I always thought I'd live near them. I always imagined having kids and all the cousins playing together, and Coop and I helping each other out and having dinner parties and minding each other's chickens when one of us is on holiday...'

'It does sound nice,' Cherry admitted. 'My sister moved away last year and I really miss her, especially now with all this.' She gestures around at the house.

'But of course that was all meant to have Mitch in the picture. I'm unlikely to have kids any time soon now. So who knows?'

Cherry looks glum. 'I'd love to say this is a great place to meet single men, but honestly it's not. Lots of stoners, lots of pensioners. I don't really see you hooking up with someone from either of those categories.'

'I'm not looking. It's too soon after Mitch. I want to be over him but I'm not – yet.'

Cherry frowns in sympathy. 'Is it as bad as ever?'

I hesitate. *Is* it? I've thought about him a lot less since I started work but perhaps that's just because I'm too busy to think about it. Then again, isn't that the point? To be busy in a life you enjoy, taking pleasure in the people and places that fill your days, instead of wallowing in a fog of darkness and tears?

'No, it's a lot better actually. He's... *receding* but not completely gone, if that makes sense? And as you said, it's early days. Too soon for soul-searching. I just want to enjoy this lovely interlude for now and take the stress off.'

'Fair enough. I won't ask again. Top-up?'

CHAPTER 20

A few days later, something happens that dislodges Mitch a little further from my mind and heart. There's a viewing on another house I haven't seen before, a perfectly normal, perfectly lovely semi on an ordinary street close to where I live. Because Roly knows I'm round the corner, he arranged the viewing for 9.30 a.m. so I can do it first thing and have a slightly later start. It's these little things that make him employer of the century in my book.

I celebrate the extra half hour with a second cup of pre-work coffee, sunshine pouring in and landing on the kitchen counter in thick, buttery pools. Then I stride the three streets to Park Rise with caffeine in my veins and a spring in my step. According to the notes I read last night, the vendor usually does the viewings, but she's not at home today. I arrive ten minutes early to familiarise myself with the place before the viewers arrive.

It's certainly not the most spectacular house I've seen since I started the job, but it has a friendly aspect, unpretentious. Again, I can't help but think how grateful I would be to own it. It has a bright blue door and a large back garden. It looks approachable, somehow, somewhere an ordinary person like me might live.

I unlock the door and walk in. I discover a lounge and a TV room on one side of the hall, a dining room and a downstairs loo on the other. Good selling point. Everyone likes a second loo.

In the kitchen, there's a half-empty pot of coffee on the counter and the air smells of a delicious rich blend. I breathe in appreciatively. The vendor, a Mrs Lydia Hudson, is obviously a kindred spirit. She must have only just left; that coffee is fresh. I wonder if she left it with me and her viewers in mind? But even for me, three coffees before 10 a.m. would be a lot.

A movement through the window catches my eye and I notice a big, sandy-coloured dog romping in the garden. She's left her dog outside? What if it rains? That shaggy coat would get drenched. Well, maybe he hates being indoors, what do I know? We usually make a note if there's a dog on the property in case viewers are scared of them. I don't *remember* reading about a dog on the file – maybe I missed it. I take another longing sniff of coffee-air and wander up the stairs.

An airy landing has family photos dotted all along the walls, and a window lets the sunlight tumble in and flood the place with light. *Gorgeous*. If it were mine, I'd have an armchair here to catch the light and I'd sit and read... but I don't have time for daydreaming.

The first door I open is a bathroom, and I jump when I see a dark figure looming through the steam. A second later my caffeinated heart slows down again. It's only a wetsuit hanging from the shower rail. Phew!

Wait a minute though – *steam*? I must have missed Lydia Hudson by only seconds! And there's a trail of sand across the floor. That doesn't look very good for viewers. I adjust my mental image of Lydia from a fifty-something woman to a younger Mrs, like Cherry, fit and toned and into surfing.

I leave the room and walk slap-bang into a person. I scream.

I'm wired from coffee and she's meant to be at an all-day meeting in Cardiff!

I spring back, my heart clattering. To my further horror, I see that the person is not, in fact, a she. It's a he, and there's not one scrap of doubt about that because he's stark naked.

In a swift movement indicative of admirable presence of mind, he snatches a framed photo off the wall, using it to cover his private parts.

'Ohmigod, ohmigod, ohmigod,' I chatter, covering my eyes. 'I'm sorry. I'm really, really sorry. I didn't know there was anyone here!'

'No worries,' he says. 'I didn't either. I'm not a flasher, I promise. I heard a noise and came to investigate – I'm just out of the shower.'

I peep between my fingers. Now the important bits are covered, he seems quite relaxed. He doesn't *look* like someone who'll make a complaint to my boss. He's tall and very tanned and – oh my God – his body is unbelievable; he looks sort of *sculpted*. There's something dreamlike about his shape, making me want to run my hands over the contours of his chest and arms... Like *that* wouldn't get me fired.

'I hope you don't mind me asking,' he goes on. 'I'm not, y'know, being all hostile or anything, but... who *are* you?'

'Oh! Yes, right. I'm Kitty Roberts. I'm from the estate agent. I have a viewing any minute. I was told the house was empty this morning or I'd never have... Actually, who are *you*? I thought a Lydia Hudson lived here. And that she was out today.' Did I look up the wrong property by mistake?

'Cory Hudson,' he says amiably, taking a step forward.

The photo slips ever so slightly. I feel my face flame.

He holds out his hand so I gingerly shake it. *My God, he's beautiful.* His hair is longish, judging by the way it's starting to dry and curl against his neck. His eyes are sea green and his mouth is wide and full. And did I mention his body?

'Lydia's my mum. I'm sorry, I didn't know about the view-ing, and she didn't know I was coming. I rock by, y'know, when I'm in town. Use the old homestead for the creature comforts and Mum's good coffee.'

Right. That makes sense.

Just then the doorbell sounds.

He grins. 'I'd better put some clothes on. Keep them down-stairs a minute, will you? I don't want to scare them off.'

Oh, he wouldn't. There's nothing remotely scary about *that* sight!

'Sure. We'll start downstairs.' I keep staring.

He smiles again and bites his lip. 'Hadn't you better answer it?'

'Oh yes! God. Definitely. Good idea.'

I scuttle to the stairs then look back.

Big mistake. Cory's disappearing into a bedroom, affording me a clear view of a high, firm backside – not too big and not too small – and long, shapely legs, glistening with fine golden hairs as if he's still glinting with sand. It's a wonder I don't topple down the stairs.

CHAPTER 21

Fortunately I make it through the viewing in a reasonably coherent manner. The viewers are a mother, father and ten-year-old son, Max. They seem to like the place.

'The vendor's son is at home,' I explain when we've finished with downstairs. 'Let me just go and check he's ready for us to go up.'

I run halfway up the stairs, feeling ludicrously shy.

'Um, Mr Hudson?' I call. 'Is it OK if we come up?'

He appears above me, dressed in slouchy jeans that dangle temptingly off his hips and a form-fitting T-shirt in a soft maroon colour with a logo of a crested wave on the front.

'Sure, come on up.' His hair is drying into a mass of curls, streaked brown and gold like sand. Looking up at him, framed in light from the landing window, I can't help thinking of angels and Michelangelo and Greek gods... which is all very inappropriate. I have a wild urge to bolt to the office and sanity. But I look behind me and smile at the viewers.

'Come on up,' I repeat.

Cory stands aside to let us all crowd up the stairs.

'I'll go downstairs out of your way,' he says to me. 'Call me if you need anything.' Then he turns to the little family, smiling and shaking hands. Before he can introduce himself, young Max looks up at him and gasps.

'Cory Hudson!' he shrieks, his eyes round as saucers. 'You're Cory Hudson! You're my hero. Look, Mum, it's Cory Hudson!'

Who on earth is Cory Hudson? Apart from my vendor's naked son.

'Why so it is,' she says, going red. 'Good heavens. You're all over our son's bedroom walls, Mr Hudson. It's good to meet you.'

'Oh, call me Cory,' he says. 'And you are?' He looks down at Max, smiling.

'I'm Max.'

'Hi, Max. Do you surf?'

'Yes!' He beams, then his face falls. 'Well, I try. But it's really hard.'

'You know what though? It is hard. It has to be, otherwise everyone would do it, right? It's only guys like you and me that stick it out till it gets easier.'

At the words *guys like you and me* Max looks as if he's about to faint clean away. He leans against the walls and squints up at Cory as if he's Superman. '*You* thought it was hard?' he queries, disbelieving.

'You kidding me? When I started I couldn't stand up for two whole months. And then I fell off so much I drank half of Brightman Bay. It wasn't pretty, Max, between you and me.'

I watch the whole scene, mystified. Max's parents are standing back in that way parents do when their kid is having the moment of a lifetime, looking at each other proudly. They know they're going to hear about this at breakfast, lunch and tea for the next two years. Max's face is alight with wonder, and Cory is as easy as Sunday morning.

'How did you... get to be *you*? I mean, how did you get so good?' asks Max.

'Practice, practice and more practice. And I had some really good tips from a pro-surfer I met too. Hey, do you live around here?'

'No.' Max looks glum. 'They might buy a house here, but they haven't made up their mind yet.'

'They' look at each other and smile.

'We're here this week, looking at houses, giving it some thought,' explains the dad.

'Well,' says Cory, 'that's a coincidence because I'm around this week too. If it's cool with you guys, I'd be happy to take Max out for an hour or two. If you'd like to, that is, Max?'

The dad laughs. 'If he'd like to!' he scoffs. 'Look at his face!'

Max looks as if he could explode. He starts nodding like a donkey.

'Say thank you to Cory,' instructs his mother.

'Thank you, Cory,' he whispers.

'Hey, my pleasure. Look, you guys need to get on with looking at the house. Before you go, give me a shout and I'll give you my card. We'll fix something.'

'Um, Cory? Is one of these your bedroom?'

'I don't live here anymore, dude, so it's kinda half my room, half my mum's home gym now. But it used to be, when I was a kid.'

He lopes down the stairs and leaves us all staring after him.

'Um, I don't mean to sound stupid,' I mutter, 'but who, actually, *is* he?'

Max looks at me in disbelief. 'He's a world-famous surfer!' he tells me in a reverent voice. 'He's been the UK champion for years now and he came third in the Billabong Pipeline Masters one year and he's won Mavericks in California too. He's... amazing!'

'And so nice!' adds his mum. 'I can't believe he's offered to give Max a lesson.'

'The only downside,' observes the dad, 'is that it's going to be hard to look at this house objectively now. I have a feeling we're going to get royally nagged.'

'Dad, we *have* to buy it! It's the house where *Cory Hudson* grew up! We have to come and live here! Then I can surf where he surfed and sleep in the room he slept in and be just like him!'

'Max, you don't need to be like him, you need to be yourself,' says his mum firmly. 'But yes, it's very exciting that we met him.'

'Um, I hate to interrupt...' I try to get things back on track, 'but shall we carry on?'

We do, but now it's like looking round a museum. In the bathroom, instead of the deluxe power shower and attractive tiling, they see only Cory Hudson's wetsuit and Cory Hudson's surfboard. The views from the window aren't ocean-facing open views, they're 'where Cory Hudson used to hang out'. I'm not sure how this viewing is going at all. They're all very starstruck, but when they get home, surely the parents will calm down and consider it objectively? I'll have to ring them next week for feedback because there's no sense from them today.

I show them out, Cory gives them his card and makes a date with Max for tomorrow morning.

When they've gone, I turn to Cory. 'Well, goodbye, Mr Hudson. I'm sorry again about... earlier and thanks for being so good about it. I really had no idea.'

'Oh hey, entirely my fault. Mum always says I treat the place like a hotel. I knew she was selling, but for some reason that hadn't translated into people coming into the house and me needing to be a bit more communicative about my plans.'

'No harm done then. Have a great day.'

'Hang on a sec.'

He disappears into the kitchen and opens the back door. The big hairy hound comes skittering in and runs straight over to me, tongue hanging out, tail wagging, utterly adorable.

'This is Shenanigans.'

'Oh, he's *your* dog. That makes sense. He's gorgeous.' I can't resist crouching to make a big fuss of him, even though his long fur is still damp and sandy and smelly.

'Hello! Hello, handsome boy,' I coo, ruffling his ears while he tries to lick my face.

'Would you like a cup of coffee before you go? Like I said, Mum's good stuff.'

I'm sorely tempted. Not only by the delicious-smelling coffee and the irresistible dog but by the chance to talk more to this beautiful man.

I glance at my watch – the viewing took much longer than I expected. 'I can't. I'd love to – I mean, I love coffee – but I have to be back at the office. They'll be coming to look for me at this rate.'

'No worries. Well, thanks again, Kitty. I'll tell my mum I traumatised you, in case we have to change estate agents or something.'

I smile. 'I don't think that'll be necessary. I'm sure I'll recover.'

CHAPTER 22

I can't deny that I'm distracted that morning. Images of Cory in all his glory keep flashing into my mind, and when they do, time slows down and I get lost for a few minutes. Then I shake myself and get on with things. It's been a long time since I saw a naked man that wasn't Mitch, and this was a particularly lovely example of the species.

I text Cherry. *Have you heard of someone called Cory Hudson?*

Of course. Local boy made good. Dreamboat. Why?

I saw him naked this morning.

!!!!!!!!!!!!!!!!!!!!!!!!!

A minute later she texts again. *Please call by after work and tell me everything x*

Silly, really, to have a crush on someone I've met once. A celebrity it seems. He's gorgeous, he travels the world doing something glamorous and cool, he must have more women throwing themselves at him than you could shake a stick at. His dog's name says it all! He did seem nice though. The way he was with Max, the way he was with me. He didn't seem arrogant or vain. I think this is good for me. It's nice to think about a guy that's not Mitch. It shows there's life in me after all. Obviously a travelling heart-throb won't be my mate for life, but maybe there's hope for the future.

By the time Roly appears in the office after lunch, I've recovered sufficiently to tell him about the incident – I thought I should – with light humour and a tone of detachment.

He chuckles. 'Good Lord, Kitty. Sounds like you handled it admirably. I'm sorry you had the embarrassment.'

It's quiet, therefore tea is the order of the day. There are periods of silence when Roly lapses into one of his philosophical zones and periods of chatting. While Roly's being zen, I look out of the window too, watching the world go by and thinking about all the people I've already met through this job. Mrs Vincent and her stunning necklace, Lisa Parnell and her stunning house, Cory and his stunning... everything.

'Have you ever found any secret compartments or cubby holes in any of the houses you've sold?' I ask Roly.

'Why do you ask? Looking for treasure?'

'No,' I lie. 'Just thinking about houses like The Chantry and that lovely 1930s one with the long garden. They're like houses out of stories, aren't they? They make me think of priest holes and secret passages and that sort of thing.'

'Yes indeed. The Chantry has a hidden cupboard. It looks like ordinary wall panelling, but if you press it in just the right place, it opens. I would have shown you, but I didn't want to in front of those awful people. Sixteenth century apparently. They think it was somewhere to store the chapel valuables, the goblets and such, at times when starving locals had no compunction about robbing places of worship.'

'Wow. Cool.'

'Yes. And then there was a place a few years ago...'

I listen to a couple of fascinating stories then work the conversation around to what I really want to know.

'What about the more ordinary houses? Like the ones in the village that are oldish but not that old. Like Claremont Street – or Helena Row?'

'No, Kitty, not that I've heard of. Though there was a place in Greengrove once, nice little street – do you know it? Students were renting the house and took out a few of the insulating bricks and stuck a light box and a seed tray in there! Grew marijuana.'

'That's... inventive. What bit of the house was it?'

'I can't remember now. One of the bedrooms, I think. Thinking of giving it a try?'

I laugh. 'No, I'll stick to growing basil in the garden.'

Once again I'm disappointed for Doris.

I pop by after work to tell her about my brainstorming and its feeble results. 'I don't suppose you or Lawrence ever made a cavity to grow marijuana?'

She laughs long and hard. 'No, dear. Oh, the thought of Lawrence doing something like that!' She wipes her eyes. 'But thank you for continuing to think about it. Stay for a cup of tea?'

'I can't – I've promised to go and see my friend Cherry. But I'll call again soon. You know, about the necklace,' I add gently. 'I'd never tell you to give up, but maybe, for peace of mind, you should let it go?'

She nods sadly.

'But I'll keep thinking about it for as long as I'm here.'

'Six months you're staying, isn't it? When does that take us till? November?'

'October.'

'Right. October.'

She looks even sadder, and I feel a swoop of regret. Suddenly, with the trees bursting with green and the days lengthening and brightening all the time, the smell of barbeque smoke on the air at weekends, October doesn't feel very far away at all.

CHAPTER 23

The next day Bella takes a call for me. 'A Cory Hudson apparently,' she says; the name clearly means nothing to her. She must be the only one around here.

I called at Cherry's yesterday and she was all agog when I told her about the morning's embarrassing incident. She fished out one of Mike's surfing magazines and leafed through it to an article with a photograph of Cory – an unrecognisable figure clad in black rubber riding a surfboard through an impressive blue tube. There was a smaller inset shot of his head and shoulders.

'Is that him?' she demanded, stabbing her finger at his grinning face. 'You saw him *naked*? Wait till I tell my mum!'

I wonder why he's calling now. Maybe he's helping his mother arrange the viewings.

'Hello? Kitty speaking,' I say, trying to sound professional.

'Oh hey, Kitty – Cory Hudson here.' He hesitates as if I actually might not remember him.

'Yes, hi, how are you?'

'I'm good, yeah, and you?'

'Very well thanks. How can I help you?' My God, I sound like a receptionist at a posh boarding school.

'Oh right, well, it's this. I was wondering if you'd like to have dinner one night this week?'

'You were what?' I sound a bit stupid, now, but honestly that was the last thing I was expecting.

'Would you like to have dinner one evening? With me,' he clarifies. 'I mean, no obligation obviously. But we had kind of a hilarious meeting and you seemed nice – I just feel like there was more we could've chatted about.'

I'm taken aback – in a good way – by his straightforward manner. *No biggie, don't get all crazy about it, but I would've liked to chat longer so if you would too let's make it happen.* How very... grown-up. When Mitch and I got together, I had to suffer the whole rigmarole of him waiting days to call after every meeting, playing it cool in case I wasn't interested so I didn't know if he was interested... it was torturous. Then again, we were only twenty-three. Everyone's an idiot at twenty-three.

'Yes! That would be lovely – good thinking.'

'Cool, nice one. Don't suppose you're free tomorrow, are you? Only cause I'm leaving town on Sunday so time's a wastin'.'

'Ummm... Yes, that could work.'

'Great. Do you want to take my number then text me yours, or give me a call to arrange it?'

I scribble it down in relief. I don't really want to have that conversation on the office phone, with Bella six feet away.

'I'll let you have that information ASAP,' I tell him, trying to sound professional for Bella's benefit. 'Thanks for calling.'

'I'll look forward to it. Bye, Kitty.' I can hear the laugh in his voice as we hang up.

I glance over my shoulder at Bella.

'Is romance in the air?' she asks, her lips twitching with amusement.

'Oh no, no, nothing like that. Just a friend. Well, an acquain-tance really. Well...'

'Dinner, lunch or coffee?'

'Ummm, dinner.'

She gives a satisfied smile and goes back to her work.

I'm all in a fluster and drop the map, then swipe my computer mouse onto the floor. Embarrassed, I pretend to read a property brochure, but I'm actually practising deep breathing, trying to get my head around the fact that a ludicrously attrac-tive man has taken the time to call me because he wants to talk to me longer.

Obviously it can't go anywhere because, as he reminded me, he's only here for a few more days. Maybe he just wants a casual hook-up – I'm not sure that's really me. But I'd be lying if I told myself I didn't want to spend some time with him. OK, I'm thirty. I'm single. I'm allowed to do this.

I go and fill the kettle, texting Cory while it boils, before I lose my nerve.

The next evening, I meet Cory at Swanson's, one of the glass-fronted bistros overlooking Brightman Bay. It's not so very long since I was roaming this footpath alone, wishing I had some company and a reason to come here. It all feels a bit surreal. I'm wearing a long, sea-green cotton dress with a long silver chain around my neck and silver sandals. It's a little on the cold side for bare toes in my humble opinion, but they're the right shoes for the dress, and Cherry insisted on the dress. She came haring up the hill last night as soon as Mike got home to look after Magpie, to act as my wardrobe consultant and to drink my wine.

'How dressed up do I need to get?' I flustered, staring into my wardrobe in confusion while she sat on my bed sipping Shiraz. 'It's a long time since I've done this, Cherry.'

'You and me both, my friend. Look, the thing is, you have to look cool, right? But you also have to look like you've made a little bit of an effort.'

I frown. 'Is that helpful?'

'Yes! Now Swanson's is the nicest place in town. His idea? Yep, thought so. You can't just go in jeans. I mean, you *could* just go in jeans, it's really casual there. It's casual everywhere around here really. But you want to look a bit different. Because *he's* making an effort. But you can't make too *much* of an effort – it's a fine line...'

At that point she swung herself off the bed and started riffling through my clothes. When she came to the green dress, she pulled it out in triumph. 'Voila!'

'Are you sure? It's only cotton. Just a loose summer thing for when it's really hot.'

'That's good, that says you're not trying too hard. But it's a *dress* – and that's what makes it perfect. Now, let's see your bling. You need a bit of bling.'

Now, I walk down to the beach, shivering a little despite the long oatmeal cardigan I've wrapped myself up in. I see no Cory on the steps outside the restaurant, and I realise I'm nervous. There's something so exposing about accepting an invitation from someone you don't know. The restaurant seems buzzy, with groups of people visible through the glass and glinting lights. If he stands me up, walking home will feel appallingly lonely.

As I look, Cory walks through the door in a white linen shirt and jeans. My stomach curls a little bit. He's even more handsome than he was two days ago.

'Hey.' He smiles. 'I was just inside, sorting out our table. How are you? You look sensational, by the way.'

I can't help but smile back. He's that sort of person, so at ease, so bright – relaxing, like sunshine. 'Thank you. I'm fine. This was a lovely choice – it's such a beautiful evening.'

He comes and stands beside me for a minute, looking out to sea. No rush. It's high tide and the water is a pale jade – it matches my dress. The sky is pink and primrose, the bright sunshine of the day dimming to softness.

'Yeah, I love that pink dusk light and the sea when it's so calm and flat.' He grins. 'No good for surfing, but perfect for sitting and getting to know someone.'

We stand quietly for a couple of minutes, taking in the view. I feel my breathing start to slow in response to his steadying presence. Then he turns and offers me his arm, old-fashioned. 'Shall we?'

CHAPTER 24

It's a date. An honest-to-goodness date. We have the best table, with an unimpeded view of the ocean, in a secluded alcove that holds the bustle and chatter at bay. We order wine and begin to work our way through three courses. Cory's eyes are full of green and golden gleams, like the waves, and I feel an answering tingle in my skin. I can hardly take my eyes off him.

And still, he's *nice*. Oh, I know appearances can be deceptive and men can put on a great act when they want to impress someone, but still... it's nice to enjoy the moment.

I ask him if he's taken Max surfing yet and he has. I admire him for following through; it's important with kids – I know this from my nephews. He tells me all about the lesson and I ask him about surfing – about his *life*. It seems unimaginable to me, touring the world for months at a time, making your living in the most exotic locations on earth. California, Australia, Bali, Hawaii... When I think of where I've spent the last seven years, in that poky flat in the city, the contrast makes me laugh. I tell him all about it, evoking the grim decor and awful neighbours in grisly detail. It's easier to joke about it when I'm here, gazing out at sea like pale blue and pink silk and a horizon as soft as a dream.

'But *why?*' he asks. 'Were you happy?'

'Yes and no,' I tell him truthfully. 'I thought I was because I was with my partner and there was this whole plan... but I guess I was living for the future rather than enjoying the present and I'm starting to understand the difference.'

'A means to an end,' he says, understanding.

'Exactly. That's what it was. Except everything changed and that end was snatched away, and it felt like the end of the world for a bit, but now...'

'Now?'

I shake my head, which is ever so slightly and pleasantly floaty from wine and enjoyment, and shrug. 'I *love* it here.' I haven't said that to anyone quite so vehemently. I always hold back with Cherry – expectation management – and with Cooper for fear of disapproval. But hey, Cory's leaving on Sunday. 'It's like *The Wizard of Oz*. I was living my life in grimy black and white and now it's technicolour. Even *work* is fun. I've met so many characters you wouldn't believe!'

Cory grins. 'Oh, I would. I grew up round here, remember? There's plenty of crazy. It's great that you love it so much. You suit it round here somehow.'

I wonder if that's true.

He asks what brought me here and I find myself telling him everything about the long-ago family holiday and even my parents' divorce. In turn I learn about *his* parents' divorce back when he was fifteen.

'It sounds like your family breaking up made you want to get settled and make a home of your own,' he observes, 'get all the good stuff back maybe. I get that, but with me it did the opposite. Made me want to shake it all off, travel the world, like no other home was going to measure up to what I'd lost. Same situation, two different reactions.'

'That makes sense.'

I take a forkful of seafood linguine in a white wine sauce. 'Oh my God, this is delicious. So how long have you been travelling for now?'

He pulls a face. 'Too long. It's wearing thin at last. I went on my first pro circuit when I was eighteen and now I'm thirty-five so...'

'Seventeen years!' I exclaim, not to prove that I'm competent at basic arithmetic but because I just can't imagine being rootless for that long.

'Yeah.' He looks rueful. 'At first, it was a blast. Like, the very best existence I could've wished for. I loved everything about it, a bit like you and the estate agency here. It was a fit. I was doing what I loved, seeing the world, making friends, meeting girls, living the dream. And it felt like that for a *really* long time – I never thought about doing anything else. But a few years ago I started noticing some aspects of it were wearing thin, like never staying in the same place for more than a couple of months. Not always having the creature comforts you might like. And missing everyone's birthdays – my best friend's thirtieth, my mother's fiftieth. You can always celebrate together later, right, but it's not the same. I realised I was getting older, that's what it was. Not *old*, but there's a difference between twenty and thirty. And that's quite scary when you make your living out of using your body, your strength. I didn't want to think about the fact that I'd have to stop one day so I ignored the fact that I wasn't quite as happy as I used to be.'

'I get it.' It must be strange having a career with a shorter shelf life than most.

'Also I've never been able to think of doing anything else because the sea is my love, I guess, and surfing's my identity. People love me because I'm famous – in the surf world anyway – and because I excel at what I do. When it all stops, what then?'

'I'm sure people like you for a lot more than that,' I interject. 'I mean, I'd never heard of you before, sorry, and I know nothing about surfing. But you're instantly likeable – not everyone is. And you're smart and kind – look how you were with Max yesterday! When it stops... you'll be fine. Not a doubt in my mind.'

He looks pleased and takes a sip of wine. 'Thanks, Kitty. That's cool. I have started coming to terms with it over the last couple of years. And we change, don't we? Things shift. At first it was minor irritations, but now it's like, I'm over it. Not the surfing, never the surfing, but the lifestyle, being on the move all the time. Not being able to make friendships that last longer than a week. You're a case in point.' He tilts his wine glass towards me. 'And Max. Nice kid. I'd help him out again if I was going to be here. But I'm not.'

'So what's next for you?' I ask. I can't imagine Cory in an office or a garage or on a farm.

'I don't know. I know a change is coming, but I haven't got that far. It won't be for a few months at least. I've got Mexico coming up, then South Africa... that'll take me up till Christmas. I'd like to make it home for the holidays. I'd like to stay with my mum and watch her open her presents and eat her Christmas dinner and go to the pub with my friends. Simple stuff.'

'I know. Simple stuff but... beautiful.'

'Yeah. So, y'know, if you're still here at Christmas, maybe we can do this again!'

I smile and nod, but I still can't help thinking the most likely thing is that I'll be back in London or Surrey by then. Considering I've only met him twice in my life, the fact that we're essentially ships passing in the night is sadder than it ought to be.

The conversation moves on and we order dessert – bread

and butter pudding for Cory, berry panna cotta for me. Around us, the restaurant has emptied out and the bartender's wiping down glasses. A glance at my watch tells me that we've been talking for four and a half hours.

Reluctantly, we get to our feet, replete, and he walks me home. I wonder if I should invite him in, but I don't know if I'm ready for what that might suggest, and I have work in the morning. He doesn't seem to expect anything though. He kisses my cheek and says he's had a great time, then wishes me goodnight, the perfect gentleman.

'Goodnight, Cory. Thanks for a wonderful evening.' I hope my voice doesn't sound too wistful.

He waves as he walks away then stops and turns. 'Wait a minute,' he says in a teasing voice. 'Did you say you know nothing about surfing?'

I grin. 'Yes.'

'Call yourself a Pennystrand girl, and you know nothing about surfing?'

'That's right.'

'That won't do, Kitty. I'm not sure you'll be granted citizenship unless you've tried it at least once.'

'I didn't realise I was applying for citizenship.'

'You probably should though, don't you think? To be on the safe side – keep your options open?'

I smile and cock my head. 'Maybe. If only I knew someone who knows the ropes.'

He shrugs, equally casual. 'Guess I could take you out for an hour or two. If you like.'

'Guess I could find an hour or two.'

'You're working tomorrow, right? What about the next day?'

'That's my day off. I could do that.'

'Amazing. Pick you up at eleven?'

Inside the house, I stand in the silence. I'm going to see him again. It's all pointless and probably a bad idea, seeing as he's leaving on Sunday and our paths will probably never cross again and I'm already way too smitten. Even so, I hug myself and grin. *I'm going to see him again!*

CHAPTER 25

The day in between dates with Cory gives me ample opportunity to mull over our idyllic beachside dinner, reliving every lovely moment. It also gives me a chance to start second-guessing the fact that I've agreed to go surfing with him. Wait a minute. I'm not *into* water sports! It's going to be like Mitch all over again. Well, it *won't*, because Cory's leaving so it can't turn into a relationship. Just as well because he'd be all about the waves and he'd want a woman who was crazy about surfing too – he must be used to an endless string of sassy surfer chicks. I'd feel this huge pressure to fake enthusiasm about something that's just not me, and he'd end up leaving me for someone more adventurous.

Then I catch myself. I'm being ridiculous! There's no question of it going that far. It was just an invitation, and I said yes. In the heady delight of last night, I was just excited to see Cory again and try something new. Honestly, if Beyoncé offered to give me a singing lesson, would I turn it down because I'm not really into singing? I would not.

The next morning he picks me up in a battered, dark blue van and I feel my heart do a cartwheel. I'm a little bit infatuated, which means I'm perfectly prepared to spend the next two hours cold, wet, exhausted, uncomfortable and embarrassed, making a complete fool of myself. I sigh and go outside.

Cory leans over from the driving seat to open the passenger door. 'Good morning! Climb in!'

I do and my stomach flips when he kisses me lightly on the cheek again.

'Your chariot,' he adds with a grin.

I look around. 'It's... lovely?' It's ancient, with peeling surf stickers on the windows, a stack of ancient-looking boards in the back and a few empty Coke cans rolling around on the floor. Two pink fluffy dice dangle from the rear-view.

'You should see what I drive on the circuit. In fact, I hardly ever drive – I get driven. Brand-new everything, all branded with whatever I'm advertising at the time, and my name plastered all over. It's embarrassing. Like driving through town shouting *Look at me! Look at me!* Which of course is what the marketing people want. This is the old van I drove when I was a kid. She lives ten or eleven months of the year in Mum's garage, and Mum takes her round the block once a week to keep her going. I used to drive round Pennystrand picking up all my mates to go surfing in this van when I was seventeen years old.'

I smile, picturing Cory at seventeen. The school heart-throb no doubt. Precociously gifted. Same wide grin, same passion for the waves. 'Has she got a name?'

He fumbles with the ignition and makes a big show of checking all the mirrors even though my street is a cul-de-sac and has no traffic whatsoever. 'Hmm?'

'The van? Does she have a name?'

'Well, yes,' he confesses. 'It's Claudia. As in Schiffer.'

I laugh. 'Isn't she a bit before your time?'

'Christopher's ten years older than me. She was his pin-up.' Christopher's his big brother, I learned last night. There's a sister too – Danielle.

In fifteen minutes, we're parking at a beach I haven't been to before.

'Traeth Haulwen,' says Cory. 'It's got nice easy waves and it's off the beaten track. If we went to Brightman or Lemon Cove, they'd be full of guys I know, and I don't want to have to stop and chat every two minutes. I think it's better for beginners to build confidence without an audience anyway.'

'Thanks for that. I have a strong feeling I'm going to make a huge fool of myself.' I chuckle to show I'm easy with this scenario, but Cory looks at me seriously.

'Don't think like that – it's counterproductive. If you think about it, what does that even mean? You mean that you won't be able to do it, right? That you'll keep falling off and choking and never catch a single wave.'

'Umm, yes.'

'So that's, like, everyone's first surfing lesson. Like I said to Max, it's hard. How is not being able to do something you've never done before, the first time you try it, making a fool of yourself? It's not – it's just having an experience.'

'Huh,' I say. 'When you put it like that...'

'I do,' he says firmly, jumping out of the van. 'Come on.'

Wow, we're not even at the water yet and he's already a really good teacher!

I climb down and he's already wriggling out of his T-shirt, a wetsuit splayed across the tarmac like some weird squid creature.

'Jump in the back. There's a wetsuit there that'll fit you – it's my sister's. I'll shut the door to give you privacy, and I promise I won't peek. Not like *some* people.'

'It was an accident...' I protest, though I did peek a little bit.

Alone in the musty space, I strip down to the bikini I've worn instead of underwear and start to pull the wetsuit on. It smells, and it feels weird. It's a bit like squeezing sausage meat into skins. Is it supposed to be this tight?

'It's supposed to be tight.' Cory the mind-reader's voice floats through a crack in the door. 'Keep going.'

When I climb out, I stand barefoot in the car park while he zips me up. His own wetsuit has a long tie attached to the zip so he can do it himself.

'Take your shoes if you want. There are pebbles on the beach.'

I slip on my shoes and we walk to the sea, Cory barefoot at my side.

It's a bright, blowy day. The sea is crayon blue with white caps, and the sun is steady. Even though this is supposed to be off the beaten track, there are still a fair few folk with surfboards.

'Hey, Cory! How's it hangin', bro?'

'Cory, whaddup, man?'

It's like being in an American high-school movie but with faint southern Welsh accents.

Cory waves and smiles at everyone but keeps walking until we're far enough away that we're alone. Then we get started.

To my utter amazement, I have the time of my life. We start off on the beach, lying on surfboards on the sand, covering the correct way to paddle and the technique for going from lying to standing. We practise over and over again until I'm gasping for breath. But pro champ though Cory is, he doesn't take it too seriously; he jokes around, making me laugh. We carry on chatting like the other night and return to the topic of him needing to retire one day.

'I'm slowing down.' He grins, leaping to his feet in a single fluid bound that I am very far from mastering. 'There's this championship, right – well, it's the biggest in the world basically, and I only came in second last time. There's this new kid – Eric Scoby, from California – he's just unstoppable right now.

Hungry the way I used to be. He beat me last year and I cared but not much. Things are a-changin', Kitty Roberts.'

'Wait a minute.' I sit back on my heels, covered in sand, and frown. 'In the biggest championship in the whole world... you only came in *second*?' I make a face. 'What a loser. I thought you were cool or something.'

'No, not me, definite has-been.' Now he's balancing on the front of the board, toes hanging over the edge in what he tells me is called a hang ten, miming the motion of waves underneath him, taking the micky out of himself.

'I might just go then.' I get to my feet and pretend to leave.

He runs after me and hauls me back.

'The gratitude! I show you all my secret lore and you *bail*? No way, Roberts! We haven't even been in the water yet.'

Despite the wind and the cold sand, the wetsuit and the exertion have kept me warm. All that changes when we go in the water.

'Oh my God, it's like *ice*!' I splutter, jumping out of the waves.

It doesn't help. My feet and ankles are wet now and seem to be encased in cooler packs that I can't shake off.

'That bad?'

I nod.

'Then I'm sorry, Kitty, but this is basically the only way.'

He picks me up and runs into the waves then throws me in. I go down shrieking and come up spluttering, hair plastered across my face like seaweed. Cory's laughing and dragging two surfboards now, remorseless.

'It honestly doesn't get any better. You could have stood there ducking in and out for an hour. I did you a favour.'

'Some favour!' I gasp, outraged. The worst of it is there's no way to get him back. I can't splash him or duck him because he's like a fish – I can see it at once. He's graceful on land, but in the sea, he just belongs.

'On you hop,' he instructs, holding one board steady in the water for me while the other bobs beside him, leashed to his ankle.

'Don't I get a leash?' I ask, heaving myself inelegantly into position. The waves lap the board and brush my face. I cling on for dear life; the board rocks from side to side.

'No. They're useful when you're chasing big waves, where your board could get swept to the middle of the Indian Ocean, but they're not safe for learners. A leash can snap a board back at a funny angle. We don't want it coming down and cracking you on the head.'

'Appreciate that.'

'Now paddle, like I showed you.'

I paddle for dear life towards the horizon, but my God, it's hard work. My shoulders already ache. The water resists every stroke. Cory shoots steadily ahead while I splash and struggle without moving. It's ridiculous!

When he's little more than a blob on the horizon, Cory sits up and crosses his arms across his chest. 'Come on, soldier,' he roars. 'Put your back into it. Do you think the enemy care that you'd rather be sunbathing? You're weak, soldier, you're weak!'

His parody of a drill sergeant is so utterly un-Cory that I burst out laughing and promptly fall into the water. I come up sputtering, my toes still only grazing the sandy bottom of the ocean bed. Even from here, I can see Cory laughing. Then I realise the board is floating away from me.

'No!' I wail, turning to swim after it.

'Wait, Kitty, chill.'

Cory sails past me, standing up now, slipping back into the water when he reaches my board. He swims back out to me with both boards, his face lit up with delight, then slips the end of the leash off his board and hands it to me. 'Grab this and I'll tow you. Save your strength – you'll need it.'

'Is that a threat?' I grumble, but I'm grinning too. His joy is infectious and, somewhere along the way, I've realised that I'm in the sea. I haven't swum in the sea for several years, not since a holiday in Spain with Mitch. My feet no longer exist, but other than that, it's fantastic!

I flop back onto the board like a landed sardine and crane my neck awkwardly to look at Cory. He slips the loop of the leash over my wrist then bobs beside me in the water, holding my wrist for longer, I'm sure, than is necessary.

'I've got you, OK?'

I nod. Although my extremities are frozen, I feel my hand and wrist pulsing with a warm glow.

'Hold the board.'

I clutch it and Cory slips onto his board and paddles away, the other end of the leash around his ankle. That's when I realise how strong he is. I'm not especially unfit, but when I think how hard I found it to paddle against an incoming tide, it blows my mind that he can do it so swiftly and effortlessly, while towing me and my board as well. In moments I'm way out to sea, further than I would ever go normally, and Cory, again, is sitting astride, looking around.

'Try and sit. It's incredible out here. A feeling of peace you just can't get anywhere else.'

Incredibly, I manage to sit up on the board and he lays a hand on it, which makes me feel safe. We fall quiet, jokes forgotten, and take in the immensity of the ocean around us. Sharp cliffs rear into the sky, and I can see a coast path and the tiny figures of walkers. Above, the sky is vast and blue and white, an endless canopy. The most hypnotic thing is the lap and hiss of the water retreating and renewing, sighing and seething. And here we are, two small people on the back of it. I sigh.

'Get it?' he asks, and my eyes fill suddenly with tears because I do.

I nod.

'Cool. Ready to try a wave?'

I smile through my tears. I never thought I would love this so much. 'Yes,' I croak.

'OK. So you can just ride it on your stomach if you want. You'll feel the swell and the power; you'll feel it carry you. That's all I really want for you. If you want to try standing, you know what to do.'

He lies on his front on the board and I follow suit. I still feel like a dead fish in this position; Cory looks like a crouching panther, every sinew of his body alert, looking back to watch the waves roll in behind us.

He nods. 'Couple of nice ones coming in. Remember what I taught you? Good. Ready? Let's go for this one. Start paddling... keep paddling... When you feel the swell. Not yet, not yet... *now*!'

In a second, he's on his feet and gliding away from me, as easy as falling in love. Too late I remember I'm supposed to be doing the same, and I try to leap up the way I learned on the beach. It was tricky to get the technique on land, but I did OK I think.

It's altogether different with nothing solid beneath you. My feet press down, the board tilts, I slide backward into the water and the board shoots up into the air like slippery soap. Mindful of what Cory said about cracking my head, I duck under the waves, and when I come up, my skull feels like it's going to break like an egg from the cold. The further out we've come, the icier and inkier the water.

Cory's back at my side and we try again. And again. The next three times, the same thing happens, but with his steady encouragement I do eventually get to my feet! For about three seconds. I can't centre my weight at all, and I wipe out yet again.

'Aaaargh!' I shout in frustration. 'I want to d-d-do it, C-C-Cory!'

'And you definitely will, but not today. You're too cold. It's time to go in. Lie down again and we'll body surf in together.'

This time, instead of me clinging on with both hands, Cory takes one of them.

'Don't do anything,' he says. 'Just lie there and feel the ocean.'

A moment later a gentle swell lifts and carries us. Hand in hand with Cory, I glide to the shore. I'm amazed by the feeling. It's not flying or floating – it's more powerful than that, because I'm being carried by something so much bigger than myself. It's *spiritual*!

The thought stuns me, and I wonder if this is what Cory feels, why it means so much to him that it's become his whole way of life. I can't ask him though; my teeth are chattering too much to talk at all as we're washed onto the sand and stumble up the beach.

'Dry yourself hard,' he orders back at the van, handing me a thick towel.

I'm so frozen it takes me ages to peel my wetsuit off and dress. When I eventually crack open the van door, Cory's dry and dressed in a hoodie and jeans, his wet brown-gold curls clinging to his neck.

'Here.' He passes me a girl's hoodie and pulls it down over my head, then takes my hands and rubs them between his own.

'I remember what it felt like the first few times. I'm used to it now.'

I can tell. It's like there's no difference between land and sea for Cory; he's equally at home in either. Just being. I realise that's why he's so calming to be around; he's simply at one with himself all the time. It's the loveliest thing.

'OK, K-K-Kitty.' He grins at me. 'I know just how to warm you up.'

At the far end of the beach is a café-kiosk, very basic, and we head towards it, me with my silver bag slung over my shoulder. I'm determined to buy him a drink at least, for teaching me so much. We buy hot tea, baguettes and Dairy Milk; as well as being cold, I'm ravenous.

We sit on some concrete steps, and Cory draws a black hip flask from his pocket. 'Whisky,' he says, tipping a glug into my tea. 'Warm you up.'

'Th-Thanks.'

My skin tingles, my blood hums, and bread and cheese have never tasted so good. If life in Pennystrand is like living in technicolour, then time spent with Cory is like living with all your senses turned up to a level you didn't know they could go to. As the blood flows back to my hands and feet, and my jaw gradually relaxes, I smile at him. 'Thank you,' I say, holding his gaze, wanting him to know how wonderful this was for me. 'Truly.'

He leans forward and rests his head against mine for a minute. I close my eyes, fleetingly, then he sits up again.

'You're welcome,' he says. 'I had a great time.'

CHAPTER 26

I don't sleep well that night, my mind still somewhere back in the waves. I can't help wondering what it all means, meeting someone who makes me feel like this only a few months after Mitch left me, someone who's *leaving*. Is it a message? A sign? If so, what's it saying? And I keep thinking about what Cory said, that I suit this place, that Pennystrand and I are a fit. Is he right? Should I stay?

The next morning I'm almost late for work. After fretting through most of the night, I finally dozed off at five and woke at eight. I'm damned if I'm going to let a guy affect my performance at the job I love, so I race through my morning routine, skipping several steps, and make it to the office at five to nine, reasonably together, hair still damp. Hopefully it'll dry before any customers come in. I'm surprised Roly's not here ahead of me – he usually is.

I get the kettle on then the phone rings. It's Roly.

'Bad news, Kitty – I'm sick.'

'Oh no! What's wrong?'

'Gastroenteritis according to my mate Dai the Doc. I'm

going to be laid up for the next week or so. It's contagious and I feel like shit. No pun intended. Sorry.'

'Roly, I'm so sorry. Can I do anything? Bring anything round to you?'

'I've got plenty of everything, just a case of waiting it out now. Thanks for offering though.'

I reach back and lift the diary off Bella's desk, then leaf through to today. 'Oh no. Roly, you've got *four* viewings on the Parnell house today. I'll call Lisa right now and explain. I'll rearrange them all for next week.'

His feeble voice floats down the line. 'I've already spoken to Lisa myself this morning. I thought I'd save you the grief.'

'Thanks, Roly, that's really sweet of you, but you shouldn't worry about things like that when you're ill. We're here to take the weight.'

'Looks like you'll have to. Lisa wants the viewings to go ahead. She wants you to do them.'

I laugh. Even when stricken down, Roly's a blast.

'No, seriously.'

'Roly, don't joke. You'll be better in a few days – surely she'd rather wait.'

'Apparently not. She was very clear, Kitty. Her exact words were, *If you're laid up, I suppose that new one is the next best thing.* Don't mention that bit to the others. If you've got other appointments today, rearrange those or let Nerys do them. And don't worry, you'll be great. You're a natural at this.'

'I hope so,' I mutter. Of all the days – when I'm sleep-deprived and fuzzy-haired.

'Look, I know you understand the importance of this client, so I won't belabour that. For the purpose of today, think of it as just another viewing. You know the house, you know what to say and what not to say. You're doing great – there's no problem.'

Right.

Nerys comes in at that point so I let her speak to Roly while I return to the all-important business of making tea then I try to get my head around the diary. *Well, if nothing else it'll take my mind off Cory!*

I only had two viewings today and one of those was just Stacey wanting to see her house again. The sale is ticking along nicely and she's starting to think about colour schemes and furniture. Lucky girl... We easily arrange for Nerys to do them, leaving me to concentrate on Fortescue Crescent. There are two viewings this morning and two this afternoon. The after-noon ones are back-to-back, but the morning ones, inconve-niently, are an hour apart. I feel stupidly nervous about them. No matter what Roly said, it's not just another house.

I gulp my tea, then make a coffee for good measure. In the little mirror over the loo I see that my hair's dry, but it's wild and bushy. I look like a grown-up Hermione Granger. I do what I can with hair clips, glad at least that Lisa won't be there to see me.

But when the front door opens, Lady Parnell is there, in a pale blue blouse and tight jeans, with gold, jewelled flip-flops. I can't believe my bad luck. I know my eyes look pinched and my hair's mad. At least my summer trouser suit and shoes are smart and I'm caffeinated to the max.

'Good morning, Ms Parnell. Lovely to see you again. Are you staying for the viewings today?' The thought crosses my mind that maybe she doesn't trust me.

'Yes. That is, no. I was going to go out as usual, but I have some urgent work to see to. I'll do it in the garden office to be out of your way. When you show the garden, please tell them they can't see inside the summerhouse today. They should get the idea from the outside, and if they're serious, they'll come back, won't they?'

'Yes, I'm sure that'll be fine. We'll leave you in peace, don't worry.'

She's staring at me, and I wonder if she's filing away my less-than-perfect state to complain about later.

'And there's another viewing at 11.30 a.m.?'

'Yes, but I'll go back to the office in-between. I'll let you know when I'm leaving.'

'Good. See you later then.'

And she's gone. Elegant and unhappy, tense and tired. She needs to go surfing. She looks fit enough, but somehow I can't imagine this brittle woman kicking back enough to mess about in the sea for hours. Surely she went when she was a kid though?

Despite our best efforts at screening in the office, the first viewers are clearly there for a gawk, not with serious intent to buy. They're local, and spend more time looking at the family photos and the corkboards in the kitchen than they do at any of the permanent features. Although I haven't warmed to Lisa Parnell, I don't like this so I hustle, telling them the next viewing is sooner than it is. I show them out after twenty minutes.

When I go to wave at Lisa, she comes to the summerhouse door. 'That was quick.'

Twenty minutes is often plenty for a viewing but not here, where there's so much to see.

I explain and turn to go but she calls after me. 'Wait, it seems silly you going all the way back to the office then having to come back so soon. You can stay and have a drink if you like.'

I hesitate. I am tired, but the last thing I want is to be in Lisa's way. 'That's kind... I don't need a drink though. I could just sit quietly somewhere out of your way and catch up with emails on my phone, if you're willing.'

She sighs. 'No, don't be silly. I need a break, if I'm honest.

Let's have a drink for half an hour then I'll get back to it and you can do your emails.'

'Thanks very much.'

Bemused, I follow her to the kitchen where she offers me an endless choice of drinks. I choose a herbal tea because, really, any more caffeine and I might explode.

She gestures at the comfy chairs in the corner and I hover until she sinks gracefully into one of them then I follow suit.

'So,' she says, beautifully manicured hands wrapped round a flowered mug, 'time-wasters, were they?'

'I'm afraid so. We screen like crazy in the office. We must turn down about half the viewing requests that come in. But it's impossible to know every time. Becomes very apparent once you're actually in the property with them though.'

She shudders. 'I'm sure. Oh well, I know you do your best. Roly is excellent. I couldn't do this if I had to go with the other lot.'

'Roly's a star. And he'll be back next week, but I'll do my very best for you meanwhile.'

An uncomfortable silence stretches. I can't ask what I really want to, which is why she's selling, so I just look around and eventually say, 'This really is such a beautiful house.' Which is self-evident and an understatement.

'I've been very fortunate,' she acknowledges. 'How are you settling into the job and the area, Kitty?'

'Very well – I love it all.'

'Have you any connections here? You look somehow familiar. Forgive me if I look at you oddly. I keep trying to work out who you remind me of.'

'No I don't, but two other people in Pennystrand have said the same thing. I must have one of those faces.'

'Maybe. So no family here?'

'None. I didn't know anyone when I came, but working for Roly is a great way to meet people.'

'I'm sure.'

She lapses into silence again and I rack my brains for a question that isn't overly personal and intrusive. 'What do you do? You said you were working from home today.'

'I own a boutique. Well, a small chain in fact. Have you seen The Sea-Change in the village?'

'Oh yes! God, I love that place – it has stunning things. That's yours?'

She nods, her face miserable. 'We have branches in Long-ford and Cardiff too. Longford is a lovely little market town. Have you been?'

I shake my head. 'I've been too busy with work since I came. I'm afraid I only know the immediate area.'

'You should make the effort to go when you have a day off. Have lunch in The Plough and tell them I sent you. They'll make a fuss of you.'

'Thanks, that's so kind.' I can't figure her out. She's as stiff and remote as ever yet she's clearly making an effort to be kind. 'I'll definitely check it out before I leave.'

'You're not staying?'

Gosh, am I really going to go into all this with Lisa Parnell?

I keep it brief. 'I just came for six months for some time out. I took the job to make it more sustainable financially but now I...' Having said it to Cory the other night makes it easier to say it again. 'I love it here, so it makes me wonder. But I should probably go back at some point. My sister and I are very close. She lives in Surrey.'

She gives the ghost of a smile. 'Ah, sisters. Life's biggest bane and brightest light. I have three. You?'

'Two. Cooper, in Surrey, and Cassidy, who's in New York.'

'Pretty names. And why did you need time out?'

I tell her about Mitch. She leans forward and squeezes my hand. Actually, it's more of a fleeting death grip.

'Infidelity is the worst pain. You don't know until it happens to you – you can't understand. I'm not surprised you needed to get away.'

Then she leans back and looks at the clock. 'Look at the time. I'd better get back to the accounts. Do stay until the next lot arrive. Make yourself another drink if you'd like to.'

CHAPTER 27

The rest of the viewings go well. One lot are genuine but can't afford the asking price. They ask if the vendor would consider a low offer and I can answer that one easily enough. Another couple are discussing it seriously and say they're considering making an offer. The third viewer, a well-to-do barrister with a number of building projects on the side and pots of money, according to Nerys, wants to barge into the summerhouse and make an offer to Lisa there and then. With difficulty, I persuade him that all offers must go through the office. When I tell Lisa there's a serious offer on the way and that another is distinctly possible, she sighs.

The next day there's only one viewing at Fortescue Crescent, in the afternoon. Lisa's working in the summerhouse again, and when I say goodbye, she says, 'Oh, Kitty, you must pop into The Sea-Change when you're passing. If there's anything you like, tell the girls who you are. I'll tell them to give you staff discount.'

'Wow, that's incredibly generous. But there's no need really. I'm just doing my job.'

'It's not forever,' she says, expressionless as ever. 'Just a one-time thing. Why not? What's the point of having a shop if you can't give a treat to someone now and then?'

'But, but...' I want to say, *Why me?* She hardly knows me.

She strides out of the summerhouse, leaving me to close the door and scurry after. 'No buts. Treat yourself. Come on. Have another cup of tea before you go. Christ, it's after four. Scrub that, we'll have a gin.'

I think she's joking, but she power-walks up the lawn, and when I join her in the kitchen she's standing in front of the bar. 'Are you a Tanqueray girl or a Hendricks? Don't even speak to me about Seedlip!'

'Oh, uh, I didn't know you were serious. Ms Parnell, I'm not sure I should...'

'Call me Lisa. Come on, you'll be back at the office by what? Five? You can manage half an hour with a gin inside you. It's Friday, after all.'

'It's Thursday.'

'Christ, is it really? Well, Thursday's the new Friday.'

She tips gin into two crystal tumblers, adds a tiny splash of tonic and a sprig of rosemary, then settles herself on a stool, setting the second glass on the counter with a determined air. I'm clearly expected to sit, so I do.

I take a sip. God it's strong. Delicious but strong. It doesn't seem very professional to go back to the office half-cut, but sitting in this stunning kitchen, drinking gin at this oh-so-cool bar is a tempting prospect. I justify it to myself as keeping an important client happy.

'So your partner was a dick and you needed to get away. Why Pennystrand?' she asks, frowning.

Oh, we're back to my life story.

'I'd been here once as a kid, on a family holiday, and I had fond memories. I wanted to be by the sea.' I'm not going to tell Lisa that I saw a psychic – she might think I'm a nutter and decide not to trust me in her house.

'And why did your family choose Pennystrand for the holiday?'

I shrug. 'I don't know. It's a lovely place. Lots of people have holidays here.'

'That's true. And your parents' names?'

'My parents...? Uh, Steve and Tilly. Roberts. Why?'

'Oh, no reason, just making conversation. Getting to know you.' She drains her glass and refills it, topping mine up without asking. We're having a second one then.

'So what was it like growing up in Pennystrand?' I ask. 'I absolutely love it here. I grew up in Surrey, which is very pretty, and great for trips to London, but there's something so free and wild about this place. So many people I've met seem to have lived here forever, or left and came back.'

'Yes, it gets its hooks into you, that's for sure. Growing up here was... well, it was good.' She nods slowly as if loath to admit it. 'I complained plenty at the time – I was a spoiled, stroppy teenager. But we were so lucky. Plenty of money for holidays and the best schools, huge parties here at the house, beach fires and barbecues and swimming. Smoking and drinking and snogging outside the beach huts when I was a teenager. It was idyllic really.'

'So you're not... leaving the area then? When you sell this place?' It's as near as I dare come to asking the burning question. But just then the front door opens and we hear voices, calling out hellos. A small crowd piles into the kitchen and stop short when they see me.

'Hello, who's this?' asks the woman leading the charge.

'This is Kitty Roberts. She works for Roly Rowlands. She's been doing an excellent job so we're having a little gin. Kitty, my sister Meredith.'

'Pleasure to meet you,' says Meredith in a smoker's baritone. She shakes my hand and grabs a glass.

'Never too early for a gin, and Thursday's the new Friday.'

She pours a liberal measure and downs it. She looks very like her sister except bigger and more buxom.

'This is my husband, Mark, my daughter-in-law Ashleigh, and her evil kids Thomas and Francesca.'

I say hi to everyone, daunted by this sudden onslaught of Parnells, and then get up to leave.

'Oh, don't worry about it,' says Lisa irritably. 'You're fine. Have another.'

She pours yet another stiff measure and Meredith drags a stool out so we're sitting in a little triangle.

'Go and do something useful, Mark,' Meredith orders. 'Ashleigh, want one?'

Ashleigh shakes her head and follows her father-in-law out of the kitchen.

'Course not,' mutters Meredith. 'Wouldn't say boo to a goose. God knows what Owain saw in her. Still, at least she gave him some good-looking children.'

The children in question, both exceptionally beautiful teenagers, gravitate towards the gin.

'Don't even think about it,' barks Meredith. 'Not until you're fifteen.'

Thomas swears, kicks a stool and stomps into the garden. Francesca sulks and stares at me. 'You're quite pretty,' she says.

Because I feel uncomfortable, I babble. 'Thank you. You're *very* pretty. Wow, lucky you!'

'Well, duh.' She pouts. 'I *am* a model.'

OK then.

'Don't brag, Fran,' says Lisa. 'No one likes a conceited bitch.'

I glance at Meredith in case she takes offence on her granddaughter's behalf but she's savouring her gin, eyes blissfully closed. 'Fair play,' she says, nodding. 'Never a truer word.'

Francesca rolls her eyes and leans on her elbows, sliding up and down along the counter in a hypnotic motion like a snake.

Lisa's back is towards her and Meredith's eyes are shut. Softly, softly Francesca reaches out a hand and pulls the bottle of Hendricks towards her. She silently takes a tumbler and sloshes in half a glass, holding my eyes as she does so. Then she picks it up and saunters after her brother.

I *really* think it's time for me to go, but I know I won't be let out before I've finished my drink and I don't want to down it because it's my third and I'm supposed to be working.

'What's the latest with Arse-Face?' Meredith asks. 'Is he still raising hell?'

Lisa gives a warning glance in my direction. 'He's being quiet for now,' she says.

'Good, let's hope he's dead,' says Meredith. I'm guessing subtlety is not her strong suit.

'No such luck,' mutters Lisa. 'I saw the Jag the other day, caught a glimpse of his stupid bald head behind the wheel.'

'Pity he didn't crash it into a brick wall.'

'So!' I say brightly. 'Is Francesca really a model? Does she do much?'

'Oh Christ yes,' says Meredith. 'So many offers coming in she hardly has time for school, not that she's any good at it anyway. She was in *Vogue* last month. She'd have run off to London by now if we didn't basically keep her under house arrest. But they've got to have a wholesome influence at that age, don't they?' She downs her drink, reaches for the bottle and makes to pour me a fourth.

'No, really,' I say, putting my hand over the glass. 'I have to get back to work and I've had three!'

'Aw, Roly won't mind, will he? Is he seeing anyone just now?'

'Oh! I don't know. I've never asked.' It's never occurred to me to wonder about Roly's private life. Is he single? In love? Straight or gay? I couldn't guess. I just turn up to work and there he is, the world's best boss. And I'm not about to start gossiping about him.

'Lisa, I do have to go. Thanks so much for the drinks. It was... really unexpected. And a treat.'

'You're very welcome. Goodbye, Kitty. Can you see yourself out?'

'Of course. Goodbye. Lovely to meet you, Meredith.'

As I weave my way rather swimmily to the front door I hear Lisa murmur something in her subdued tones and Meredith retort in her more strident way, 'Bloody hell, yes! She's the spitting image.'

Are they talking about *me*? Something about all of Lisa's questions and the intent way she keeps looking at me – even Francesca did it too – is trying to add up to something in my brain, but I'm highly unlikely to make sense of it after consuming half a gallon of nearly neat gin. My God, those Parnell women can drink!

CHAPTER 28

That evening I'm capable of nothing except ordering pizza and watching one episode after another of *Buffy the Vampire Slayer*. I'm jolted from my stupor when my phone rings. It's Cory.

'I had an idea to help you have the full Pennystrand experience,' he says when I pick up, his voice containing that already-familiar smile.

'What's the full Pennystrand experience?' My stomach flutters in a very uncool manner. He *had* said after surfing that he hoped to see me again before he left, but I knew he had loads of people to catch up with so I didn't count on it.

'Well look, you were here as a kid with your family. You're here now. But you were never here as a teenager! Teenage Pennystrand is arguably the best Pennystrand. I want to recreate it for you.'

I remember what Lisa said about snogging by the beach huts and my stomach does a full-on body-roll. 'That's very kind of you. What does that involve?'

'You'll have to wait and see. Are you free tomorrow?'

'Well, I'm working...'

'And after?'

'Afterwards I'm free.'

'So how about I drop by at 7.30 p.m. and we recapture our youth for one evening? Have dinner first.'

I smile and sink back into the sofa cushions. I kind of feel like a teenager already! 'Sounds great, Cory. So... how've you been?' I want to keep him on the line just a little longer.

'Oh crazy. Been running round seeing old friends, doing some errands for Mum – it's nice to help her out while I can, you know? Haven't even started thinking about packing, but it's kind of second nature by now.'

'I'm sure.' For a minute I feel the gulf between us acutely; he's about to go on such a big adventure, but for him it's just another day in the office. 'What time do you leave on Sunday?'

'Early. Six, I think. Gotta be at Heathrow by noon.'

'And do you feel ready to go? Are you looking forward to it?'

'Yeah, yeah I am. The call of the wild and all that. But part of me wishes I had longer to do more for Mum, make plans here. My best mate turns forty next month and I'll miss it. But hey, I'll be surfing in Mexico. Don't feel too sorry for me. How was your day? You sound sleepy. Roly working you hard?'

I giggle, still a little heady. 'No. I'm sleepy because I put away half a bottle of gin with Lisa Parnell this afternoon!'

'No kidding. She's thawing then?'

'I guess. It was a bit weird really – her sister turned up and I wasn't sure what I was doing there, but they wouldn't let me go! It didn't feel very professional, but they wouldn't take no for an answer.'

'Hilarious. I want to hear that story tomorrow.'

'Deal. Night, Cory.'

'Night, Kitty.'

The next day there are no Parnell viewings, thank goodness, but two offers come in – from the barrister and from the other interested couple. I call Lisa and Roly to keep them up to date. Lisa sounds despondent. My brain has recovered remarkably well and I ponder what Meredith said yesterday, about Arse-Face making Lisa's life a misery. It sounds as if a nasty divorce is behind her having to sell.

The day passes in an ordinary sort of way – at least, what passes for ordinary around here. Stacey, the buyer of Sunset Terrace, calls in, bubbling, to show us the sofa she's ordered and the paint colours she's chosen. Francesca Parnell walks by with a gaggle of long-haired, bare-legged girlfriends. When she sees me and I wave, she flips me a V-sign. Matthew from over the road calls in to speculate on whether gastroenteritis is the true nature of Roly's illness and to muse over what his early demise would mean for the Pennystrand estate-agency business. 'You'd all have to come and work for me!' he concludes gleefully. And shortly after that we're both roused from our admin by a loud, frenzied honking.

'That is doing my head in!' exclaims Derrick. He goes to the window. 'Oh my God, Kitty, you have to come and see this!'

The sad bit is that a funeral procession is coming up the hill. They're doing it the old-fashioned way, with men in top hats walking soberly before the hearse. Passers-by stop respectfully. The crazy bit is that a red Ford Fiesta is stuck behind the procession, apparently unwilling to be patient. It's truly shocking.

'I can't believe it! Can't he *see* it's a funeral?'

'Drunk?' Derrick speculates.

'At eleven in the morning?'

But sure enough, the Fiesta pulls out to overtake at last, careering up the hill with three mop-haired youths just visible inside, whooping and cheering. All the pedestrians stare in shock.

As the noise of the engine recedes and the procession

continues, Derrick shakes his head ruefully and sits down. 'Another day in Pennystrand.'

Soon enough, it's another evening in Pennystrand – another evening with Cory. I still have no idea what it entails. I change into my favourite skinny jeans, a cami, long-sleeved T-shirt and blue jumper. When in doubt, layers are good.

I listen out for the van, but Cory calls for me on foot. I reach for my mac – the weather's so unpredictable round here – but Cory shakes his head. 'We're teenagers tonight, remember. Did you ever think about sensible clothes when you were a teenager?'

I laugh. 'Never. My sisters and I never learned.'

'Exactly. That's why I said to eat first. We never went out for dinner back then. Now, have you got money?'

'Yes, I've got my wallet, and my card.'

'No bank cards – it's cash all the way. Pocket money, change jars. Scavenge your coat pockets if you have to. I've got' – he pulls a handful of change from a pocket – 'twelve pounds eighty-three.'

'Oh wow, you *are* being authentic. Hang on.'

I empty my purse, go through my coat pockets and scoop a few silvers out of a little bowl on the kitchen counter. 'Eight pounds forty-seven.'

'No way! Between us, we've got over twenty quid. Just think how drunk we can get on that! Come on.'

'No, wait! Come in for a second – I've just thought of something.'

I run upstairs and consider my make-up – mascara and lip balm. When would teenage Kitty ever have made so little effort to go out with a boy she liked? Entering into the spirit of the evening, I dig out some sparkly eye shadow and add lipstick and my wet-look lip gloss, hitherto only used for big nights out. I find two quid in my other handbag. Then I run downstairs again.

'Never warm enough and always in make-up,' I tell him. 'That's being a teenage girl.'

'Now you're getting it.'

We walk down the hill to the village off-licence and choose our cans of lager. There's a fine selection of local craft beers so we make a classier choice than we would have fifteen years ago because our inner adults, who insist on crashing the party, can't resist. Cory grabs a large bottle of cider as well: the universal drink of adolescence.

Then we walk to Brightman Bay, past the smart restaurants and the sandy-floored café, out to the beach huts that overlook the sweep of the bay. Most are occupied now that summer's here, but the farthest row, away from the hub of things, is still locked up. From here the figures still running and walking on the beach look like living toys, and only faint shrieks reach us from the waves. Cory sits on the ground, stretching out his long legs, and leans against the closed front of number eight. The air is warm, and a salty breeze ruffles the palm trees behind us. I sit beside Cory and he twists open the cider. We pass the bottle back and forth; the tangy sweet bubbles tickle my nose and I sputter.

'I know, right?' he says. 'I haven't drunk cider for about ten years.'

'I haven't either. Why is that? When and how do you grow out of it?'

'Haven't a clue,' he says happily, taking a long swig and wiping his mouth with satisfaction. 'But posters Blu-Tacked to the bedroom wall seem to disappear around the same time.'

'True.' I take the bottle, remembering again what Lisa said yesterday: *smoking and drinking and snogging outside the beach huts when I was a teenager*. I feel a thrill of excitement in my tummy that distinctly reminds me of the school disco where I had my first kiss. 'Who was your first kiss?'

He laughs. 'Oh God. Melissa Duckworth. We were ten. She had long blond hair like a mermaid. We went out for a week then she dumped me to concentrate on her studies. I kid you not, that was the phrase she used.' I guffaw. 'Yours?'

'Joe Bates. I was fourteen. It was at the school disco and I'd fancied him for a whole year. It was the *best* feeling!'

'And was this Joe Bates good enough for you?'

'Almost certainly not. He worked his way around most of the girls in my year, and he went to juvie later on. But look, he had cool hair and blue eyes and that was honestly all I cared about back then.' I smile, remembering when love was that simple.

'Shallow,' he sighs, shaking his head.

We reminisce over more teenage memories while the violet summer dusk deepens around us and the temperature drops. We finish the cider then start on the beers. The stars come out, pricking the dark velvet sky like tiny diamonds, and when I start to shiver, Cory puts his arm around me. I snuggle in close, soaking up his warmth.

'Parasite,' he says.

'I make no apology.'

Eventually we run out of beer. The people walking past on the cliff path below don't see us sitting on the ground above them, in the shadows. At one point a gang of teenagers comes across us.

'Urgh, old people!' exclaims one in disgust.

'Tennis courts,' another decrees and they veer away. We burst into slightly tipsy laughter.

'*That* never happened back in the day,' says Cory.

We laugh and laugh, and when we finally stop, I look up at him. Even the silver starlight can't mute his gilded glow, and the darkness doesn't hide the strong line of his jaw and full mouth. His longish, curly hair dances in the breeze, and I'm full of cider and beer and teenage dreams, and I can't help reaching up to touch his face. His skin is cool, but beneath the air's chill, there's that warmth that Cory always seems to emanate, even in the depths of the ocean. I swallow hard. I'm falling for this guy who's leaving.

He holds my gaze, long and intense, and everything else falls away. There's only Cory and me, and this incredible excitement between us, when he bends his head towards me.

I catch my breath. If I kiss him I'm lost, but of course, it's inevitable.

I close my eyes because the sight of him is making my head spin. A second later, I feel his lips on mine, and a swirling, tingling feeling spirals all the way through my body. A great warmth floods through me as his arms wrap around me, and I turn to face him properly, throwing my arms around his shoulders, knotting my hands into the hair at the nape of his neck. And we kiss and we kiss like teenagers. We kiss as if we're running out of time. Which, of course, we are.

CHAPTER 29

When we stop, we still cling to each other – his hands clutching my jumper, my hands still in his hair. I feel a sense of wonderment that I hope I see reflected in his eyes, but it may just be wishful thinking. This can't be it for us, can it?

'What are you doing tomorrow?' I breathe. I have work and in the evening I've promised to go to Cherry's, but in the moment, I'm fully prepared to pull a sickie, to bail on my friend... I can't think beyond the immediacy of me and Cory.

He looks stricken. 'My sister's arriving first thing tomorrow and staying the night. I'm not free, Kitty. I haven't seen her for a year.'

'Well, that's important. We'd better make the most of tonight then.'

He looks at me. 'I want to, Kitty, I do. But I can't change the fact that I'm leaving. I don't know when I'll be back or for how long.'

'I know.'

'It's just, I'd hate to... You know, a one-time thing isn't what I'd want for us if I lived here... I want you to be OK, after I've gone. I don't want to do the wrong thing.'

'It's not the wrong thing. I'll be OK, I promise.' It's a wild promise, rashly made, in a moment when I feel buoyed up and invincible from his kisses. He cares about me, he doesn't want to hurt me – that's all I need in that moment.

A slow pattering begins around us: summer raindrops, big and fat. We laugh, the intensity broken.

'Come on.' He leaps up and pulls me to my feet, then we start to run. The hill makes me stop, panting, even as the rain speeds up. Cory isn't even slightly out of breath, reminding me again that he's a top-class athlete. We are very different beings, living very different lives.

He shrugs. 'It's only rain.' We walk the rest of the way hand in hand, arriving at my place absolutely drenched. We stumble inside, still laughing, and strip off our outer layers in the hall. This is only going one way unless we make a firm decision to stop it.

He kisses me again and I ache with longing. I can already sense how I'll feel when he's gone, a little puncture in my invincibility. But I want this anyway. 'Come on.' I take him by the hand and lead him upstairs.

In the bedroom we undress each other, and I feel pure joy at the sight of his naked body. I sigh and run my hands over his skin, lean against him and rest my head on his chest for a moment.

The summer storm has made the air in the little room hot and cloying. Cory kisses me and goes to crack open the window. Wind and rain blow in, and we sit side by side on the bed for a minute, listening to the thunder. Then there's no holding back any longer.

CHAPTER 30

The next morning I hate tearing myself from his arms, I hate showering the smell of him off me, I hate making breakfast knowing that scrambled eggs are the only meal I'll ever cook him. We eat in subdued silence. I dread the devastation that's waiting for me when the afterglow of our incredible night fades. What was I thinking? I'm not the sort of person who can be detached and philosophical about falling for someone hook, line and sinker and them disappearing for good. But do I regret it? Watching him gather our plates and wash them without a word, seeing his long, rangy form and ruffled-up hair, his sad smile when he re-joins me at the breakfast bar, I decide that I don't. It's just that there's a huge price to pay.

His phone buzzes, breaking the spell. He reads the text. 'Danielle came home last night to surprise me. She demands my immediate presence.'

I kiss his cheek. 'Go – don't miss a moment with your sister. I have to go to work anyway.'

He picks up his rucksack. It rattles with empty cans and the bottle, a nostalgic sound that reminds us of how last night started out. The best fun.

At the door, he takes my hands. 'I had an amazing time with you, Kitty. I always love a week at home but this... it was tremendous.'

'Thanks,' I manage. 'Thanks for everything. You're... great.'

'So are you. So look, I'm off obviously, but can we keep in touch? Text? Email? Or would you rather not? You might feel it's not worth it, because I'll be thousands of miles away. But I'd like hearing from you now and then, if that's OK.'

'Sure. That would be good.'

'Here's my email.' He scribbles it down on a notepad on the hall table. 'That's probably best because I do lose my phones fairly often – occupational hazard. Drop me a line with yours. Please don't be all like, *Oh, he's busy, he won't want to be bothered.* Because I will.'

'OK.'

'Good. OK then. You take care, Kitty Roberts.'

He kisses me goodbye and I watch him walk away. I stay staring after him, at the quiet Saturday street, for a long time, then I brush my teeth, grab my bag and go to work.

The absence of Cory, before he's even left the neighbourhood, is palpable. Both Bella and Nerys are working today – just as well because I'm operating at chocolate-teapot levels of usefulness. I'm forgetful, can't string a sentence together, tell one caller that a tiny one-bed chalet with ten-month occupancy is £850,000 because I'm looking at the wrong info. When Bella goes out on a viewing, Nerys brings me tea and cake and asks, 'Man?'

I nod. 'That obvious?'

'Yep. Cory Hudson?'

'How do you know?'

'This is Pennystrand. Everyone knows. If you need to talk, I'm here. Go for a drink after work if you like.'

'Thanks, Nerys, I'd love that. I'm going to a friend's today but next week?'

'Definitely. I've never met him but I've seen pictures of course. My God, what a heartbreaker.'

'Yeah.'

Somehow I struggle through the day and go home before going to Cherry's, so I can have a good cry and get it out of my system before I see her. It's torture. The house is the last place I saw Cory. The bed is still ruffled and mussed. The towel he used is still thrown over the banister. I touch the bed, I touch the towel. I want to bring him back. The window's still open as he left it. The flashbacks start coming – his smile, his touch. Our conversations and laughter. I remember how bold and expansive I felt when we were kissing by the beach huts. 'We'd better make the most of tonight,' I'd said. 'I'll be OK, I promise.' Wow. Lust really does make you crazy.

But Cherry won't let me succumb to despair. She proves unexpectedly tough on the matter. 'Yes, you feel like shit now,' she concedes. 'And that's fair enough. It sounds like you guys had an amazing connection. But you were loving your life here before you met him and it's still the same life – great job, great place, finding yourself and all that jazz and, of course, me. This is good, Kitty. It shows you're well and truly over Mitch. It shows that part of your life is opening up again. It's actually good that he's gone if you think about it, because if he was staying, it would become all about him. Whatever you do in October, you need to do it for *you*, not some guy. The universe has kindly removed him so you can continue to make your decisions in peace.'

'It doesn't *feel* kindly,' I mumble. 'It feels brutal. How could I be so stupid, Cherry? I'm not a casual-sex person. And he's the only guy apart from Mitch I've slept with in *years*. It's a big deal for me! And he asked me, he *checked*. And I told him I'd be fine! What was I *thinking*?'

'You weren't thinking. You were feeling. And that's OK, Kitty – don't beat yourself up. And it doesn't sound like it was casual for him either, just... isolated.'

'But now I'm just like all the other girls.'

'What other girls?'

'Oh, Cherry, come on. He's a champion surfer, travelling the world. He's gorgeous and sexy and easy-going. He must have girls chucking themselves at him everywhere he goes.'

Cherry raises her eyebrows. 'Well number one, you don't know that. Plus, sex does *happen* between adults, you know. Say you stopped at the kiss last night. You'd be here now, telling me you miss him, same as you are now. You'd be telling me there was a moment, a definite moment, when it might have gone further, but you didn't want to get hurt. And you'd probably be regretting *that*! Don't you think?'

I take myself back in my mind to that kiss, the rain slowly splattering onto the ground around us, the stars glittering and his arms around me. Cherry's right. It would have felt so incomplete. '*Yes*,' I grumble. 'Oh wise one. It was always going to hurt, no matter what. Wow. Anyone I meet in the future will have a very, very high bar to live up to.'

'And that's a good thing too,' says Cherry, slapping me bracingly on the thigh and getting to her feet. 'I'm getting you medicine. Red wine and chocolate cake.'

I nod gratefully. 'Can't fault it,' I say, sounding like Derrick.

CHAPTER 31

Thankfully I have the next day off. It wasn't a late night with Cherry and I'm not hungover, but I do need some time alone to digest all that's happened recently, and it's a relief not to have to put on a brave face. I stay in bed and cry a bit, I daydream and regret, then I get up and get on with it. I make a delicious breakfast of avocado and poached eggs on sourdough and take a long walk by the sea. When I get back, I tidy away the reminders of Cory – the two mugs, the two plates, sitting on the draining board. I tuck away the piece of paper with his email on it inside a drawer in the bedroom. I will email him, but not yet.

That afternoon, my dad calls.

'Dad! It's so good to catch up with you finally. Have you been crazy busy?' Because he has a restaurant, it's not always as easy for us to connect; the service industry keeps stupid hours, and I've always done office hours. Dad might want to call me after midnight when he finishes a busy shift, but I'll be in bed ready for my 9 a.m. start. He works a lot of weekends too, so a Sunday afternoon chat with him is a real treat.

'So busy. We *want* the restaurant to be busy, but Claude's

still off and I'm covering a lot of his shifts. It's full-on.' Claude,
Dad's head waiter, hurt his back in a motorbike accident.

'Maybe you should get someone in for a month or two. It
doesn't sound as if Claude'll be better any time soon, and you
don't want to burn out.'

'Hey, don't worry about me – I'm tough. But yes, if he's not
back in a week or two I'll do that. But never mind about me!
How's my girl? I feel as if I haven't talked to you in ages. How's
Wales?'

'I'm good, it's all good – I really love it here.'

'You always did. But you sound subdued or tired or something? What's up, poppet?'

I tell him about Cory – just a little bit. I don't need my dad
to know *all* the gory details. 'So he's gone,' I conclude. 'Left at
six this morning. I'm fine, it's just that he was nice, and I miss
him. But I've still got my brilliant job and Cherry and summer
by the sea to enjoy.'

'How are the houses? Did you find the pearl necklace yet?'

Dad's the only person I've told about Doris's necklace. I
wanted to tell Cory, but a confidence is a confidence. Dads are
different though. And mine is hundreds of miles away so it's not
like he can let anything slip here.

'No sign of it,' I sigh. 'But plenty of entertainment. We had
drunk teenagers tailgating a funeral procession the other day...' I
fill him in and enjoy hearing him laugh. From my earliest little
girlhood, it's been a treat for me to hear that laugh. Then I tell
him about the huge quantities of gin I consumed with the
Parnell sisters. And he goes quiet. I thought he'd find that hilarious. 'Dad? You OK?'

'Yes, fine, just thinking. Well, they certainly do sound like
characters. And you're selling a house for them, you say?'

'Yes, well, for Lisa – she's the eldest sister. God, you should
see it. It's this ginormous mansion on a crescent at the top of the
cliff. It looks out over the ocean and it's just... well, it's sensa-

tional. Everyone nicknames it Fortune Crescent because you have to be so rich to live there.'

Another pause. 'Gracious. And why is she selling?'

'Unknown. She hasn't even told Roly, and ordinarily she'll only deal with him. But he's off sick for a few days and I'm the next best thing apparently.'

'You mean she asked for you instead?'

'Yes. I was super surprised. She didn't seem to think much of me when we first met. But she must have reconsidered.'

'Well of course she did. My girl is splendid in every way! I'm glad you're still enjoying it there.'

'Dad... do you *know* the Parnells or something? You sound a bit weird?'

A longer pause. 'Of course not. Maybe I heard the name when we were on holiday there or something. It sounds a bit familiar.'

That's unlikely. Out of all the snatches of local conversation he would have heard that week, why would one random surname stay with him through the years? I know my dad – there's something he's not saying.

Cooper's theory that he had an affair snakes into my mind, unwelcome. I don't even want to *think* about that. Then again, now might be the perfect time to do a bit of fishing.

'Dad? When we were all here on that holiday... did you and Mum fight a lot? I mean, did being here somehow cause the problem between you?'

'Why on earth would you ask that?'

'Something Cooper said. That she heard you and Mum have a row or two. She's older, right, so she remembers it differently from me.'

'Right. We might well have had a row of course – it happens. But no specific one that I can remember all these years later.'

And yet he can remember the name Parnell. Fishy. 'And she

said that you weren't always with us during the day? Why would that have been?'

'Why were you and Cooper talking about this? Is everything alright? Does she need me to call her?'

'No, we're both fine. We were just reminiscing.'

'Oh gosh, I can't remember. Maybe I was taking care of the errands so your mother could totally relax. That was probably it. She was very tired and tense back then.'

'Why?'

'Stress at work, taking on too much. She felt very torn about taking time off.'

'Huh, I never knew that.'

'No, well, she didn't want to worry you girls. You know your mother – always keeping her cards close to her chest.'

It's true – Mum is very like that.

'Anyway, poppet, I have to go, but look, I'm off on Thursday. Can we catch up again then? I hate when we miss each other for weeks at a time.'

'Me too, and yes, for sure.'

'I'll look forward to it. Meanwhile, try not to miss that fella too much. He sounds great, but you deserve the best of everything, not some guy who's just passing through.'

'OK, Dad. Don't work too hard! Love you.'

'I love you, Kitty.'

When we hang up, my mood is lower than ever. Cory's gone and my beloved dad is lying to me. I know it because I know him. We've always been the best of friends; I know every tone of his voice. The long pauses, the heaviness in his voice: classic Dad when he feels uncomfortable. He sounded the way he did when he forgot to pick up the cake for my tenth birthday and we had to make do with doughnuts from Greggs instead.

Guilty.

CHAPTER 32

As the days pass, I set my worries about Dad aside. Next time we talked, we avoided the subject and everything was fine. I don't mention our weird conversation to Cooper.

I try asking Mum about that holiday when we talk but she's unforthcoming and brisk. Unlike Dad, that's nothing out of the ordinary for her. 'Come and visit me in Bath when you get a weekend off,' she says. 'There's a wonderful new Thai restaurant you would love and a fabulous photography exhibition in the gallery. I'll treat you.'

I guess whatever happened between them is water under the bridge now. And it's their business. I just don't like to think of Dad being less than honest with me and I don't like to think of him treating Mum that way.

Still, I don't want to spoil my time here with thoughts about events in the past that I can't change. It's now full summer and apart from occasional downpours, the sun is hot, properly hot at last, day after day. The beaches are packed with holidaymakers, the roads in and out of the village get congested, the car parks are packed with cars that glare in the sun. I'm over halfway through my time here. I don't need to make any decisions yet, but the time when I will is on the horizon. For one thing, I'd want to give Roly the full month's notice, so if I *am* going in October, I'll need to tell him at the beginning of September, and it's just into July now. It feels alarmingly close when I think about it like that. I make the most of every minute I'm not in the office to swim, sunbathe and picnic. I don't quite have the spirit to try surfing again, not without Cory.

At work there's plenty to keep me busy. Everything goes smoothly with Stacey's purchase of Sunset Terrace, and I know I'll never have an easier sale. It was a straightforward completion – no hitches or hold-ups; ten weeks to the day after I first showed her the house, I hand her the keys to her new life.

On the Friday of her first week in residence she invites me to go up and have a glass of Prosecco on the doorstep with her, just as she dreamed. It's lovely up there, with the sea winking below. Seeing how thrilled she is with everything rekindles in me that bittersweet longing for a home of my own. When will it be my turn? And *where*? That's an equally pressing question now.

Of course there are more than two places in the world. I don't *have* to choose between Wales and Surrey. But why would I go somewhere random and start all over again when I've only just started all over again here? Surrey still has a lot going for it. Family, the sure knowledge that I'll always have a warm welcome in my sister's lovely home, the chance to watch the boys grow up at close quarters – that's hard to set aside. But Surrey is more expensive. My buying-a-house dream is more reachable here. And is the Surrey countryside really as *me* as I always thought it was? I do love living on the coast. I love that Pennystrand is laid-back and casual and windswept. I love that it's quirky and, well, a bit weird. I love feeling part of the community, which has happened thanks to my job. Would I find another job like this one, another *view* like this one, anywhere else?

Sunset Terrace really is a lovely little spot, tucked away and quiet. The bowl of Pennystrand Bay is blue as blue can be under the cloudless sky, and it's catching the late afternoon sun. Stacey's already in shorts and a vest, and I kick off my shoes and hitch up the skirt of my summer dress to get the sun on my legs.

'How's it going working at Rowlands?' she asks.

'I love it. It really is the perfect job.'

Stacey sighs. 'That's lovely. It sounds as if you've found your true calling. My job's so dull.'

I already know that she works in a big firm of accountants half an hour away and that it's just a way to pay the bills.

'But you've got the dream house,' I say, smiling. 'Maybe we can't have everything.'

'That's true.' She stretches languorously. 'I still pinch myself every day. I never thought I'd be able to live somewhere like this, that I'd be able to do it all by myself.'

'So you're really, properly happy here?'

'Oh my God, yes! I've got my little routines, you know?'

'Like Prosecco on the doorstep after work?'

'That's the best one. Just sitting here, taking it all in. It's perfect.'

'I'm really glad.' And I am. It's lovely seeing people happy. But I wonder if I would make the trade that Stacey's made again: a soulless job to pay for the perfect house. That was my plan through all those London years. And yet, I'm happier now than I've ever been. Five days a week of boredom is a high price to pay. I'm not sure I could do that anymore.

Which is exactly what I love about a job where you meet so many people all the time. You don't just learn about *their* lives – they make you think about your own. Doris Vincent has me thinking about a life well lived, about the memories that sustain you when life moves on. Lisa Parnell shows me that all the material blessings in the world can't make you contented. Cory made me try new things and remember what it's like to kick back and have fun. I think my job is making me a better person. To anyone else, it might look like just a job. Not the best paid, not one you need any special qualifications for. But right now I wouldn't swap it for anything in the world.

CHAPTER 33

The next day, to my delight, Roly's finally back at work and perfectly well.

'So you obviously got on very well at Lisa's?' Roly asks. 'She didn't burn you at the stake or anything?'

'No, on the whole she was much friendlier than I'd expected. And the viewings were all fine. But she... she...' I suppose I don't really need to tell him, but I still feel slightly guilty.

'What? You're worrying me now, Kitty!'

'She made me drink gin.'

'The bitch!' gasps Roly without missing a beat.

I burst out laughing.

'That's vile.'

'Well, no, it was nice of her, and it was very good gin. But it was in the afternoon and I said I should get back to the office, but she wouldn't take no for an answer.'

Roly shrugs. 'It could be worse. I won't start disciplinary proceedings.'

This afternoon, the barrister wants to look around for the

third time. Because I've dealt with him until now, I do the viewing. Lisa's not at home. Before he leaves, he lingers in the hall, maybe imagining himself in black tie welcoming guests. As I try to chivvy him politely, we hear a key in the lock and Lisa comes in, helping an elderly lady over the doorstep.

'Oh, you're still here, are you, Stuart?' she says coldly. 'You do know you actually have to buy a house before you move into it?'

I wince. He's our only serious potential buyer so far and I don't want him put off by her rudeness.

'Take a chill pill, Lisa,' he says. 'Thank you, Kitty. I'll be in touch.'

He strides down the drive and I'm about to follow when the old lady stumbles. Lisa catches her with an arm around her shoulders.

'Do you need a hand?' I ask.

'Could you take her other arm? Help me take her into the sitting room – she likes the view from there.'

'Sure.'

The elderly relative, Lisa's aunt Agatha is my guess, is bird-like in stature, but she's swaying and her eyes are clouded. I take her arm and together we settle her in the pale blue and gold sitting room, in an armchair facing the window, which frames a magnolia tree. Lisa looks at me with worry in her eyes.

'Would you stay with her for two minutes while I make her some tea?'

'Of course. Don't worry, Lisa – take your time.'

She's back in a few seconds with a packet of triple chocolate cookies and a china plate edged in rosebuds.

'Can you chuck a couple of those on the plate for her while I get the tea? She probably needs some sugar.'

She disappears again, and I rip open the packet.

'Hello. Are you Agatha, by any chance?' I ask, passing the biscuits to her. 'My name's Kitty.'

She doesn't answer but takes the plate, stuffing the first biscuit into her mouth. She eats the second one more slowly, gazing into the meandering patterns of the magnolia branches then holds the plate out for more. I stick another two on it and they disappear too.

At last her eyes clear, her expression brightens and she looks at me. 'Jessica!' she cries. 'Why, you're just as pretty as ever! Where've you been all these years?'

'Oh, I'm not Jessica – I'm Kitty.'

She frowns. 'Did you change your name?'

'No, I really am Kitty. I've never been Jessica.'

Her lined face crumples into a paper ball of confusion. 'Well, that's uncanny, but I'll take your word for it. It's nice to meet you, dear.'

'You too. And you're Agatha?'

'Yes. I'm surprised they haven't told you all about me. Crazy Auntie Ag, they call me. But I'm not crazy, Kitty. I just have moments where my attention slides away and I lose track a bit. Do you ever get those?'

'Truthfully, yes. Like if I'm overwhelmed with things or sad. My mind wanders off... Is that what you mean?'

'Exactly. The problem is, when you're my age and live in a home, they don't accept that. They flap and panic and think you're going to set fire to yourself. It's very tiresome.'

'I can imagine.'

'You're kind too, like her, like Jessica. And the spitting image, if you don't mind me saying so.'

'If you don't mind me asking, who *is* Jessica?'

'Lisa's sister. Do you know Lisa? Well of course, this is her house, so if you don't, you probably shouldn't be here. Mind you, you seem lovely, so I don't much care.'

'Oh, I do know Lisa. I'm her estate agent – or one of them. I thought her sisters were Meredith and Emily.'

'Yes, and Jessica. And the two boys, Francis and Griff. I say boys, but they're all grown up now. All grown up, and look at me, I'm ancient.'

At that point, Lisa comes back with tea on a tray and a few sandwiches. 'Here we are, Auntie Ag, something nice and hot to drink. Are you feeling any better?'

'Any better than what? I'm fine. I've been chatting to Kitty here, though I must say she's the absolute spit of Jessica, isn't she? I embarrassed myself at first by calling her Jessica. She probably thinks I'm as loony as you all do now. But the resemblance is uncanny, don't you think?'

Lisa stops abruptly and the tea things slide. I leap up to steady the tray.

'Thank you, Kitty. Would you pull out that side table?'

When everything's safely positioned, Lisa pours tea, ignoring her aunt's chatter. There are two cups, two plates; obviously I'm not invited to stay this time.

'I should get back to the office,' I say. 'Can I do anything else to help before I go?'

'No, but thanks for your help, Kitty. I appreciate it.'

'That's a shame,' says Agatha crossly. 'I like her, Lisa. Can't she stay and have some grub with us? I haven't told her about the mermaids yet.'

Lisa rolls her eyes. 'No, Auntie Ag, Kitty has to go. She's working today.'

Actually, I would love to stay and eat chocolate biscuits and hear about the mermaids. But I can see Lisa wants me to head off.

'Bye, Lisa, all the best. And goodbye, Agatha. It was lovely to meet you.'

'*Au revoir*, Kitty. Come and see me sometime. I'm at the Willows nursing home for the loose-screwed. I have a stash of jam tarts I could treat you to.'

'That would be lovely,' I say, at the same time Lisa says,

'Don't be silly, Auntie Ag, of course Kitty won't be visiting you. That wouldn't be appropriate at all.'

CHAPTER 34

The next day, on my day off, Cherry holds her long-promised coffee morning so I can meet her friends. I go early to help her set up. It's a Saturday, so Magpie is at large, running around making aeroplane noises, trailing a coat over her shoulders like a cape – or wings. Despite that minor trip hazard, we get the table laid, the china stacked and the cakes displayed in plenty of time.

I tell Cherry about my encounter with eccentric Agatha Parnell and her calling me Jessica.

'Jessica?' says Cherry at once. 'As in the long-lost sister?'

'You know about her? I wasn't sure if there really was one or if she was just... a bit confused.'

'Oh no, Jessica's real alright. There were four Parnell girls and two Parnell boys, and I know because Jessica was my mum's age. They weren't at the same school of course, but they did ballet together. Mum talks about it a lot. I think she's sad that Jessica disappeared. They weren't close, but she liked her a lot. They bumped into each other over the years after the ballet finished and always had a nice chat, she said.'

'Why did Jessica vanish? It wasn't anything horrible like an abduction, was it?'

'Pretty sure not. Nobody knows of course, but there was a rumour of some big falling-out with the mother over her *career choice*, of all things! Who knows with that lot? It seems like a daft reason to become estranged from your family forever, but they're a mighty force, aren't they? Maybe a clean break was the only way. Funny she thought you look like her though. I'll have to show a pic of you to my mum and see what she thinks.'

'If you like. Funny thing is, remember how I told you Lisa was really stiff and cold at first?'

'Before she thawed and force-fed you gin – yes.'

'Well, back then she used to kind of *stare* at me. As if I looked familiar, I suppose. And when I was leaving after the famous gin session, I heard Meredith say something about an uncanny resemblance. I'd forgotten about that till yesterday.'

'Ha! Maybe you're an illegitimate Parnell! Wouldn't that be hilarious? What? Kitty, I was only kidding. Don't look so horrified.'

But I haven't told Cherry Cooper's theory about Dad having an affair here. *God, what if he did and the woman got pregnant and... no, wait a minute, I was already alive. Oh, thank heavens.* 'No, obviously you were joking. It was just the thought of being part of that scary clan.'

'Anyway, on to more important things. Have you heard from Cory?'

I shake my head.

'But you have emailed him, like he asked you to, haven't you?' Cherry looks strict.

I pick a strawberry from the bowl on the table and bite it from its leafy hat, nodding. 'I did. Just a short one – I thought he wouldn't want long missives to read while he's on the move.'

'And when was that?'

'Two weeks ago.'

'Hmm, not that long in man years. And you got the right email address?'

'His handwriting was very clear.'

'OK, well you've done your bit – that's good.'

'I'm glad you approve,' I say, wondering where to put the strawberry hat, glad of an excuse not to meet her eyes. I know Cherry's excited, still hoping there might be more for me and Cory. But I think two weeks is a long time. It's not 2005. Everywhere has Wi-Fi; everyone has email on their phones. It's not as though he has to wait till he gets to a town with an internet café to catch up with his emails.

I still miss him. When I walked past the tennis courts, I wondered if Cory would fancy taking a lesson or two with me. When I saw a couple on Lemon Cove having a picnic, it was something I wanted to do with him. When my favourite café, Time and Tide, started selling a new chocolate brownie with orange and whiskey, Cory sprang to mind. But hey, I have Cherry. She said an emphatic no to the tennis but an enthusiastic yes to the picnic and the brownie. Two out of three ain't bad.

Her friends arrive and I push thoughts of Cory from my mind. There are four of them – her schoolfriends Annest and Cerys; an art friend, Emma; and Diane, who's 'just from around'. They're a nice bunch, chatty, delighted to take the piss out of themselves for having a coffee morning.

'We're so grown-up!' Cerys says, laughing.

'We're boring,' argues Annest.

'We're our mothers!' marvels Diane. 'How did that happen?'

They're all very interested in why I'm here and the tragic backstory that brought me. Cherry, to her credit, says nothing about Cory, and I don't mention him either. I don't want to reduce him to an anecdote.

'So you're single?' Annest clarifies.

'Well then, we need to find you someone!' cries Emma.

'Come on, girls, put your thinking caps on! Who can we fix up Kitty with?'

'No, really, I'm fine—'

'You think I haven't tried?' demands Cherry, ignoring me. 'I've been wracking my brains! I don't want to harp on about it, because I want Kitty to stay in Pennystrand, but this is not the best place in the world for single men, is it?'

'No,' says Cerys glumly. 'It is not. There's the short, fat and bald variety. There's the hunky but married variety and the hopeless variety, which includes the following categories: A) on drugs, B) in prison and C) alcoholic. All those sub-categories, needless to say, are unemployed.'

'That's very scientific,' says Cherry, impressed.

'Rubbish!' cries Annest. 'You guys are depressing. There must be some lovely eligible men. What about Morgan Freeman? No wait, he's the actor. Who am I thinking of? Morgan Westman.'

'Are you kidding?' Cherry looks outraged. 'He's a slimeball with a comb-over and the conversational ability of a slug.'

'Really?' Annest frowns. 'I remember him as really fit!'

'Maybe fifteen years ago, but times have changed, my friend.'

Annest pulls a face. 'Right, ew. Sorry, Kitty. OK, how about Richard Brannen? Not *super*-hunky maybe, but a really nice guy.'

'He got back together with Sophie Davies.' Emma looks regretful.

'*Again?* Jeez, leave them to it.'

'What about my second cousin, Jason?' wonders Diane. 'You know him, right?'

Heads shake all around the table.

'Wait, I'll show you.' She fishes out her phone and starts scrolling through photos. 'Here he is. It's a bit unclear, but you get the idea.'

She passes it around; I see a laughing young man with dark hair.

'He's definitely single, because the Welsh network of aunts immediately informs all family branches if someone changes their relationship status. What do you think, Kitty?'

'Um, it sounds very efficient.'

'Not of the *network*! Of *Jason*!'

'Oh, right. He looks great. But honestly, I—'

'Excellent, I'll set it up.'

CHAPTER 35

The next day I'm back at work and it's just me and Roly. Apparently the barrister made an offer on Lisa's house yesterday. It's not far off the asking price, but Lisa is playing hardball – full asking price or nothing.

'Thanks again for all you did while I was off sick, Kitty You're doing an excellent job here, you know. You're clearly in your element. I was wondering, have you given any thought to whether you might stay any longer in Pennystrand?'

'Endless thought actually. And I still don't know is the answer. I'm sorry, Roly.'

'Nothing to apologise for – it's your life. I said this job is yours for six months and I meant it. But just so you know, if you did decide to stay on, I'd be very happy to make you permanent.'

'Wow! That's amazing to hear. Thank you, Roly – it means the world. If I do stay, of course I'd love to keep working here. In fact, this job is one of the biggest factors making me want to stay.'

'Well, I'll say no more about it for now, but keep an open mind, eh?'

A little later Lisa rings, asking me if I can pop in that afternoon. 'Only for ten minutes,' she adds. 'I don't want to hold
you up.'

'Of course! I've got a viewing near you at three, so I can
come by after that? Is anything wrong?'

'No, nothing. After three is perfect.'

When I tell Roly, he's intrigued. 'That woman is an enig-
ma.' He shrugs. 'I think I'll be half sorry if we do sell that house,
though it'll make us a stack of money of course. But there's
something very sad about severing her from her kingdom, isn't
there?'

'Severing,' I repeat with a shiver. 'It does feel that way,
doesn't it? Yes, it's all very peculiar. I met her aunt the day
before yesterday and it was a bit of an odd encounter.'

'Agatha? Most encounters with her are a little odd, but she's
a dear woman, as open-hearted and whimsical as Lisa is
guarded and poised. I suppose she said you look like Jessica
Parnell, did she?'

I stare at him. 'How did you guess?'

'Because I thought so the first time I met you. I remember
Jessica well. We dated once, in fact. Agatha was very close to
her; she was bound to notice it.'

The day passes quickly, and I head out at quarter to three to
walk up to the big houses on the cliffs. The property I'm
showing is in a prime spot – corner plot, sea views – but it's
rather depressing in itself, a large bungalow where an elderly
couple lived until recently. Now they've both died and their son
is selling the family home. He had tears in his voice the last time
I spoke to him. There's quite a bit of damp, and no alterations
have been made in the last twenty years bar the installation of a
great many disability handles and rails. It would need a lot of
work, as the couple viewing it point out, and whilst I know
that's practical, something in me balks at the thought of that old

couple living there for so many years, then their lives being obliterated without a trace.

I'm in a melancholy, reflective mood when I walk round the corner to Lisa's house. I could do without her brittle energy today.

'Thanks for popping by, Kitty,' she says when she opens the door. Today she remains standing in the doorway, as she did the first day we met. It's one of those days, is it?

'It was no trouble. How can I help?'

'I just wanted to check that you were OK after meeting my aunt the other day. Obviously she gets extremely confused sometimes and it can be disconcerting. I apologise.'

'Oh, there's no need. I was fine, honestly, and she didn't seem confused at all after she had a couple of biscuits. I liked her very much.'

'Well, I hope you won't try to visit her at the nursing home. She may be doling out invitations, but they're actually very strict about visitors there – family only. I'd prefer you didn't – best keep the boundaries clear.'

'I quite understand. I wasn't going to anyway – I got the impression you weren't that keen.'

'Very good. Well, that's all I wanted, Kitty. I promised not to detain you today.'

'Take care then – have a good evening.'

As I walk back down the hill, I'm exasperated. Honestly! One minute it's all gin and chit-chat, the next it's all standing on the doorstep and being told to keep my distance. The cheek!

As with everything else about Lisa, it's confounding. Roly said he didn't think Agatha got many visitors so I can't believe the home would be anything but pleased for her to have a bit of company. No wonder she doesn't get many with Lisa acting as her guard dog! Is there some secret she doesn't want me to uncover? Or is she simply ashamed of her eccentric relative? Whatever. Sometimes I really get tired of thinking about that family.

CHAPTER 36

The next day I'm off again and Cherry and I take Magpie to the beach. Her nursery is closed for the summer holidays. It would be idyllic under any circumstances with long-legged teenagers tossing their hair and parading, surfers dipping in and out of the waves, families sprawling with sunshades, windbreaks and picnic blankets. But being there with a child gives everything an extra gilding – the fairy dust of childhood. We go rock-pooling and build sandcastles and draw ice lollipops from the cool box like magicians drawing flowers from a hat, laughing at her round, dazzled eyes. We swim in the sea and splash each other and count the different types of seaweed.

If I lived here, I suddenly think, Cooper and David and the boys could come and visit. The boys would love it here. What about Mum? Dad? Would *they* want to visit me? I feel a chill of disappointment like a cloud going over the sun when I realise they really wouldn't. If Cooper's right about Dad, then this is probably the last place either of them would want to visit. If I want my parents ever to visit me again, I'll have to find some-where else to settle. As this strikes me, I realise quite how far down the path of staying my mind had strayed. I don't want to leave.

I push these thoughts away, so they don't mar our sun-filled afternoon. We brought a ton of food but somehow we manage to finish it all and still feel hungry. Cherry runs up to the beach hut to get us trays of salty chips and bottles of cold water from the kiosk. My phone pings: a message from Diane's cousin Jason about meeting up. My phone pings again: an email from Cory.

Ohmigod! Hastily I flip the cover closed and plunge my phone deep into my bag. I can't read that now, with Magpie arranging seaweed over my toes and my legs, and the sun glare on the screen, and Cherry nearby with her high hopes.

Somehow I get through the rest of the afternoon without dying of curiosity, but when we wend our way home, salt drying on hot, sandy skin, I can't resist ducking into the public loos en route. As I sit on the cold seat, I fumble for my phone and nearly drop it down the toilet in my eagerness to open the email.

Hey Kitty,

How's it going? It's been a while. Had my first big comp yesterday and I won. Another day, another peso, right? Perhaps there's life in the old dog yet! Tacos to celebrate tonight with a couple of mates. Shenanigans says hi – I think he really took to you. He wants to see you again and I've tried explaining to him that our lifestyles make it tricky, but he's not really accepting it.

Mexico is beautiful. The colours are all so rich and bright, and the light... it's like the sun's made up its mind that if it's going to shine, it's really going to shine, you know? The beaches are white and the surf is perfect. Have you been surfing again? I saw definite promise there!

It's nice to ramble on to you. Hope you write back and tell me all the news from Pennystrand. I hope the Parnells aren't giving you too much grief. Have you decided anything about how long you're going to stay? Pennystrand can be pretty hard to leave once it's got its hooks into you.

Stay cool, Cory xx

PS check out the attached link. Seems like something you should see x

I don't open the link now but hurry out to re-join the others.

'What?' Cherry demands. 'You look like you've got news. For God's sake, you only went to the toilet!'

'Are you psychic or something?' But really I'm not surprised she can tell something's up. I can feel the bounce in my step. My whole body feels as if it's filled with big, rainbowy bubbles. 'I just had an email from Cory.'

'Oh!' she shrieks, then clamps her hand over her mouth as people turn to stare at her. 'Sorry, that was a bit loud. I'm just excited, that's all. What did it say? Was it a good one?'

'Yes, it was really nice. Friendly.'

Her face falls. 'He didn't declare his undying love and say he's giving everything up to move back and be with you?'

I snort. 'If he did, I'd think he was a lunatic. But yeah, as I said, it was really friendly.'

'Can I read it?'

It's taken me a while to get used to Pennystrand ways when it comes to other people's business. Things that would be considered intrusive or rude or even a little sinister at home are par for the course here. I could say no – but actually I want Cherry to know what he said. How else are we going to dissect and analyse it in minute detail?

'Sure – here you are.' I open it up again and pass her my phone.

She reads it, pressing herself into the shade of some bushes and squinting. 'Oh, you're right, that is nice. Really warm. Obviously Shenanigans is code for Cory – *he's* missing you and not happy that he can't meet up with you again.'

'You think? You don't think he's just saying that his dog liked me?'

Cherry gives me a look. 'What's the link? Did you open it?'

'Not yet.'

She glances at the screen. 'It's a link to the Wilton-Granger website.'

I shrug and hold out my hand for my phone, but Magpie starts getting restless, tugging at her mother's hand.

'Mumma! *Home!*' she whines in that insistent toddler way that always amounts to, *I will wear you down.*

'I'll look when we get back to yours.'

Back at Cherry's, we take off sandy shoes and troop upstairs. She runs some warm water in the bath, and we sit side by side on the edge to wash the sand off our feet. When we've dried them in fluffy lilac towels, she rinses it out and runs it properly for Magpie then dunks her daughter in a cloud of lemon-smelling bubbles. While Magpie splashes in the bath, with a variety of rubber marine life and a waterproof picture book, I sit on the linen bin and Cherry perches on the toilet with the lid closed. The link is to a property for sale with Wilton-Granger. At first, I think it must be related to something I've told him about work, but as I read through properly, I realise what it is.

It's my dream home.

'What is it?' nags Cherry.

'It's a house. Wait a sec. I just need to...' I scroll through, taking it in, and the weirdest swell of excitement rises up inside me like a wave. I feel just as I did that day with Cory, when the wave lifted me up and carried me back to shore.

I'm excited for two reasons. The first is, it really *is* my dream house. It's an old fisherman's cottage on the far side of Lemon Cove. It stands alone on the edge of the beach, but there's a very small housing estate of pleasant semis built around the road leading down to it, so it's not *too* isolated. The outside walls are painted pale blue, and the internal pictures look divine: wooden floors, a log burner, gauzy curtains at low picture windows, beams in the ceiling. For a minute I can't breathe, it's so perfect. Not only that, it's not on a bus route to any schools, which means the price is not too outrageous. I'm too agitated to do the maths now, but having worked in the industry for these few months, I know my savings would make a halfway decent deposit.

The other reason I'm excited is because I told Cory my dream and he remembered it. I don't know why that should make me so excited, but it does. Here's my house, in my hand, on a small rectangular screen.

'Hand it *over*!' orders Cherry. 'I want to see. Why is he sending you a house?'

I look at her and hand her the phone. 'You'll figure it out if you read it properly.'

In fairness, Cherry twigs faster than I did. 'Oh my God, Kitty, this would be *perfect* for you! It's *everything* you've told me you'd love in a house. By the sea, an old cottage, really pretty... Oh my God, it's round the cove from me! You have to buy it, Kitty, you have to!'

'But I haven't decided to stay here. I mean, I haven't decided to *go* either. I worry about my parents. How could we have relaxed, happy get-togethers in a place that holds difficult memories for them. Cooper too, come to that?'

'Well, yes, I see that. I do. But you're tempted, right? You'll have to sleep on it. It's not a small decision, is it? Moving permanently, buying a house. But whatever you decide, make sure it's for *you*, not for your parents or your sister. Not even for me! Family's important, *I* know that. But if you *don't* move here, you have to go somewhere that you feel at least as excited about as you do about this place. Don't choose second-best to keep everyone else happy.'

I nod. I know she's right, but I feel really daunted at how this might play out. 'You're wise, oh oracle,' I tell her.

'Like Yoda I am,' she agrees and stands to fish Magpie out of the bath.

'Come on, Mags, or you'll be pickled like a prune.'

Magpie laughs hysterically, and Cherry makes a great show of searching through the water. 'Oh no! I can't find my little girl! I can only find a wrinkly prune.'

'I'm not a wrinkly prune!' shrieks Magpie with some indignation.

'No, sorry, my mistake. You're a crinkly old raisin! Excuse me, crinkly old raisin, have you seen a little girl in here, three years old?'

'I'm not a raisin! I'm Magpie. Magpie! Magpie!' she shrieks, breathless, slapping the water so that droplets and bubbles fly everywhere.

'Well why didn't you say so?' says Cherry, laughing as she lifts her out and wraps her in a towel. 'Wrinkly little Magpie...'

I smile, watching them, wondering if I'll ever have a child, be such a wonderful mother. If I did buy this house... *if* I did... would everything else I want from life follow? Or would I stand a better chance of meeting single men in London or Surrey? Imagine living round the cove from Cherry though! It would be so much fun.

To counterbalance it, I imagine living the next village over from Cooper. That would be lovely too. Aside from Cooper's family though, does the prospect of living in a quiet Surrey village appeal to me? Yes, it does. Does it appeal as much as living here and going home all salty and sandy after a day on the beach?

My stomach gives a sick little swoop because I'm not sure that it does.

CHAPTER 37

That night, when I get home, I shower the sand out of my hair and heat up a pizza. Then I call my sister. I know I don't need her permission for anything, but one of the voices in my head cautioning me against making a permanent life here is definitely hers, so I think it's time to talk to her. While it rings, I find the house on my laptop so I can see the pictures on a bigger screen.

'Kits! It feels like ages. How are you?'

'I'm good, Coop, really good. How are you?'

'I'm well! Missing my little sister, being driven slowly round the bend by my two sons. Planning a holiday with David, during which Mum will babysit said sons. Honestly it can't come soon enough.'

'That's brilliant! You guys deserve some alone time. When? Where?'

'October. Italy, not sure which part yet. Oh wait, October's when you're coming back. What if you need me? Should we push it back a month?'

'Cooper, you're crazy. You and David haven't been anywhere for three years but you're thinking of postponing it in case your thirty-year-old sister might need you? Get a grip, woman. Go and enjoy yourself.'

She laughs and it's good to hear. 'So, you are still coming back in October, right? You can come straight here if you want. You can babysit with Mum, have some quality time with her.'

'Actually, Cooper, I wanted to talk to you about that.'

'Oh yes?' Immediately her voice sounds wary, and I feel apprehensive. I'm too old to have to justify my choices, but Cooper and I have always had that sort of relationship. In readiness for this call, I've prepared both a camomile tea and a glass of white wine. I reach for the latter and take a slug.

'Cooper, you know I love you more than anyone on the planet, right? I want your honest opinion on something, and your support. OK?'

'OK.' The word is long and drawn out.

'Good. I think I want to stay on here. Permanently. Cooper, I've never felt so happy in my life. You know how much I love my job, how great all the people are. Cherry's a really good friend. And the lifestyle is just... well, it's *me*, Coop. Being so far from you is the biggest negative about this place, but if you take that out of the equation, Pennystrand is where I want to be. I've been on the beach all day with Cherry and Magpie. I can't wait to go to work tomorrow. My chest feels kind of expanded all the time. I just love it. I worry that Mum and Dad will be devastated if I move here, I worry that they'll never visit me, but there's a house for sale... it's my dream house. I want to try to buy it. I want my life to be here.'

After this impressively long monologue, I take a deep breath and another gulp of wine.

'Coop? Are you there?'

'Yes of course. Hang on a sec. This is important, isn't it? So I'm thinking.'

'OK.' I drain the wine glass.

After what seems like an interminable pause, during which I start on the camomile tea and burn my mouth, Cooper speaks.

'So obviously I've been looking forward to having you nearby for years, and not just for the free babysitting. I'm not being negative, I'm confessing my bias! I'm totally, totally biased in favour of you coming back. *But* the important thing here isn't me. It's you, Kitty. *Your* happiness. I'm not selfish, I'm just bossy, so I have to say, it sounds very clear to me what you should do.'

'It does?'

'Kits, this is what you said to me: you've never been so happy in your whole life. That you want to buy the house and carry on your life there. That's it then, isn't it? If all your reasons for leaving are about keeping other people happy then they don't count.'

Ridiculously, my eyes fill with tears. I hadn't realised how much I was preparing myself for an onslaught of reasons why I shouldn't stay.

'Thanks, Coop,' I croak. 'That *really* means a lot.'

'You know, at our age, we shouldn't need each other's blessing, but I get why you do – I feel the same about you. Well, you have it anyway.'

'You're the best sister. I miss you so much. Coop, would you come and visit me ever? I know you have some memories... but the boys would love it, I'm sure. You could all come for summer holidays and have a fortnight on the beach and you'd love Cherry and...' I gaze at the photos of the little blue house with its sweeping sea views and cottage garden.

'Kitty, you don't need to sell it to me! Of course I'll come! With the boys, yes, but also on my own for some sister time. Actually, now that I think of it, this could work well for me. It'll give me a cast-iron reason to get away from time to time.'

'Oh, Coop! I'm so, so pleased. But what about Mum? If

you're right, and this is where she got cheated on, it feels cruel to expect her to come back to the scene of the crime.'

'Look, for one thing, we don't know that's what happened. For another, you have to live the best life you can, irrespective of the past – especially when it's someone else's past. I'm sure Mum will understand. But ask her – both of them. It may put your mind at ease.'

'You're right.'

'Do it now, when you hang up from me. But first, I need to ask bossy-big-sister questions. Are you sure you can afford it? What about the fact that your job is temporary and part-time? Are you sure you're not all misty-eyed about the hot surfer? Have you taken enough time to decide? You could always extend your lease, see what it's like in winter...'

I smile. I like bossy-big-sister questions. 'Roly's already said he'll make me permanent if I want to stay on. On a rough calculation yes, I can afford it, but I have to run the numbers properly before I do anything. I'd be lying if I said I never think about the hot surfer, but I'm not staying for him, no. And no, I don't need more time.'

I hear her take a big breath. 'OK. Go and phone our parents. And I meant what I said about coming to visit.'

'Good. Bye, Coop.'

I can't quite believe how amazing she was. Not because she's *not* amazing, but because I know how much she worries about me and how much she was looking forward to having me nearby. I'm going to send her some flowers.

I gaze into space for a bit, letting it sink in. Am I really going to try to buy a house at last? Of course there's the small matter that I haven't actually *seen* the house yet – I must arrange a viewing. What a shame it's on the market with the Wilton-Granger mafia. I don't really want Matthew knowing my business, my hopes.

I drum my fingers for a bit then call up Mum's number on

my phone. Then I clear it. I'm really nervous about calling her. I call Roly instead, on his mobile.

'Kitty? Everything alright?'

'Everything's fine. I just wanted to ask you something. Remember you said that if I wanted to stay on in Pennystrand, you'd keep me on at Rowlands?'

'Yeees.' I can hear the satisfaction ripe in his voice. 'And yes, the offer still stands.'

'*Thank* you, Roly, that's amazing. Would there also be any way I could work full-time instead of the four days?'

'Of course! We're as busy as we've ever been, and when Nerys qualifies in her psychology programme next year, she'll be off. It would be good to have you on board full-time then. Why though? I thought you liked the time to yourself.'

'I do, but... Roly, I want to buy a house!'

'Anything I'm familiar with?'

'I don't know. It's on with Wilton-Granger unfortunately. I don't like the thought of dealing with them, but it's perfect. At least, it looks perfect. I know you never can tell till you've had the survey.' A lesson I've amply learned during my time in the job. Only last month one of the many, many Parnells wanted to buy a flat overlooking Brightman Bay and subsequent investigations threw up problems with the roof, the leasehold and the plumbing, as well as a mouse colony beneath the floorboards.

'Where is it, Kitty?'

'Lemon Cove. Round the far side. It's a tiny little—'

'Blue cottage? I know it. Don't arrange a viewing, Kitty – leave it with me. I may be able to help.'

'Seriously? Thanks, Roly, I really, really appreciate everything.'

'I'm delighted to think of you staying on. It's not easy to get people of the calibre I want working for me. Between you and the others, I feel very fortunate. See you tomorrow then.'

'See you tomorrow.'

. . .

When I end the call, I see that I've just missed Dad. I hit dial
straight away. He's so hard to get hold of – if he's available, I
want to seize the moment. As it rings, I feel a coil of excitement
in my belly over everything Roly said. A full-time permanent
job is one step closer to making me the perfect buyer.

'Kitty darling, how are you?' Dad's voice is warm and fills
me with an overwhelming urge to rush into his arms for a hug.

'I'm good, Dad. You?'

'Fine, fine. I've got a really busy spell coming up, ten double
shifts back to back, so I thought I'd try you before it all kicks off.'

'Good thinking. Any news on Claude?'

'Yes! He's back at the end of the month, thank God. So I
don't have to recruit, which I'm ecstatic about, because it's such
a royal pain in the backside.'

'I'm so pleased! Will you take a holiday then? Or at least a
break?'

'I'll have to. I'm so tired that I can't sleep, if that makes
sense. Too wired all the time. I love my restaurant, but I'm
getting too old for this pace. In fact, I was thinking I might come
and visit my youngest for a few days, if I wouldn't cramp her
style.'

'Are you kidding? I would *love* that! Totally, totally come. In
fact, I wanted to talk to you about something, Dad.' Quickly I
outline the situation, as I told it to Cooper. His silence is even
longer than hers was.

'Poppet, you have to do what makes you happy. You know
that's all I've ever wanted – your mother too.'

'But will *you* be happy?'

'I'm always happy if you're happy.'

'But you don't *sound* happy,' I persist. 'You sound worried.'

'Do I?' His airy denial is fooling no one, and he obviously
realises it because he caves right away. 'Alright, look, I do have

certain... reservations. Not on your behalf – I can tell how happy you are there.'

'So on *your* behalf then?'

Another long pause. A sigh. And then he says, 'I think you'd better talk to your mother.'

'What?'

'My darling, my reservations aren't about me either. But I can't explain it – you need to talk to Tilly. You haven't mentioned this to her yet?'

'No. I was going to, but I saw the missed call from you, so I rang you first.'

'Right. Well, she might have her own reasons for not wanting you to be there. But as I say, it's not my story to tell you.'

I pick at the hem of the sofa throw. If Cooper's right and Dad cheated on Mum, this is a bit weird. After all, if he was the one in the wrong, it's his confession to make, his story to tell.

'Dad, can I ask you something?'

'Sure.'

'When we were all here before, did you have an affair?'

He's obviously sipping something because I hear a splutter. 'Did I what?'

'Have an affair? Cheat on Mum?'

He laughs. 'In the space of two weeks, whilst on holiday with three small daughters? Er, *no.*'

'No?' *That's Cooper's theory exploded then.*

'Categorically no. Why on *earth* would you think that?'

Oh God, how do I answer this one without dropping Cooper in it? Still, I've come too far to back down now. On my laptop, the internet is still open on the little house by the sea. It's everything I ever wanted. But is there some deep dark secret that means I shouldn't have it? 'You know I said Cooper and I had been talking about that holiday?'

'Yes.'

'Well, she heard some rows between you guys. She heard Mum shouting at you for going to see some woman. So she... sort of wondered.'

Dad groans. I can picture him rubbing his hands over his face the way he always does when he's agitated. '*Cooper* thinks I had an affair? For all these years?'

'No, no! She's not *sure*. I mean, it was just a theory...'

I hear a deep breath in Edinburgh. 'Kitty, please talk to your mother. Have this conversation with her. I can't tell you what's not my business to say. But let me assure you that I did *not* have an affair, in Pennystrand or anywhere else. And it's high time all this was cleared up so that my daughters don't think I did, and so that you can move on with your life. Buying your first house is a huge deal. Especially for you, Kitty, with how much you've always wanted it. I want you to be excited, not conflicted.'

I'm certainly confused. 'Thanks, Dad. I want you and Mum to be excited too. I want to send you the link to the house so you can see why I love it.'

'Then send it, poppet. I'd love to see it. But talk to her. Soon.'

'I will. So I'll see you in a couple of weeks?'

'I'd love to, but I think you'll want to see your mum with some urgency so you may not have time. Keep me posted.'

I can't stand all this mystery! Why would I need to see Mum urgently?

I dial Mum's number before I can lose my impetus, even though this is my fourth phone call in a row and my head's spinning.

I get voicemail and leave a message. Only then do I remember that she's out for dinner with her friend Sally tonight. *Aaaargh!* I let out a quiet scream of frustration.

CHAPTER 38

I sleep badly that night, torn between longing and worry, tormented by the heat, and the next day I arrive at work tense and slightly squinty-eyed. Roly, by contrast, is simmering with exuberance. It's glinting in his eyes and shining out of his round cheeks. 'I've got us a viewing,' he announces with great aplomb as I walk in, wiping sweat off my forehead.

'Where?' I ask, wondering which of our houses needs me and Roly to go together.

'*Where* she asks! Oh, Kitty. Don't tell me you've changed your mind about your house of dreams!'

'Oh! No, I haven't. Only, how...?'

In fact, my enthusiasm *has* been tempered by the weirdness with my parents, but Roly has more than enough for us both. He recounts how he went there this morning on his way to work, intending to pop a note through the door but coming face to face with the owner instead: 'A *very* charming woman of fifty or so.' Apparently she was standing outside in the summer dew enjoying her morning cuppa when he rolled up. He explained the situation, she was very amenable and I'm to go at four this afternoon, with no need for an estate agent from The Enemy to get involved. Roly will come too if I like, he adds casually. I can hardly believe it.

'Roly, that's *wonderful*! It's so kind of you to go to this trouble for me. I wouldn't have dared be so cheeky. And it's lovely of you to offer to come with me, but... why? I mean, you don't *have* to.'

'Ah but I do, my dear. Three reasons. Number one, we Welsh, as you know, are nosy. I want to see the house and be all in your business, as they say these days. Number two, Miss Alton may move the house over to Rowlands, so I'd be there in a professional capacity. And number three, well, you don't have your parents here to view it with you and it's a big step, so I thought I'd function as a sort of parent proxy, if you wanted one.'

'Oh, Roly. Very much so. I want to hug you now, but is that really unprofessional?'

'My dear girl,' he says, beaming and holding out his arms.

I give him a big hug, and we hear a tapping on the window-pane. Matthew's standing outside looking through the glass, wagging a finger and wearing a smirk.

'Oh dear, that was unfortunate timing,' says Roly, giving him the finger. 'It'll be all over Pennystrand that we're having an affair in about five minutes. A story far more mortifying for you than for me, I'm afraid.'

'I don't care,' I retort, glaring at Matthew's oily, retreating back. 'Gossip is the least of my worries at the moment.'

'Really? I thought you'd decided to stay and all was well in your world?'

'Yes, except there seems to be some sort of ridiculous mystery in my family about Pennystrand and I'm worried it's going to spoil everything.'

Remembering that Nerys is coming in late today because of a dentist appointment, I tell him the sorry story while we're alone. I'm perched on the front of Nerys's desk, and Roly paces the office as he listens.

'I understand your reservations,' he says, 'but you mustn't let all this spoil the adventure for you.'

I smile. 'That's exactly what my dad said.'

'There, I'm doing rather well at this paternal business already, aren't I? He's right. We shall go and view the house this afternoon, and you'll talk to your mum tonight, and you'll get the mystery sorted. That will put your mind at rest.'

'But what if it doesn't?'

'It will. It will all be fine. Your mother will support you.'

'How do you know?'

'Because it's fate that you're here, Kitty. Anyone who's seen you going about your days over the last few months could not possibly doubt that you're in exactly the right place doing exactly the right thing. I can say categorically – and I have a great gift for such things – that you belong here.'

I never knew Roly's fatalistic streak ran so deep. I hope he's right and that I can stay without causing any trouble or upset to anyone I love.

I hadn't planned to tell anyone else about the house until I've actually *seen* the house. Already Cherry, Roly, Cooper and Dad know, and really, at this stage anything could happen. But the minute Nerys arrives, I find myself telling her. She brings up the web page and oohs and ahhs satisfyingly.

The hours pass slowly but at last it's time to leave.

'Walk or car?' asks Roly.

'Car please. It's roasting and I don't want to be a bath of sweat when I get there.'

'I'm so relieved.'

We jump into Saffron and drive towards Lemon Cove, then take a loop to enter the housing estate, then jolt down the rather rutty road behind it to reach the house. The walking route, down the hill past Cherry's house and around the cove, is more direct but inaccessible by car. We step out of the car, and I instantly hear the wash of waves and the sound of gulls. A shimmering blue horizon drifts into the sky.

The owner, Miss Alton, all smiles, is a pretty woman, which I don't believe has escaped Roly's notice.

'You must be Kitty,' she says, shaking my hand. 'Welcome. Shall we look indoors first?'

We go inside. This side of the house, facing away from the sea, is cool and peaceful, a welcome relief from the glare of the sun. I wonder if it might be a little dark and dismal in winter.

'The front of the house gets all the light,' says Miss Alton, reading my mind, 'but the back rooms are very cosy with fires. Would you like to see them first?'

There's a lounge with an open fire and a small dining room with a log burner. They both have wooden beams and low ceilings. She tells me this is the original part of the house and that it dates back to the eighteenth century. Some cottages, as I've seen recently, can feel poky and a little depressing, as if they've got lost out of time, their charm and function obsolete. This isn't one of them. These two rooms feel as if they're holding out their arms, waiting to welcome you in and tell you stories. I gaze around, imagining living here, and it's ridiculously easy to do so.

'What's the history, do you know, Shelley?' asks Roly.

First-name terms already, Roly? Oh ho!

'I do indeed! I'm a keen historian, you know, Roly, and when I first came here, I looked into it very thoroughly. It's rather wonderful, in fact. Are you of a romantic bent, Kitty?'

'Well, yes, I suppose I am.'

'I thought so. I can tell by looking at people. Then you'll love this. Back in the old days, Lemon Cove wasn't called Lemon Cove. It was called Traeth Ceiniog Wen.'

I look at her enquiringly and she looks at Roly, smiling.

'The beach of silver coins?' he hazards.

'That's it! Very good, Roly. And do you know why it was called that, Kitty?'

'Um, because the sand shines silver in the sun?'

'No, although that's a good guess. Because it once was used by smugglers!' She makes the announcement with a flourish, and I give a little gasp, which seems to please her.

'Really?' marvels Roly. 'What a fabulous history. I had heard there used to be smugglers hereabouts. Weren't the Parnells mixed up in all that way back, once upon a time?'

'Yes, absolutely. They got up to some very shady dealings by all accounts. So yes, Traeth Ceiniog Wen, because of all the treasure.'

'Oh, that's marvellous,' I breathe. History and character have always been on my wishlist for my house, and this place has it in spades.

'That's not all,' Miss Alton goes on. 'That rough little road you just came down was the start of the smugglers' route up from the beach, over to the big houses and taverns where sympathetic landlords and estate owners would let them hide their booty. So it's still to this day called Llwybr Dihiryn – Villain's Way. This house, now, is known as Seafoam Cottage, which is very pretty admittedly. Some previous owner must have renamed it. But I rather like the original name, which I came across in some wonderful old papers in the archives. Ty Dihiryn – Villain's House!'

'Oh my God.' I'm not very eloquent, but I can't believe I haven't even got to the 'good' bit of the house yet and already I'm head over heels. This is it, this is the feeling that will stop me being a house whore like Nerys and settle down, a one-house woman forever. Anywhere you can hear words like treasure, smugglers and villain within five minutes of arriving is magic, in my opinion.

'Splendid, Shelley, splendid!' booms Roly. 'You can see

Kitty is quite dumbstruck. She loves old houses. I think this might be a match made in heaven.'

She looks at me closely. 'That's what I'm looking for. It's not easy for me to pass this place on. I want someone who will love it and appreciate it as I have done. Anyway, come and see the rest.'

In a daze, I follow her to the front of the house.

'And this is the extension of course,' she says.

We find ourselves in a modern kitchen that reminds me a little of Lisa Parnell's, except a fifth of the size. But it's a decent size for a little cottage, and it has a scrubbed-pine table and French doors that stand open, letting in the scent of roses from the square cottage garden, which is a riot of summer colour. Off to the side is another sitting room, also with French doors. Whilst the back of the house is low-ceilinged, atmospheric and cosy, the whole front is airy, bright and sun-filled. It's like two houses in one!

Even though I'd intended to explore the whole house before going outside, I find myself pulled irresistibly to the French doors and through them...

The garden has a picket fence around it, barely containing the roses and lupins and hollyhocks that brim up and over exuberantly. I've never had a garden, but I'll have to learn about gardening if I live here. I can't be the owner who lets this gorgeous, old-fashioned profusion fall to wrack and ruin. That dreadful London flat has never seemed so far away.

Between the flowers, there are small triangles of lawn, narrow paths of white gravel and a stone fountain fashioned as a nymph sporting with swallows, a jet of water shooting up from her cupped hands. There's even a bench beneath a trellis burdened with clambering honeysuckle. I can't speak.

'And there's the gate of course, if you want to take a look?' says Shelley.

I nod and walk after her. She clicks the latch, and it swings open. We step through onto a sandy path winding through the dunes. The swish of the sea is louder now. I look at Roly and bite my lip.

'Come on then,' he says. 'Let's see the rest of it.'

He's right. There's nothing more to be learned from standing here. It's perfection. What else is there to say? We go back inside.

'There's no downstairs loo of course,' Shelley says apologetically, leading us towards the stairs. 'The Wilton-Granger agent did say that would be a disadvantage – seems everyone likes a second bathroom these days.'

'Oh, who cares about that?' I explode. Yes, a downstairs loo is useful, but who cares about *useful* in a place like this? Where's the poetry in *useful*? I realise I should probably be trying to play it cool, but really, I'm not that good an actor. And I can't honestly see Miss Shelley Alton, with her love of a juicy history, her youthful figure and her pretty grey hair – held off her face with pearly clips – trying to extort extra money out of me because I love it here.

The two bedrooms are lovely, with patchwork quilts and low windows, a window seat in one. The solitary bathroom is fine – not large but spotless, with a window hooked open and a claw-footed bath and separate shower. On the landing, a small airing cupboard houses the boiler.

'Can I have another look at the bedrooms?' I whisper.

'Of course, dear. I'll go downstairs and give you some privacy.'

'I'll join you, Shelley.' Roly rushes after her.

I take a couple of deep breaths. Both bedrooms face the sea, with the bathroom at the back. The larger room with the window seat would be mine. The smaller one is a perfect guest room. I imagine Mum or Dad or Cooper coming to stay, waking up to that view of dunes and marram grass and sparkling sea. Cass too, if she ever comes back from New York. If Cooper brings her family, we'd have to be a bit creative. Maybe a sofa bed downstairs.

I reflect on everything that's brought me here. Mitch's betrayal and my subsequent devastation. My family encouraging me to move on. Angelique! Goodness, I was in such a state the only constructive thing I could think of to do was see a psychic! I haven't thought of her in a long time, but her words come back to me now, across all these months.

'You will be a great many things to a great many people. You will have choices – many choices. You must make them one at a time. And you will have a full and wonderful life.'

Her prediction has proved startlingly accurate. I think of all the things I am to different people in Pennystrand: employee, colleague, friend. Facilitator of dreams to so many people buying and selling houses. Goodness knows what I am to Lisa. And of course confidante and failed treasure-hunter to Doris. I compare it with before, and although I no longer have a partner, there's no doubt that this life is richer and fuller and happier than my old one ever was.

I go downstairs to find Shelley and Roly standing close together in the kitchen, Roly smiling in a way that can only be described as flirtatious. Goodness!

'Well?' asks Roly. 'I don't think we need to ask what you think, do we?'

'It's perfect, Miss Alton. I need to do the maths in a bit more detail and run some things by my family, but I really, really want it.'

'Of course you do, my dear. You look exactly as I did when I first came here. You go and sort yourself out and get back to me.'

'Thank you! I won't take long. Only, I should make an offer, shouldn't I? Oh my God, I do this for my job and it's all gone out of my head. Roly, help!'

Thank God for Roly. He nods, serious now. 'Well, Shelley, Wilton-Granger made a sound valuation. It's definitely worth the price they're asking, and as professionals, neither Kitty nor I would expect you to take a low offer. But if you're happy to instruct me instead, I'll waive any agency fees, and that will help Kitty.'

'Roly! You don't have to do that. I don't expect it!'

'Oh yes I do, Kitty. I assure you I'm being entirely selfish. If I help you buy Seafoam Cottage, I ensure your future at Rowlands. I get to work with this delightful woman, and I get to steal business away from Matthew Granger. It's a no-brainer, as they say these days.'

CHAPTER 39

That night I phone Mum. My trepidation is at an all-time high because now that I've actually *seen* Seafoam Cottage – Ty Dihiryn – the stakes are higher than ever.

'Kitty!' she answers after just two rings. 'I was literally just going to call you. Are you alright? You sounded a bit flustered on your message yesterday. I was out with Sally.'

'Yes, I remembered afterwards. Did you have a nice time?'

'Oh, glorious. There's this wine bar in the gallery and they do tapas – it's a lovely ambience. I'll take you when you visit.'

'I'd love to. Listen, Mum, I need to talk to you.'

'I'm all ears.'

'OK. So remember how I was in bits after Mitch, and I came here because I needed somewhere temporary to sort my head out?'

'All too well, darling. I hated seeing you like that.'

'Well, it's worked, and my head's sorted, and I know exactly how I want to move forward. Only I'm afraid you won't be happy about it, and I'm really worried.'

'You want to stay.'

'Yes. I've found a house I want to buy. Oh my God, Mum, it's... I love it. Anyway, the point is, I need to know how you feel about it.'

'Have you spoken to your father?'

'Yes, last night. Look, I know something happened here when we were all on holiday together. And I'm worried that me moving here permanently will be a bad thing for you. But I have no idea how or why. Dad won't tell me anything, and he told me I have to speak to you.'

'Bless him.' Mum's voice sounds wistful, sad even. 'He's right – we need to talk, Kitty. In person would be better. I suppose... I'd better come and see you.'

I can't miss the note of reluctance in her voice.

'Well that would be great – I'd love that. But, Mum, we're both busy with work and this house is so perfect. I need to put the ball in motion – things move *so* quickly in this market – and I'm afraid that if we wait till we can conveniently get together, I'll lose it. But I can't go ahead if I think it'll make you unhappy.'

She groans. 'Oh, I have made such a mess of things. Such a monumental mess. Go ahead with the house, Kitty, with whatever you need to do. I'll come to you this weekend. I can amuse myself while you're at work, and we can talk when you're not. Don't worry about me, OK?'

'OK, Mum, thanks. But... are you sure? I mean, will this make you unhappy?'

'No. I can't say it's not awkward, but I've been a coward for a long time. As the saying goes, you can run but you can't hide.'

'God, Mum, I don't know if I can wait till the weekend to find out! This is seriously weird! Are you sure it's nothing awful? Will you visit me if I live here?'

'I'm coming this weekend, aren't I? It's fine, Kitty, go ahead. I'll text you with arrangements.'

I hang up the phone none the wiser. In fact, I'm more confused than ever. She's given me the go-ahead, she's told me she'll be fine, but if that's the case, what's all the fuss about in the first place?

I groan and knock my phone gently against my forehead. Why are my parents so unbelievably, maddeningly cryptic?

Everything happens very quickly after that. I stay up all night doing maths and offer very close to the asking price. Shelley Alton tells Wilton-Granger that she's found a private buyer for Seafoam Cottage. It's basically true, since Roly isn't charging her. I appoint a solicitor and book a survey. Roly draws up a memo of sale.

When he prints it out and puts it on my desk, I take a photo on my phone and type a hasty email to Cory. I've been longing to email him but I wanted to wait till I had news.

Huge congratulations on your win. I'm so proud of you. Imagine, I once drank cider with the legend that is Cory Hudson! Good luck for your next – I hope you're enjoying every minute.

By the way, thank you SO MUCH for sending me the house link. Now it's my turn to say... I thought you should see this xx

Then I attach the photo of the memo of sale.

Between work and buying the house, it's so busy I don't have time to talk to Cooper. We communicate via hasty texts.

What did Mum say?????

She's coming here this weekend. Will tell me everything! X

Tell me IMMEDIATELY! X

Will do x

I follow that with: *Um, I appear to have bought a house x*

Great! Nathan has a Lego propeller stuck up his nose. Don't have kids x

CHAPTER 40

Plans with Mum are all settled and the week rushes to a close. She'll arrive on Saturday at four and make her way to my house. I'll be at work, but I'll leave a key under the potted bay tree for her. By the time she's let herself in and made a cup of tea, I'll be home. I did suggest that she come and meet me from work. I thought we could kick off with a cuppa in Tymorau or even a celebratory vino in Fathoms. 'You could meet whoever's working with me that day,' I said, excited. 'I'd love you to meet them.'

But Mum put a very firm stop to that line of thinking. She's going to stay in my house until I join her there. I'm disappointed – I want to show my family everything about my lovely life here. Does she think the locals are going to stone her or something? But then I remember that this particular visit was always going to be an odd one, with its great mystery to be revealed. I may as well go with the flow a little longer.

The day before she comes, I do a viewing at The Chantry. It's lovely to see it again after all this time. Even the drive is a treat. Whizzing over the open expanse of the Burrows, I grin at the sight of sheep and wild ponies scattered over the tussocky landscape. I have the windows open, fresh air blows through the car and it's good to be getting out of Pennystrand for a while, away from everything that's happening. It's all good, but it's overwhelming and I could do with some perspective.

The Chantry gives me that. The old grey stone, the bell tower looking across the moors, the rambling, secretive garden all make me breathe more slowly. *What are you worrying about?* they seem to say. *We've seen more extraordinary things than you ever will and we're still standing.* The stained-glass window blazes in the sun, throwing red and orange splashes over the gallery landing. I wander round, reminding myself of how very special it is before the viewers come.

They're quite late though. I look at my watch. Quarter of an hour. Well, that's not much. Maybe they got lost?

I go into the garden, leaving the back door open so I can hear the doorbell when they arrive. I drift towards the holy well, crouch in the tufty, dark green grass that grows around it. I remember Roly saying it brought good fortune, granted wishes. I wonder if it would work for me.

I look around. I'm completely alone.

I lay my fingers on the cool, mossy stones; they are rounded and sunken with age. 'Please,' I whisper, 'if you still have magic, let everything work out for me in Pennystrand. Let Mum's secret not be too terrible and let us all be happy, our whole family. Please look after Cory. Please let Roly and Shelley get together. And please let dear, lovely Doris find her necklace. Thank you.'

Feeling sheepish, I stand up and brush myself down, double-checking that no one has seen me being so whimsical. I go back inside and check my phone to see if there's a message from the office, but there's no signal. I wait another half hour, but the viewers never come.

CHAPTER 41

Saturday is another glorious day – summer in full flower. Yawning blue skies, golden sunlight, beach laughter filling the air. And it's hot. So hot that our little office is very, very quiet. Time crawls. I spend the morning catching up with a ton of admin. On my lunch break, I eat a sandwich on a park bench and people-watch. I do a little desultory tidying after lunch then lapse into inactivity, riffling pointlessly through files, tapping my biro on the desk. Derrick does the one and only viewing of the day, and Roly and I wait the minutes out.

At 3.45 p.m., he rouses himself. 'Go home, Kitty. It's absolutely dead – no point two of us being here.'

'Are you sure? I can stay if you want to get on the golf course.'

'Don't be silly – your mum's coming. You can beat her home if you leave now.'

I don't hang about. Impatience has been killing me all day. I gather up my things, depart with a wave then stride up the hill despite the pulsating sun, and in about two minutes I'm a bath of sweat.

At the crossroads, I see something that makes me hesitate: a slight figure tottering aimlessly, at times straying alarmingly close to the kerb. I pause. Pennystrand is full of elderlies. The gift shop has an amazing array of cards for ninetieth, ninety-fifth and even hundredth birthdays. The theory is that the hills and sea air promote good health. Personally, I think it's so lovely here that no one wants to check out. This particular elderly, however, looks familiar.

I glance at my watch. I don't want to interfere and I really want to see Mum but... I hurry over just as she sways and clutches a lamp post for support. I was right. It's Agatha Parnell.

'Hello, Agatha, are you alright there? Do you remember me? We met once at—'

'Kitty! Hello, dear. You've come at just the right moment. I'm feeling a little...'

I put an arm around her, and she leans her slight weight against me.

'Oh!' she gasps in a little puff. 'I thought my legs were going then. They're not as reliable as they used to be. Damn things.'

'I saw you stumble. Come on – let me help you over to that bench.'

When we're seated, I give her a moment then ask where she's going.

She turns to look at me with a look of annoyance. 'I'm going home,' she says firmly. Despite the heat, she's wearing a long scarf made of some slippery-looking fabric in iridescent rainbow colours, shot through with silver threads. She plays with it as if the feeling is comforting to her.

'To the Willows?'

'No! That's not home. That's just *the* home, where they put me because I'm an embarrassment. *My* home is Fortescue Cres-cent. It's where I grew up; it's where I belong. And now stupid Lisa is selling it just to get one over on her horrible husband. I won't have it, I tell you. Why won't she take the money?'

'What money?'

'*My* money! I'm loaded, dear. The mermaids saw to that – you heard about my time with the mermaids, yes? That's why I wear this scarf – it was a gift from Neptune. These are his colours, you know. No one seems to know these things. I don't understand why people aren't more interested! It was the adventure of a lifetime, and if someone told me a story like that, I'd be *full* of questions. I'd want to hear every little detail. But they all just brush it under the carpet. They think I'm crazy of course.'

I bite my lip. I know Lisa doesn't like her aunt talking about the mermaids, but really!

'I would love to hear about the mermaids, Agatha. I don't have time now because my mum's coming to visit, but one day, perhaps when work is less busy, you can tell me the whole thing?'

Once the house is sold – and I'm sure it will be, whatever Agatha says – there'll be nothing to stop me visiting her.

'That would be lovely, dear. But what was I saying? Oh yes, I've offered the money to Lisa to buy her filthy pig of a husband out of his half of the house. *He's* offered to buy *her* out, but he only wants it to spite her. He wants to torture her by living there when she loves it so much. No doubt he'll make all sorts of horrific changes to the place and have horrible parties with his cocaine-snorting banker friends. Over my dead body, I tell you! She reckons selling to a stranger is better than that at least. Together, Lisa and I could make him an offer he can't refuse, but she won't take it!'

'Why? I hardly know her and even I can see how unhappy it's making her to sell.' I'm almost certainly crossing some boundaries now, but this is ridiculous!

'Because then I wouldn't have money left to pay for the home, would I? I'd have to go back to Fortescue and live with her, and she'd have to deal with me every day, the crazy old aunt who makes up nonsense about mermaids. You'd hope I would be the lesser of two evils, but apparently she'd rather sell the house.'

'I see.' *Well then, she doesn't deserve to keep the house*, I nearly say, but I can't talk about her like that; I have to maintain some shred of professionalism.

'Look, Agatha, I have to get home, but I need to see you safe first. Can I walk you somewhere if you're strong enough? Or shall I call a taxi? Or Lisa?'

'Whatever's easiest for you, dear. I don't want to put you out. But I'm not going back to the Willows. I have to keep trying to talk some sense into Lisa. Which is hard to do,' she finishes with a sigh, 'when they all think you're batty.'

'I'll call Lisa.' She'd want to know about this, I realise.

She picks up immediately. 'What?'

'Er, hi, Lisa. It's Kitty. I'm sitting on Carpenter's Corner with your aunt. She's on her way to visit you and had a bit of a wobbly turn. She's feeling better now, but I don't want to leave her alone.'

'Oh God, not again. Stay there. I'll drive down now and pick her up. Stay where you are and don't talk to her about anything. Thanks.' The phone slams down.

I look at it, startled. I understand that an elderly relative who wanders off and has funny turns is a scary and unsettling thing to live with, but really! Don't *talk* about anything indeed. What are we meant to do? Sit here mute? I had been softening towards Lisa, but now I revert to my first impression, which is that she's a thoroughly unpleasant woman.

'Um, she's coming down for you,' I tell Agatha. 'Um, perhaps don't mention that you told me about the money. I don't think she—'

'Of course. I'm not stupid. She doesn't want anyone knowing her business or helping her, because of her stupid Parnell pride. We all have it – it's a family trait, but it's run riot in Lisa. She's her own worst enemy. I wouldn't care except that if she sells that house, it's the whole family that'll be deprived, not just her, not just me. Her father would turn in his grave. Oh, here comes her car. Keep mum!'

Agatha zips a finger across her lips, her eyes filled with a conspiratorial twinkle. Here's another mystery, as if Pennystrand doesn't have enough of them. Agatha's meant to be nuts – she claims she was kidnapped by mermaids – which is certainly... startling. But other than that, she seems perfectly sane. The sanest of the Parnells in fact. Her wanderings aren't random befuddled escapes, as Lisa seems to think; Agatha's like a cat, trying again and again to go home. She's a woman with unfinished business. Yes, she gets faint and weak sometimes, but she's old, and it's a very hot summer. And far from being fuzzy headed, she seems unusually perceptive to me. What a puzzle.

Lisa pulls up in front of us, face like thunder, and we get to our feet. I'm relieved to feel that Agatha is steadier now.

'Thank you very much, dear,' she murmurs to me. 'I appreciate your help. Please give my love to dear Jessica.'

'Jessica?'

'Yes, your mother. You said she's coming to visit. It's high time she was back in Pennystrand if you ask me.'

'But my mother's called Tilly...' *Just when I was starting to think that, mermaids or not, she's perfectly sane.*

'Get in, Aunty!' barks Lisa through the open window. 'I'm holding up traffic.'

I open the door nearest us and Agatha climbs in. Lisa immediately pulls off and drives away. And I stand there, watching the burgundy estate disappearing in the stream of traffic, utterly confounded.

CHAPTER 42

Mum and I arrive at almost exactly the same time. As I walk down the road, I see her get out of her car and check the number on the door before gently lifting the pot with the bay tree.

'Mum! Talk about timing!'

She whirls round. 'Kitty! You're early.'

I grin. 'You're late.' And despite the heat, I run the last little way into her arms. It's so good to see her, despite everything.

I get her overnight bag from the car and usher her inside, glad to be there to witness the pleasure on her face as she looks around the homely space. 'It's not like a rental at all, is it?' she says, beaming. Then her face shifts into a more reflective gaze. 'It's as if you've always belonged here.'

'I kind of feel that I do,' I say gently. 'Anyway, you've had a long drive, Mum. What do you want? Tea? Wine? Food?'

'Something cold and non-alcoholic please. Lemonade or something like that. And I wouldn't say no to a biscuit.'

I open the back door and brush fallen petals and cobwebs off the two garden chairs. I find sparkling apple juice, put cookies on a plate and carry them all outside.

In the tiny courtyard we sit with the crowding buddleia and honeysuckle rustling around us and the sound of the little boy next door singing tunelessly. A quick peep over the fence shows that he is singing to a worm. We don't talk about anything deep and meaningful at first. Now that she's actually here, it's nice to chat about normal things – our jobs, friends, music. She tells me I look well, contented.

'You're brown for the first time since you were a kid!' she says.

It's true; I have that sort of very white skin that sometimes goes with dark hair; it takes ages for me to develop any sort of a tan. But because I've spent so much time outside this summer I have, if not a tan exactly, a sort of pale caramel glow. And a few freckles.

After an hour or so in the sunshine, we go inside and I open a bottle of red wine and throw together some pasta, the easiest thing I can make. This isn't the occasion to spend ages concentrating on something elaborate.

'So I need to tell you some things,' says Mum halfway through the meal.

I nod and lay down my fork.

'Gosh.' She gives a nervous laugh. 'This is really hard. I've been thinking about what to say to you, how to explain it, since we spoke last. Look, it's nothing terrible, no great suffering or tragedy to tell you – you and your sisters will probably wonder why I didn't tell you a long time ago, that's all. I should have. When you came here in April, I knew this moment would come. When you got the job and you met... some of the people, I thought maybe it would help you understand why I've been so...'

She's twirling her tagliatelle miserably and I can't bear to see my normally cool, poised mother at a loss for words, twisting on a hook. I just want to get through this horrible bit, make it easy for her. For both of us.

'Mum.' I reach for her hand and stop the twirling. 'I'm just going out on a limb here but humour me. Are you Jessica Parnell?'

And my mum – Tilly – nods slowly and says, 'Yes, Kits. Yes I am.'

'Wow. OK. So... how? Why? Just tell me, Mum – it's all OK.'

She nods, leaning back in her chair. 'Right. So, you've met my sisters, Lisa and Meredith, which would seem extraordinary except that it's Pennystrand. You know the thing about seven degrees of separation? Here it's only ever three or four at the most. I loved it here, for all the reasons you do. And I meant what I said: there's no big drama to tell you, but my family, they're... well, they're not easy, Kitty. And I don't have *anything* in common with them. Sometimes families are close, you know? Like you and me and your sisters. Your dad too, even though things between us didn't work out – and *that* was my fault. When I was growing up, I used to feel like a... cow in a field of sheep or, actually, a lamb in a field of wolves. I don't want to colour your opinion of them because they're your family too after all. But I have to tell you how my experience of them was back then, because otherwise you just won't understand why I cut contact with them the way I did.'

They're my family too? Oh my God, for some reason that particular penny hadn't dropped.

'Lisa's my aunt!' I exclaim in some horror, taking a slug of wine. 'Oh God, so is Meredith!'

Mum actually smiles. 'Yes, and Emily, whom you haven't met.'

Another aunt! I remember hearing that she lives in Paris.

'And Francis and Griff, my brothers, are your uncles.'

I realise that my mother grew up in Fortune Crescent, that I've unwittingly been showing people around her childhood home for weeks!

'This is seriously weird,' I mutter. I skewer a pile of pasta in a futile attempt at normality.

'Poor Kitty,' Mum murmurs, patting my hand. 'So. Imagine growing up here, plenty of money. I had a great childhood, of course I did. But I started to feel uncomfortable around them when I got a bit older, twelve or so maybe. The prevailing family deity was money. I started noticing how they treated others who didn't have much of it, and I didn't like that. I hated the way people looked at us, the things they said about us, that we "thought we were better than everyone else". I hated it because it was true. Once I asked if I could go to school in the village. I'd made friends with a local girl one summer and I wanted to be in her class. My mother hit the roof – wouldn't hear of it.

'The girls are older than me, the boys are younger. My sisters were fun as kids but total horrors when they hit their teens. Always in trouble, always behaving badly. I wasn't a goody two-shoes – I don't think – but they said I was. If ever someone was caught smoking pot or stealing or flashing their boobs, it was always Lisa or Meredith or Emily.'

'Wow!' I say again. I really can't imagine Lisa flashing her boobs.

'You know what it's like being a teenager. Everything matters so much it hurts. Their behaviour made my life hell because everyone expected me to be like them. I couldn't go to a party without getting badgered for hours to "loosen up a little", or "come out of my shell". Boys assumed I was easy because they were, so I got harassed quite a lot. I always felt like a disappointment because I wasn't "like a proper Parnell". My sisters were really loud, always shouting and swearing, and, Kitty, you know what I'm like. I like books, I'm quietly spoken, I care about people's feelings. It's like I was from a different planet. I know you shouldn't be embarrassed by your family, but I was, a bit. And they always complained that I was dull. When the boys got older, they got crazy too – there was hardly a month when one or the other wasn't arrested. They – we I suppose – were all so *spoiled*! I started dreaming about when I could move away and be known for myself, instead of as one of the Parnells.'

I remember Francesca taking the gin behind her grand-mother's back, flicking me a V-sign on the street. That sense of entitlement and arrogance is still alive and kicking in the clan. It's hard to get my head around the fact that I never knew where Mum came from. It's even harder to believe that she came from *them*.

'Things got worse with my parents too. We disagreed on everything. They kept trying to fix me up with sons of their friends, from "good" families. But they were all wealthy and arrogant and pushy and thought I was weird. When I was nine-teen, I dated Roly for a while—'

'Oh my God, yes! He said! That he'd dated the other sister, I mean... no wonder you weren't keen to come to the office today.'

'Not that I wouldn't love to see him again. But I had to tell you all this first, didn't I?'

'Yes. Oh my God, Mum, you dated my boss. That's so weird.'

She sighs. 'Sorry about that. Anyway, he was lovely. It wasn't true love or anything, but we had a nice time, and he was always such a gentleman...'

'I can imagine.'

'But my parents raised ructions. A Parnell shouldn't be dating an ordinary boy like that. He wanted to be an actor then, and they thought that was ridiculous. Told me he'd never amount to anything... We didn't break up because of them; our relationship ran its course, but my family made my life a living hell until it ended. My brother Griff started a fight with him one night in the pub. Meredith spread a rumour that he was gay...

And that sums up my family really. How they were then, I should say. They'd get an idea in their head about something, get drunk, throw their weight around, bully the world into doing what *they* wanted and then carry on, oblivious to the hurt they caused. I became more and more unhappy.'

At last poor Mum tucks into her pasta again, shovelling in a huge forkful and chewing determinedly. I'm glad of the pause to digest everything I've just learned.

'I do understand, Mum. I've only met Lisa and Meredith, but I would never in a million years have imagined you could be related.'

Although Lisa's reserve is very like Mum's, I realise, with a little jolt, albeit without Mum's warmth and consideration for others. Lisa must have changed a lot over the years.

'So what happened next?'

She swallows and sits back again, has a small sip of wine. 'So then I went to uni, a year late because I missed my deadline the first time round – I'd spent months arguing with Dad about what to study and where. He wanted me to do law at Cardiff. I wanted to do history or languages as far away as possible...'

'So you did history at Durham?' It's a relief to find a fact about my mother's past that I *do* know.

'That's right. I loved it. I was the only student there who dreaded the holidays. In the final year, I met your dad, and we were exclusive pretty quickly. We knew it was something special. When we graduated, my father wanted me back in Pennystrand where he could keep an eye on me and interfere. I knew I couldn't go back – I missed the place, but I needed to keep a distance from the family.

'Your dad and I both found jobs in Cardiff, and for a while I thought I could have my independence and still spend time in Pennystrand. I took him home to meet the clan, and of course they were shitty to him. He was the butt of all their practical jokes and raucous teasing. I used to get *furious*. But family meant a lot to him, and he wanted to support me to get along with mine as best I could. The difference was that his were *nice*. Can you imagine how your grandparents fared with my lot?'

'Oh dear.' Grampy Roberts was a railway worker, and Granny left school without a single O level. I know that side of the family inside out and love them dearly. I hate to think what the Parnells of old would have thought of them.

'Exactly. So my parents tried to stop me seeing him, put loads of pressure on, threatened to cut off my allowance. I was working by then, albeit earning a pittance, so I told them I didn't care. I stopped going home for visits – I just got on with my life. The way they saw it, I'd rejected them, so they got very offended and left me to it.

'Another year passed. Your father proposed. You know most of this about your father and me. What we didn't tell you was that your father – bless him – went to see my family to ask for their blessing. They wouldn't give it. By then my sisters were both married. Lisa had married an alcoholic who used to knock her around, so at that point she was in the middle of a divorce. Meredith had married a colourless accountant way older than her, just because he was loaded. She'd already had two affairs that I knew of. But *my* choice of fiancé they had a problem with. No money, living a quiet, happy life away from the mighty Parnells and all their stupid dramas... they couldn't handle that.

'One evening Francis turned up on our doorstep, drunk, beating his chest, metaphorically speaking, and threatening to ruin the ceremony if we did get married. Up till that point, your dad had entertained fond hopes that they'd come round and that I might have a better relationship with them when we were all a bit older and wiser. But after that night even he knew it was hopeless. We didn't tell any of my family where or when we were getting married.'

'Oh, Mum, I'm so sorry. What a nightmare. Thanks for not being like that.'

'Cheers!' She clinks her glass ruefully to mine and takes another sip, calmer now. 'Anyway, I'm rattling through the events of many years. Long story short, Steve and I had long talks about how best to handle things going forward. I was adamant I wanted nothing more to do with them. You know, long years of hurts, big and small, pile up until you reach breaking point. That's what happened with me. I had no toler-ance left for them anymore. Your dad got offered a job in London and it was a really exciting opportunity. So we went, without telling my family. It was time for a completely fresh start, and I never wanted to open my door again to a drunk rela-tive thinking he could push us around. That's when I started going by Tilly, instead of Jessica.'

'Why Tilly?'

'It was a joke from a book we read together as students. Tilly was a bosomy beauty on the run from her dastardly father who was lord of the manor. Your dad often used to call me Tilly when he was teasing me, so it stuck very easily. It was a name that reminded me of laughter and freedom and the time when I met your father.'

'It suits you.'

'When I got married, I wanted no trace of Jessica Parnell – I can't describe how sick I was of that identity by then. I changed it by deed poll. I'm sorry, Kitty. You must think I lied uncon-scionably to you girls for all those years. But it didn't feel like lying – it just felt like walking away from a situation I found unbearably toxic and choosing the life I wanted. But I should have told you where I came from, because indirectly you do too. Although, when we were bringing you up, I never regretted that your Parnell relatives weren't around to stick their ten pence worth in.' She runs her hands through her hair and takes a shaky breath.

I smile to reassure her, and we fall quiet for a bit. We finish our meal and I push my plate aside.

'Mum, I do get it. I mean, is it a shock to realise I have this whole enormous family I never knew about? *Yeah!* And I wish I'd known *you* better, all these years. But I understand why you had to break from them, and I understand why it would've been really painful to look back. I'm sure we girls would have asked you a million questions about them... we wouldn't have understood then; we might have wanted to meet them... I get it.'

'Are they the same? Lisa and Meredith?'

I consider. 'Meredith I think pretty much, yeah. What was the name of the colourless accountant she married?'

'Garth Jenkins.'

'Right, well she's on another husband now. Mark. I only glimpsed him, but she seemed pretty bossy towards him too. Ha!' I grin wickedly. 'Maybe Cooper has her aunty Meredith's genes.'

'Kitty Roberts, hush your mouth! Cooper may be... opinionated, but she's nothing like Meredith.'

'I know. I can still tease her though. And her grandkids seem pretty messed up. But Lisa? I think she's probably different from when you knew her. She's still fond of a G&T, and snooty, but also very glamorous and understated – I really can't imagine her flashing anyone. She's not wild now, more like sad and jaded, you know?'

Mum sighs. 'Poor Lisa. And obviously she's getting divorced again. My family aren't gifted at lasting relationships. So are we really alright, Kitty, you and me? I've spent these last few months living in terror that this would all come up and that I'd lose you.'

'Never. Mum, you've been the absolute best mother us girls could wish for. Loving, patient, encouraging. A little distant sometimes. I think I always instinctively knew some areas were off limits...'

'I'm sorry.'

'But now I guess that'll be different too.' I frown. 'Which brings me to the next question. What happened to you and Dad? And why on earth would you come on holiday here when you'd stayed away all that time?'

Mum groans and heads over to the sofa. I top up our wine glasses and follow with them as she sinks into the cushions.

'I questioned the wisdom of it, all through the run-up to that holiday. I hadn't seen my family for fourteen years. Sometimes I'd think of them; Steve and I would chat about how they might be, what they might be doing. And we both had qualms about keeping them a complete secret from you girls. We wondered about making contact several times over the years and decided against it every time. In the end, Cooper was pestering us for a beach holiday, we couldn't go abroad that year because money was tight and we decided we could kill both birds with one stone. Take you girls to the coast, and I could scope out my family, see if I felt I might want anything to do with them after all.

'We got there and you all fell in love with it, especially you, Kits. I've never seen such a beach baby. You were a Pennystrand girl through and through, just as I was. God, I miss the sea. Anyway, on the third day here, I went up to the house – the house you know rather well now – and knocked on the door. My mother answered it – and slammed the door in my face. I tried again and this time Lisa answered. Her first words to me were, "Oh you've got a nerve. Don't tell me you're tired of slumming it."

'It was like a wall, Kitty, between me and them. I walked away. They were always so black and white. *I'd* cut ties, so *I* was bad and had to be punished.

'To be fair, Lisa came running after me. I'd gone quite a way, so I guess she'd spent a while arguing with herself – or with Mum – but she came running down the road. She called my name – Jessica – and it was like she was calling a stranger. That's when the Parnell in me took over. I could be black and white too. I'd had that horrible reception from them and I couldn't be bothered. So I told her to go away – well, I was a bit ruder than that – and stormed off.

'I wanted to go home, but you girls were smitten with the place. Your dad persuaded me to stick it out. It was bittersweet of course. I wanted to share my childhood memories with you girls, but I couldn't open that can of worms. Then your dad stopped coming out with us. He said a pile of urgent paperwork had come through from work... but eventually he told me he'd been meeting Lisa. He was trying to do what I hadn't been able to – get through the initial shock and find some sort of mutual understanding.'

'Oh I *seeeee*!'

I get up and pull a tub of ice cream out of the freezer, grab two spoons then flop back onto the sofa, handing a spoon out to Mum.

'*That's* who you were talking about when you said you didn't want him seeing her again – *Lisa*! He wasn't having an affair – he was trying to smooth things over!' I suck thoughtfully on an icy-sweet spoonful. Now it all makes sense.

'An affair? Your *father*?' Mum looks horrified. 'Why would you ever think that?'

Quickly I fill her in on Cooper's side of the story – her memories of that holiday and the arguments between them.

'Oh no,' Mum groans, burying her face in her hands and getting a bit of ice cream in her hair. 'Poor Steve. I did have a rather shirty text from him during the week saying I'd better tell you everything or else. He must be devastated that his daughters have been thinking that.'

I reach for a tissue and wipe the strand of hair. 'Yeah, poor Dad. We should have known. But then, Cooper heard what she heard. She was a teenager. She put two and two together and made four-ish. She only told me when I came here because I couldn't understand why she was so down on the place.'

'Poor Cooper. I'll talk to her of course. As well as Lisa, I think he saw my brother Griff once as well and Meredith. They all said they'd been a bit hasty and that they'd love to see me again and meet you girls. That's when he had to tell me what he'd been up to. And I hit the roof, Kitty. The divorce was all my fault honestly. I was Parnell through and through at that point in my life. I felt betrayed, so I was unforgiving and furious. I was terrified that I couldn't trust him and that he'd let them into your lives and they'd mess you up. I said terrible things, and we couldn't come back from it. And that, my darling, is the whole story. You can ask me anything you like, and I'll tell you anything you want to know, but those are the basics, and again, I'm very sorry.'

I nod slowly. 'I think I'll have a million questions, Mum, but they can wait, right? Now that I know the bones of it, I can phone you whenever, so no, we don't have to talk about it all weekend. I'd quite like just to enjoy having you here for a couple of days.'

'Enjoy being mother and daughter together in this place, the way we always would have if things had been different,' agrees Mum, looking fragile. 'I'd like that, Kitty.'

'Good. Just one question for now then. Will you see Lisa and the others now? Do you think enough water's finally gone under the bridge?'

'Would you like me to?'

'It makes no difference to me, Mum. It's your call. I'll love and support you no matter what.'

'Well maybe. But not this weekend. I have to think about it. As long as you're OK and not furious with me, I don't really care about anything else.'

'I meant what I said, Mum – I get why you did it. Let's just relax for the rest of the weekend. Go and see the house I'm buying – I'd love you to see it. Go to Tymorau or Time and Tide for hot chocolate, pop into the office and say hello to Roly...'

'My darling.' She reaches over to hug me. 'I never thought I'd say this, but I'm really happy you came here.'

CHAPTER 43

The next morning I wake up early and tiptoe downstairs. It's quiet – I can see the sun brimming behind the long curtain that covers the back door. I pull back the drape and open the door. Sitting in the worn red armchair with a coffee, the cool morning breeze stealing over me, I stare into space, listening to the riot of birdsong and remembering last night. I'd been dreading Mum's revelations all week and now a cloud has lifted. Dad didn't cheat on her. Me moving here won't destroy anything. There's a new honesty between me and Mum. It's all good.

Except... I'm a Parnell. That's going to take some getting used to. Wait till Cherry hears *this*! I'm not sure if I want to own it or not. If I go ahead and move here for good, my sprawling, outrageous, often-unpleasant maternal family will be right on my doorstep. Might they try to interfere in my life the way they did in Mum's? I toy with the possibility of never telling anyone and living here in contented anonymity as the daughter of Tilly, from Bath. But I want Mum to visit often, and someone's bound to recognise her. I just won't *let* them push me around, that's all! They have no claim on me, and I'll make that clear. Seafoam

Cottage, former home of my villainous Parnell ancestors – how fitting! – is too delicious a dream to let slip through my fingers.

When I hear Mum get up, I start up the stairs. She's on her way down to see me, and we meet halfway for the most enormous hug. 'I love you,' we both say at the same time, and this time there are no clouds in her eyes, no secrets standing between us.

We both have a holiday feeling that Sunday, unburdened and happy. It's too soon to say goodbye so she texts her boss to take an impromptu day's leave on Monday. When we tumble down the hill after a massive breakfast in the house, I ask the same of Roly, and of course he says yes. He's over the moon to see Mum and gives her a huge hug. I introduce her to Bella and Derrick, then we go to Time and Tide for hot chocolate, and Roly comes with us. Between us all, we see at least six people we know and spend about an hour talking. No, this was never going to stay secret. Then Roly goes back to work. Mum and I go home for swimsuits and towels and go to the beach.

The day goes on and on. I've texted Cherry with a succinct update and invited her to call up. She arrives for tea, wearing a navy headscarf with pink spots. Her mother, Rhian, is with her, Mum's old childhood friend.

'Oh my word, it's so good to see you, Jessie. Please let's not lose touch again,' she cries – and there are more hugs all round.

'Kitty, it's so lovely to meet you at last. Cherry's thrilled you'll be staying. My word, you look like your mother!'

On Monday morning, Mum and I visit Seafoam Cottage together – Mum loves it – then she leaves after lunch. I promise to visit her soon. I call in to my solicitors with some paperwork for the house then go home to spend the evening on the phone with Cooper and Dad. I even find a succinct email from Cory in response to my house news.

!!!!!!!!!!!!!! 😊 😊 😊 *More soon xx*

Then on Tuesday I'm back at work. Roly has his hands full negotiating back and forth between Lisa and the barrister, both still stalling over a negligible amount. There are no viewings at Fortescue Crescent thankfully, so I don't have to deal with Lisa until I'm ready. And everything goes back to normal.

Two days later, Roly takes another call about The Chantry. This time, it's the owner, who's come back from Colombia unexpectedly.

'Well, that was very strange,' says Roly, setting down the phone. 'Morgan Valentine's back in Wales and staying in The Chantry for a few weeks. He still wants to sell – he just wanted to warn us he's in residence for when we arrange viewings.'

'What's strange about that?' asks Derrick. 'Makes perfect sense.'

'That wasn't the weird bit. He says he has something of a sensitive nature to discuss and wants me to go out there this afternoon. He wouldn't even give me a clue. He said it's incredibly important and we might have to involve the previous owner, and he can't discuss it over the phone.'

'Who was the previous owner?' asks Derrick.

'I can't remember offhand. It was years ago. Fish out the file, one of you. I'll take it with me in case I need it. Kitty, do you want to come? I know you love the place.'

'Not me.' Derrick shivers. 'Creepy.'

I retrieve the paperwork from the filing cabinet. 'Yes, always. But will he want me there if he's being so cryptic? What if it's confidential?'

Roly makes a face. 'He didn't say to come alone. I'm not paying a ransom demand.'

'Go in case Roly needs backup over something,' suggests Derrick. 'You can be his bodyguard.'

The thought of bodyguarding six-foot-tall, rugby-built Roly, with his foodie's belly for added bulk makes me smile.

'If you're sure.' I leaf through the file, back to when Morgan

Valentine bought it. His name was Kevin Morgan then, I note. 'The previous owner was a Mrs S. Thomas,' I tell them. 'She sold in 2006.'

Derrick shrugs. 'Before my time, mate. I was a mere babe in arms.'

'Thomas, Thomas...' Roly mutters. 'Come on, Roly, man, remember! It had to be a Thomas, didn't it, not something memorable? The old brain's not what it used to be.'

I'm amazed he remembers all he does. His brain is like a living rolodex of Pennystrand property history and this was over a decade ago.

'Oh *yes!*' he exclaims with satisfaction. 'Oh, she was a nasty piece of work. Let's hope we won't need to get in touch with *her.*' He looks glum then brightens. 'Unless maybe he's found her dead body somewhere.'

I'm a little bit concerned that I did something wrong when I was there last week for the no-show. Did I leave a door unlocked or a cupboard open? Surely he would discuss something like that over the phone.

As we drive over the Burrows, Roly and I speculate, our guesses becoming wilder and wilder. Mrs Thomas was a heroin dealer and Morgan Valentine's found a wad of drug money under a floorboard. She was a dominatrix and he's found some seriously dodgy equipment at the back of a bedroom cupboard...

When we pull up in the drive, the door flies open and a small, stocky, good-looking man with straight dark hair tied back in a ponytail comes out. He's wearing jeans and a white linen shirt, leather thong sandals and a necklace of turquoise beads. His appearance is more Native American than South Wales. He looks jittery enough for any of our crazy stories to be true.

Roly greets him with his usual poise and good humour and introduces me. 'I hope it's OK I brought Kitty along.'

'It's fine, it's fine. Come on through. Let me show you the... er... issue.'

He hurries us inside, disappearing at pace down the hall, through the kitchen and into the garden. I close the front door after us and leg it after the two men.

'So how long are you back, Morgan?' Roly's trying for small talk. 'How's Colombia? How's the art world?'

'All good, good. I'm back for a month or so. My agent wanted new material and I had an idea for a series inspired by the Burrows. All I want to do is paint, Roly, just work and get the paintings out and go home. Conchita's expecting again, and she's not happy with me being away. But you have to go where inspiration takes you – you have to strike while the iron's hot. I can't get caught up in anything, Roly; I can't get distracted. I need you to take care of this. I'm here for a purpose, and any interference could be catastrophic to the artistic process. And to my marriage,' he adds, biting his lip.

'I'd love to reassure you, Morgan, but until I know what it is...'

'I know, I know. Here we are. Sit.'

We're at the holy well. Roly looks dubiously at the grass; he's not the niftiest bloke in the world. 'Can I stand?'

'Yes, yes, sure. We'll stand. Whatever. Right, so I slept off the jetlag on my first day here and yesterday started to prepare myself to work. I came to the well to ask for its blessing on the project – I need to do my best work yet and make a fortune and prove to Conchita why I had to come. I have a small ceremony I do to invoke the elements at the start of every new undertaking. At one point, I put my hands in the water and the strangest thing happened. I felt as if they were being moved, guided.'

'There was something in the water?' asks Roly. I can see that he's imagining a mini Loch Ness monster. Perhaps a Burrows seahorse. I shiver. I knew there was something about this place.

'Nothing corporeal. But my hands moved as if they had a will of their own, as if there was a current in the water. They moved to the left-hand side and I felt the edge of the pool, the moss and the weed and the old stones. And I found something.'

'What?' ask Roly and I in unison.

'Well, I put it back! I didn't know what to do. I swear I just *found* it...'

I start fidgeting with curiosity. 'So... it's still there? In the well?'

He nods. 'Unless I was hallucinating.'

I'm not sure whether that's just a figure of speech or whether it might actually be a possibility. It'll be a tremendous anti-climax if he was.

'Might you bring it out for us again then?' suggests Roly with admirable patience.

Morgan Valentine drops to his knees in the grass and bows his head. He doesn't put his hands in the pool as I expect, but we see his lips moving.

Then he looks up. 'Kitty, it has to be you,' he says. 'Come kneel please.'

I glance at Roly, who shrugs. I kneel beside Morgan and plunge my hands into the left-hand side of the pool, trying not to think about slime and things that nibble. Despite weeks of baking sun, the water in the pool is cool and mysterious, other-worldly.

'Further back.' Morgan reaches in too and guides my hands. Sure enough, there's a small gap in the cold, slick stones. 'There!' He gives my hands a little nudge, then sits back on his heels, shaking the drops of holy water back into the pool, then wiping his hands on his jeans.

I experience a nervous thrill, akin to when Mitch and I visited the Bocca della Verità in Rome, the marble mask said to bite anyone who lies. Is some sort of ancient fish lurking piranha-like in the cavity? Oh God, I hope it's not a human body part!

My fingers close around something hard and compact with

a smooth covering. I pull it out and fling it on the grass, rattled now. It's an old oilskin, wrapped around a slim rectangular shape.

'That's it,' says Morgan. 'Exactly as I found it.'

'Why did you put it back in the water?' I wonder.

'I wanted you to see it exactly as I found it. I told you, I can't afford to get mixed up in any trouble. I can't be accused of anything. I need to get back to Cartagena.'

Roly's curiosity trumps his lack of athleticism. With a wince, he lumbers to his knees beside me and starts unwrapping the oilskin. My hands are too cold and trembling to do it.

Inside the wrapping is a long navy jewellery case with a slight velvety pile. Roly snaps it open and gasps. 'My word, Morgan! You're right – this is quite a find!'

'I don't understand,' says the stressed-out artist. 'When you sold me the house, I didn't know there'd be... *this* here! Whose is it and why is it in my well?'

'I have no idea,' breathes Roly. 'To either question. I see now why you thought we may need to involve the previous owner. I wonder if it's hers or something much older. It's not the sort of thing you forget, is it? Kitty? Why aren't you saying anything.'

'Um...' I say in a voice that sounds high and tinny, coming from far away. 'Because I know exactly what it is and who it belongs to.' Well, that clinches it. The holy well is definitely magic.

Roly manoeuvres himself uncomfortably to sit on the ground. He and Morgan look at me in astonishment.

I pick up the navy box and look at its contents, gleaming in the sun. It's Doris's long-lost pearl necklace.

CHAPTER 44

The three of us sit on the grass with the stunning necklace shimmering between us. Fortunately, when Doris first enlisted me to help her find it, I took a photo on my phone of her wedding photograph. I bring it up now to show the others, enlarging it on the small phone screen. The necklace is instantly recognisable. Quickly I recount the story of her evil daughter-in-law and the way she taunted Doris at the party. 'She said it was at the house. Poor Mrs Vincent has been going crazy thinking she'll leave Helena Row and leave it behind. But it was *this* house! I had no idea she'd ever lived here. *Was* it her, Roly, Mrs S. Thomas?'

'S for Siwan, yes. Good God, what a despicable way to treat poor Doris. I told you she was a nasty piece of work, didn't I?'

'Yes. I can't imagine her ever living somewhere like this.'

'Oh, it was brief. This is a wonderful house, but it's not the easiest place to live. It must have passed through my hands at least four times over the years. Siwan Thomas was *persona non grata* after her divorce from Rory Vincent so she took it into her head to move out here and martyr herself, be the pitiful, misunderstood woman on the moor. Anyway, two months later she was begging me to sell it, said the loneliness was driving her mad.'

'But this is *wonderful!*' exclaims Morgan Valentine. 'I'm delighted.'

'Isn't it incredible? Doris is such a lovely woman; she deserves this.'

'I meant that we don't have to get the police involved. I don't even have to deal with that awful Siwan creature. You two can take it back to its owner and leave me in peace. Thank God I called you, Roly.'

Roly crinkles his brow. 'You want us to take it now? Just like that? Don't you want to verify Kitty's story? I mean, *I* trust her implicitly obviously, but you've never met her before!'

'Good enough for me. I've seen the photo. Here you go.' He tries to bundle the lost treasure into my distressed leather hand-bag, slimy oilskin and all.

'I don't think I need that!' I push it away and take just the box. 'But wouldn't you like to give it to Doris yourself? It was found on your property?'

'No, no, I told you, I just need to paint.'

'He just needs to paint,' says Roly with his beatific smile. 'Come on, Kitty – let's leave him to it. Cartagena calls. Good luck, Morgan.'

He heaves and lumbers a bit, finally working his way onto all fours and from there to standing up. I take a last, grateful glance at the well before getting to my feet too.

Half an hour later, we pull up in front of number three, Helena Row. 'In you go,' says Roly. 'I'll see you back at the office.'

'You don't want to come? See her face?'

'I do, yes, but it's you she asked for help. I'll leave you to it. No rush.'

'Thank you, Roly. You are the best boss in the entire world.

Oh, by the way, she didn't want anyone to know about quite how bad it was with Siwan... I think she feels embarrassed. I probably should have said so to Morgan.'

'I wouldn't worry. He'll be up to his eyes in paintbrushes – I doubt he'll speak to a soul all month.'

'That's true. Thanks, Roly.'

I clamber out of Saffron and ring the bell of number three as my remarkable boss drives away to hunt down a parking space.

Doris answers the door, out of breath.

'Hello, dear! I'm packing boxes – horrid work. Is there a viewing I've forgotten about?'

'No, much better than that. I have some news. Well, various bits of news really,' I add, realising that she doesn't even know about Seafoam Cottage. The last couple of weeks have flown, and I haven't had time to call on her.

'How lovely – come in. Are you skiving off work?'

I laugh. 'No. Roly just dropped me off actually, so I'm here with his blessing.'

'Dear man. Will you have a cup of tea?'

'I will, yes, but can we go and sit down first, before you do all that? I can't wait.'

'Gracious, that sounds important! It feels very odd to sit down with a guest without giving them anything. Nothing wrong I hope?'

'The very opposite. Come on, Doris.'

I'm so impatient now that I grab her hand and tow her to the sitting room where we usually chat. I guide her to her usual seat on the sofa and sit next to her. She looks at me, and I can't restrain the massive beam that wants to burst over my face.

'Are you ready for some good news? Something big?'

'I'm ready, dear. Are you moving here for good?' Her eyes sparkle with hope.

'Actually, yes, but we'll get to that in a minute. This is even better.' I pull the navy jewellery box from my bag and hand it to her.

Her face is serious as she strokes the short pile. 'What's this?'

'Open it.'

She snaps the box open and her face changes, expressions scudding across it like clouds on a windy day. Her mouth opens then closes again. 'I... I...' she says at last. 'Is it a replica? Did you have it made for me as a gift?'

'No, it's the real thing. Doris, you're not going to believe where it was.' And I tell her about The Chantry, about Morgan Valentine's ritual and discovery of the box, about his summoning Roly and me going along because I love the house. 'I recognised it at once. Can you *believe* it? I guess when Siwan said to you that it was at the house, she really did mean it, only she was thinking of a different house. Did you even know she'd ever lived there?'

Doris shakes her head slowly, stroking the pearls with shaking fingers. 'I think I heard something about her moving to the wilds, but I didn't pay any attention to the details. I was just so glad she was out of our lives. Good grief. Tucked away in a holy well, all these years? There's something poetic about that, don't you think?'

'It's more than poetic, it's magic! Only last week... Don't laugh at me, Doris... Only last week I was there on my own and I made a wish at that holy well. Lots of wishes in fact, including that you would find the necklace. And here it is. That's the truth.'

'What would Lawrence say if he heard all this?' She smiles. 'He loved a good yarn, did Lawrence – always said there were more things in heaven and earth.'

'Now why don't I make us tea while you sit here? You must be stunned.'

'Yes, thank you, Kitty. Only don't make tea. I think this calls for a sherry, don't you?'

CHAPTER 45

The weeks pass. I talk to Mrs Charlton and we agree to roll on my lease month by month from October should there be any hold-ups with Seafoam Cottage. 'I'm glad you're staying around – don't be a stranger,' she says. 'But you wouldn't catch *me* living there.' She shivers. 'Too windswept. And to think, you're moving in just before winter. It'll be terribly bleak.'

But nothing can dent my enthusiasm. The sale isn't quite as speedy as Stacey's purchase of Sunset Terrace but rolls along straightforwardly enough. The survey throws up an issue with the roof, so I have to rejig some finances to have it fixed before I move in. No way I'm living in a house with a dodgy roof in Wales in winter. Although I'm impatient to start nesting in my own place, at least in my rental I'm cosy and content, enjoying the anticipation. I won't start buying furniture until I've completed and hold the keys in my hands – I'd be too afraid of jinxing it – but I start browsing online, dreaming up visions for the different rooms, realising I have expensive taste. *Well, I used to work in interior design, so sue me.*

Things move along in my friends' lives. Magpie starts infant school in September, with new red boots, a new *Frozen* lunch box and a new autumn coat with a furry hood. Doris moves into the retirement village, and I spend a weekend helping her arrange her things. I meet her old friends and new neighbours and get roped into several hands of poker and a fierce game of Scrabble. It's easy to see she'll be happy there. When her old house finally sells, I don't worry about her anymore.

Cooper visits for a long weekend and is gratifyingly enthusiastic about everything. I introduce her to my house, my Pinterest boards, my favourite places and my friends. Cherry shows her a surfing magazine with a picture of Cory striding out of the waves, wetsuit unzipped to his navel. Cooper raises her eyebrows eloquently. Dad visits too and gets the same treatment, minus the surfer abs.

The date that I was due to leave Pennystrand comes and goes, and summer reaches its end. The rain comes more often now, and the evenings are drawing in. There are still plenty of days of sunshine, but they're shimmer-shot with rainbows, and the leaves turn golden as freshly baked scones.

And the inevitable day comes when I have The Conversation with Lisa Parnell. I haven't seen her for over a month, but one Thursday, there's an urgent summons from Fortescue Crescent. Roly has a valuation on a new barn conversion – a job that only he can do – and there's no one else in the office. 'It's time,' he says in his philosophical voice. 'You can't avoid her forever, Kitty.'

When I turn up, Lisa and Meredith are both there; it turns out there's no house-related business at all. 'I own the barn conversion Roly's valuing,' says Lisa. 'I arranged it, so you'd have to come. We need to talk.'

'So Roly's wasting his time?' I bristle. He was so excited about that property and promised me photos.

'Oh no, I am going to sell it, and of course I want him to do it for me. But I wanted to see you, Kitty. We both did.'

Meredith is uncharacteristically quiet, clutching a large wine glass.

I sigh. Parnells pulling strings. I already feel weary, but I'll go along with it this once; we do need to talk.

I follow them into the kitchen and we have a tussle when they offer wine, gin and whisky, but I insist on tea.

'I never understood the whole social thing about tea,' sighs Meredith, collapsing onto a bar stool. 'It just puts your hostess to a lot of trouble – cups and saucers and boiling the kettle. Much easier to open a bottle of wine.'

'I'll do it.' After all I know my way around this kitchen pretty well now.

But Lisa won't let me. She makes it, then suggests the comfy seating area. We settle there, Meredith muttering as she hefts herself off the stool and into an armchair.

'Pretending we're all civilised now, are we? She knows what we're like, Lis.'

'Well, that's the thing – I'm not sure she does,' says Lisa. 'At least, I *hope* there's more to us than first impressions. Kitty, you know what Pennystrand's like. We heard from our neighbour Jeanette, who heard from her grandson Pablo, who heard from his girlfriend's mate Sienna that your mum came to visit you a while back, and of course we heard that she's our sister Jess. Which didn't come as any sort of surprise to be honest because you really are—'

'The complete spit,' finishes Meredith in her croaky smoker's voice. 'Chip off the old block, two peas in a pod, all that. Christ, I left my wine on the bar.'

'I'll go.' I jump up for something to do and fetch the wine – glass and bottle.

'Ah, there's a good niece, nicer than the rest of the little bastards, isn't she?'

Lisa rolls her eyes. 'Kitty, we suspected of course, because of the likeness, but you never said anything, and you didn't appear to know. It seemed too much of a coincidence that you'd turn up here *not* knowing... Is that what happened?'

'I saw a fortune teller.'

'What?'

'In London, when Mitch and I broke up, I couldn't see a way forward. So I went to see a psychic in Covent Garden. She told me I should go to a small town by the sea, somewhere I'd been before. I loved it here when I was a kid so I came, just for six months, or so I thought, to clear my head and make some decisions. And no, I had no idea whatsoever that I had relatives here till Mum told me the other day.'

Lisa takes a deep breath. 'We've also heard that you're buying a house in Lemon Cove. You intend to stay?'

'I do. But not because of you. I don't want anything from you. I was brought up not knowing about you, I came here not knowing about you and I don't see why anything should change now just because I *do* know about you. I'm staying here because I love it, because I'm making good friends and building a good life. I do *not* want family dramas or politics or anything. I want you to leave me alone and respect that I'm an adult and completely independent. And I'll leave you alone too as soon as we're done with the house.'

'Now hang on, hang on,' says Meredith in a tone of some outrage.

'Meredith, hush!' Lisa holds up a hand to quell her.

'Talk to the hand,' mutters Meredith, but she subsides.

'Kitty, that's fine. We probably haven't made the best impression on you, and your mum's story must have had an impact too. We behaved shockingly to her is the truth of it. I'd like to say we're older and wiser now, changed people and all that... we *are*, but probably not as much as we should be. I'm not surprised she didn't want to see us when she was here, but I wanted to know... does she still hate us?'

I frown and sip my tea. 'She doesn't *hate* you. I don't think she ever did. I think it's just that you all... made her life really difficult, and it was easier to move away from you, emotionally and geographically. But she doesn't hate you, and I don't either.'

'Well, thank you for that. Did she say anything about... might she ever want to see us in the future, do you think?'

'I did ask. She doesn't know. I don't think she's ruled it out – put it that way.'

'Yes!' Meredith raises her hand in a high five, but with no takers she puts it down again and pours more wine.

Lisa nods again, as measured and taut as I've ever seen her. Despite everything, I still feel a strange sympathy towards her. Meredith seems the happier of the two, even if her mood is generally induced by a sparkly haze of alcohol.

'Is that what you wanted?' I ask. 'To know that Mum doesn't hate you? Did *you* want to see her again?'

'Oh yes, of course!' Lisa looks surprised. 'We always did. It probably didn't look that way, but we never wanted to lose our little sister. But I can see that we went about everything the wrong way. I'm sure you don't want to be a go-between, Kitty, and I won't ask again, but please would you just tell her that we're sorry, and if she'd like to call the next time she visits you, we'd be very happy. But if she doesn't, we'll understand and leave you all alone.'

I scratch my neck. 'OK,' I say slowly. 'I guess I could tell her that.'

'And, Kitty, if *you* wanted to... get to know us a bit, we'd like that too. But again, if you want to live a completely separate life, I wouldn't blame you. We're a lot to take. But you're our niece, Kitty. So... we're here if you want us.'

'Ha!' snorts Meredith and it's unclear what she's laughing about.

'Right. Thank you. Can I think about it?'

Lisa nods at once. 'Yes. I meant it – no pressure. We shan't make the same mistakes with you that we did with Jessie.'

'Good. It's not that I don't *want* to know you, but I have a really nice life here. I don't want any trouble or drama and... well, it seems like being a Parnell can involve a bit of both. I just don't need that.'

'OK then. Well, that's all I wanted to say to you. I don't suppose you'd like to stay for another cup of tea?'

This was new. Lisa considerate, contrite, diffident.

I hesitate. Part of me does want to go. It's hard to talk seriously with Meredith getting steadily more pissed, and I'm not sure I can trust this new gentle treatment from Lisa. But they're my aunts! I never had aunts – Dad only had a brother. I'm here now, and I do have questions, I suppose. Although the most pressing isn't about Mum at all. Dare I bring up a completely different topic? At this point, I realise, I don't really have anything to lose.

'I'll have another cup,' I say, starting to get up.

'No, no, I'll get it,' says Meredith, rocking to and fro, working up the impetus to get to her feet. 'Fair play to her – I'll get it.' She lumbers off to the kettle and Lisa sighs.

'Perhaps I should have talked to you alone. But Jessie's her sister too.'

'I get it. There is one thing I wanted to ask you about while I'm here. Why are you selling this house? I've been wondering ever since I met you. You seem so incredibly unhappy about it, Lisa. You belong here. I see a lot of owner-house combinations in my job, and this place is *yours*. You could sell it ten times over and it'd still be yours. Isn't there another way?'

Meredith comes back with another cup of tea, which she places in front of me. 'Off to the loo,' she announces. 'Might be a while,' she adds with a cackle and wanders off.

That makes it easier to say what I want to say next. 'I was talking to Agatha a while back. Please don't be mad at her for talking to me. She said you're doing it to spite your ex but that if you and she pooled resources, you could buy him out. Why don't you do that? Wouldn't you both be happier?'

Lisa bites her lip and taps a caramel-coloured fingernail against the side of her glass. 'Look, Agatha's my aunt. I love her. But you've met her. She's old, she's frail, she's barking mad. She's better off where she is. I have enough on my plate with the business and the divorce and the grandkids... I don't think Agatha's a viable person to join forces with, to get financially tangled up with. To *live* with! I can't be involved with that.'

'*Is* she barking mad though? She seems perfectly sharp to me. She figured out who I was in five minutes. And you *are* involved, aren't you? Who do they call when she escapes from the home? Who did *I* call when I found her? You. And you came straight away. Wouldn't it be *easier* to live with her? It's a huge house. You could get a carer in... and stay here!'

Lisa looks around the spacious kitchen, the glittering bar, the granite island, the flagged floor. The French doors are closed, and outside, the weather's creating a kaleidoscope of rain pattering on the glass, sun and cloud, sweeping the garden with light and shadow. The sea in the distance is dark blue and brooding; I can see the longing in her eyes. The longing *and* the belonging – it maddens me to think she might stubbornly plough on with selling.

She turns back to me, looking almost lost. 'But you said it, Kitty. She goes wandering off. Meandering aimlessly about the place. It's not safe. I don't want that responsibility. And I think you know about the other thing? The... mermaids? She thinks she was abducted by mermaids when she was a girl. It's frightening. It's *embarrassing!*'

I take a deep breath. 'I get all that. But when she wanders off, she's *not* just meandering – she's trying to get home, back to this house. If she was already here... maybe she'd be *safer!*'

She smiles. 'The irony of this, after you said you didn't want your bossy Parnell relatives interfering in your life, is not lost on me, Kitty Roberts.'

'Well, yeah, I see that. I'm overstepping. But look – I love Agatha. I kind of like *you*, for some reason. You're both unhappy. You could both be happy. It makes no sense to me. And I'm not speaking as your niece – I'm speaking as your estate agent. I can see that you don't really want to sell. You've been stalling the solicitor for weeks. Agatha presents an alternative solution. I don't want unhappy clients.'

'You realise you're talking Roly out of a sweet commission? He won't thank you if I take your advice.'

'Roly feels exactly as I do! He hasn't been happy about this project from the start. He said it didn't feel right.'

'What a sweet. You know your mother used to date him? We created havoc of course. Dreadful.' She shakes her head ruefully. 'But, Kitty, the *mermaids.*'

'Oh so what if Agatha believes in mermaids? Let's say you're right and it never happened—'

'*Let's say* I'm right? Kitty, please don't tell me you believe in mermaids too or I'll have to disown you before I've even... owned you. That came out wrong – you know what I mean. Of course I'm right! You can't possibly think that ever happened, can you?'

'Well, no, if I'm honest. But there are still explanations. The world is really, really strange, you know. Look at the psychic telling me to come here, for goodness' sake! And...' I think of Doris's necklace, waiting in the weeds of a holy well fed by a sacred spring from the moor. But that's not my story to tell.

'Well, other strange things have happened recently. The world is bigger than we can ever grasp. Or maybe Agatha had one isolated psychotic incident when she was very young. Assuming it's a delusion, it's a pretty harmless one, don't you think? It's not like she's trying to drown herself to get back to them. It's just a story about her past. Is it worth losing your home for that?'

Lisa shakes her head. 'Incredible,' she murmurs. 'You are so like your mother. She used to see everything quite differently from us too. We're all focused on how it's a stupid story and an embarrassment. You see possibilities and love. Maybe, after all, I'll think about it...'

Meredith comes back and collapses into her chair with a loud huff. 'Sorry about that, girls. When nature calls, you know. What did I miss?'

CHAPTER 46

Things go quiet for another week, then Roly is summoned to Fortescue Crescent. When he comes back to the office it's with the news that Lisa's taking her house off the market. 'Agatha's leaving the home and moving in,' he reports. 'She's going to have a whole suite of rooms and a part-time carer. They're buying out Lisa's bastard husband. I've never been so thrilled to lose £40,000.'

'I'm sorry, Roly – I know it was going to be a really prestigious sale for us,' says Nerys.

'No, it's fine. I never felt right about it. And she's selling three other places to free up some more cash – the barn conversion, a massive detached place in Woodside Gardens and a sea-view flat overlooking Brightman Bay so we'll rake in plenty of commission, don't you worry. She's decided she doesn't need to own half of Pennystrand apparently! Wonders will never cease.'

News travels fast, and the following day Matthew calls in to crow about Roly letting the 'sale of the century' slip through his fingers. We are supremely unbothered.

Soon after Matthew flies off on his broomstick, Stacey appears. 'Hi, Kitty,' she says. 'I'm glad you're here. I've got a job for you.'

'A job? What do you need?'

'I need to put the house on the market.'

'What?' I'm stupefied. 'Not Sunset Terrace?'

'Yup. I'm selling.'

'But why? What's wrong? You *love* that place!'

'Don't talk her out of giving us business please, Kitty,' calls Roly from his desk at the front.

'Oh right, yes. Of course we'll sell it for you. Um, I don't suppose we need to value it, do we? You only bought it five minutes ago.'

'Four months,' she says. 'I've had four wonderful, happy months there. And no, it hasn't changed.'

'The market's pretty similar too,' says Roly. 'I'll just resurrect the file, shall I?'

'Yes please.' Stacey smiles at him then turns back to me. 'I'm moving in with my boyfriend.'

'Oh! Great. Where?'

'In Brenton.'

It's not a name I know. 'Where's that?'

'About an hour from here, just off the motorway, easy for him to get to work. It's got a fitted kitchen and there's plenty of room for when we have kids... we're getting married!' She waves her left hand at me, and a very pretty diamond ring sparkles away.

'Oh, congratulations!' I stand up to give her a hug. It's lovely news. I should be happy for her, but I feel strangely flat and I don't know why. But now isn't the time to figure it out. We reassure her that the house will be back on the market by the end of the day.

'Do you want a board up?' asks Roly. 'OK, I'll send the sign guy round. He'll be with you in the next couple of days most probably.'

When Stacey leaves, he fixes me with a look. 'What's up with you, Kitty Roberts?'

'I don't know. It just seems such a shame.'

He laughs. 'So many people's idea of a sad ending: love and marriage, a new house, a family. What's a shame about it?'

'I don't know! It's wonderful, you're quite right. She did *look* happy. But...' I fall quiet, trying to work it out. Stacey's a grown woman – she knows what she's doing. But I remember the feeling I got when she first set eyes on Sunset Terrace, the look of incredulous wonder on her face as she wandered from room to room. And I compare it to the feeling I got today, when she told me about the new house – a kind of cold, dull feeling.

'It's a shame she couldn't have had a little longer to enjoy Sunset Terrace,' I say. 'She was just so happy to buy that house. She wanted to be by the sea so much, and now she's going to be an hour away. Off the *motorway*!

'I know what it is!' I realise in a rush. 'There's no poetry in it. She's gone from, *Ooh, I can have Prosecco on the doorstep and look at the sea,* to, *It's just off the motorway so he can get to work.* What's exciting about that?'

Roly laughs. 'That's not about Stacey, Kitty, that's about you. *You* would rather have poetry than practicality, *you* would rather have the dream home than the dream man, at least for now. She'll be fine. You concentrate on Seafoam Cottage. That's your Sunset Terrace, right?'

He's right. I resonated with Stacey's joy all those months ago because I was living my dream vicariously through her. This new adventure of hers doesn't resonate with me at all. Maybe because I haven't met the right man yet. I'm still playing text-tag with Diane's cousin Jason. We somehow haven't been able to find a date to meet that suits us both over the last couple of months. His texts are perfectly friendly but I can't help thinking if either one of us was really enthusiastic about it, we probably would have made it happen by now. It was all so *easy* with Cory. But honestly, *just off the motorway?* Why can't *he* move *here* and drive a bit further and let her have her Prosecco by the sea? Selfish prick.

I walk home lost in thought, examining my conscience. I've been scrupulously honest with myself and it's true, I don't envy Stacey. Not that I wouldn't love to love someone enough to spend my life with them, but I wouldn't want to have to walk away from my own dreams to do it. But she probably *is* happy to do it; she certainly seems to be. As she said, she's had four happy months there, and maybe for her, that chapter is over now. Not every chapter has to be a long one. I'll ring her tomorrow and offer to take her out for champagne. I haven't seen much of her over the summer, but Sunset Terrace was my first sale and Stacey's a nice girl, and I want to cheer her on.

My thoughts turn to Seafoam Cottage. I've booked a roofer, but he can't start for another two weeks so I have that time to exchange and complete. Then, assuming all goes to plan, I should be able to move in late November, in time for my first Christmas in my own home.

Lost in dreams, I wander along Rockspell Close and I'm nearly at my front door before I see that there's a man standing there, tall, with an athletic build and a goofy smile.

'Hello, Kitty.'

I jerk to a halt. For a second, just a split second, I think it's Cory. But it's not. It's Mitch.

CHAPTER 47

I can't believe my eyes. It's like seeing a seal in the desert or a giraffe at the North Pole. *Mitch belongs in London, not here. Mitch belongs in the past.* For a moment everything spins as the new life I've been living this summer, the future I'm building and the past in which I got badly hurt all whirl around together like ingredients in a Nutribullet.

'Surprise!' says Mitch and things gradually slow to a halt, allowing me to see that his arms are flung wide in a *ta-da!* pose and that he's holding a massive bouquet of peach roses, my favourite.

It *is* a surprise. So much so that I honestly don't know what my reaction should be. Outrage? Delight? Hope?

'Mitch,' I say carefully, not trusting my voice. 'What on earth are you doing here?'

I take a small step towards the house but he's comman-deered the doorstep, and I don't want to get too close so I stop. My heart's hammering so hard I'm surprised he can't see it leaping about in my chest. With trepidation or excitement? Again, I can't tell.

'I've come to see you of course. Here.'

He comes towards me, holding out the roses, and I take them because what else are you supposed to do?

'To apologise, and check that you're OK, and talk to you, if you'll let me.'

'But... how did you *find* me?' I'm certain my family wouldn't have told him where I was without giving me any sort of a heads-up at all.

He laughs. 'You gave me your address, silly.'

The shock really is making me slow. I haven't spoken to him since Black Thursday, which seems so long ago now it's practically grey. '*When?*'

'On your *email*. The one you sent me the first night you were here.'

Oh *that* email. I'd completely forgotten about it.

'That meant so much to me, Kitty. The cracks were already starting to show with Rachel. Not her fault – I just couldn't handle what I'd done to you. And I missed you so much. I was crazy to think I could just pick up and start over again with someone new after all our history. Anyway, it meant a lot to know that you were missing me too. We've always been on the same page, haven't we?'

'I thought so. Until I found you kissing Rachel in our flat while I was looking at houses for us to buy together.'

'Yeah.' He grimaces. 'That was appalling. I'm so, so sorry, Kitty, and I really wish I could have ten minutes to explain. Not that *anything* excuses betraying you like that, but I've done a lot of reflection over the last few months, a lot of self-examination, and I didn't like what I saw. So it would mean a lot to me if you're willing to talk. No obligation of course. You don't owe me anything.'

It strikes me that if my email meant that much to him, he could perhaps have answered it at some point. That if he really doesn't want me to feel obligated, he could have called ahead instead of turning up and blindsiding me. I do feel a little obligated now that he's come all this way, made the big gesture with the roses. I sigh. I know I have a choice, but it doesn't feel like it.

My next-door-but-one neighbour passes. I've never spoken to him, but we exchange waves now and then. 'Oh, good for you,' he comments. 'Nice to have a bit of romance in the close.'

I smile weakly, knowing that this must look like one of life's perfect moments from the outside.

'Come in, Mitch. I don't have long – I'm meeting a friend in half an hour.' I'm not, but I want to give myself an out because I *still* don't know how I feel about seeing him. How is that possible? I loved him for seven years.

'Great!' he says. 'Thanks, Kitty. You need to get those in water at the very least.'

I hand the flowers back to him so I can get the keys from my bag and unlock the door. He follows me inside and looks around, taking in the cosy, open-plan interior, the leaded windows, the faded furniture and the little courtyard outside. 'It's nice!' he says. 'Very you. Are you happy here?'

'Very.' When Mum came to visit, or Cooper or Cory, I eagerly watched their faces as they looked around because I loved seeing it all anew through their eyes. With Mitch there's a massive disconnect. I feel almost defensive of the place, like I don't *want* him to see it. Because he hurt me, I suppose, and my brain is still trying to catch up with events. I did actually *tell* him where I was, I *think* I said I'd like to see him – though I can't actually remember what I put in that email. It was nearly seven months ago! So it's not as though he's completely out of line. I still feel a strange jarring though.

'Tea? Coffee?'

'Don't suppose you've got a beer?'

'No.' I've got wine, but I'm not offering him anything that might prevent him driving away.

'Tea then. So how are you, Kitty? You look well. You look amazing actually. Wales must suit you.'

'It does. I'm fine, Mitch. Better than fine. I'm happy.'

'Are you seeing someone?'

I laugh. 'Because the only way I could be happy is if I'm seeing somebody?'

'Well, no, of course not. But are you?'

'No.'

'Great! I mean, not that I don't want you to be happy, but—'

'I *am* happy, Mitch. I told you.'

I turn to face him while the kettle boils. 'So what's this all about? You're not with Rachel anymore I gather. And you regret hurting me and... what else?'

'Wow. To the point. I get it. And I desperately want you back, but I know there's very little chance of that happening because I acted like a complete dick, but I had to come and see you. I had to ask. At the very least talk to you so you know I'm deeply, truly sorry.'

I fetch teabags from the cupboard – mixed berry for me, regular for Mitch, who never got into the whole herbal thing – and pour milk into his mug while he launches into his explanation. He always loved me, but he felt we'd stagnated. He knew I wanted a different lifestyle and felt the pressure that it wasn't happening fast enough. He was so focused on what *I* wanted he hadn't thought about what *he* wanted. He should have talked to me about all that, but it felt too hard to broach so he sank into lethargy. And when Rachel came along with her outdoorsy, adventurous spirit, he had a moment of weakness. That shocked him because he just wasn't that guy. His mind tried to make it better by turning it into more than it really was. He told himself he wouldn't have cheated on me just for sex; it had to mean something. And because Rachel seemed to offer everything that was missing in our life together, she took on the enticing sheen of an escape route – from our painfully slow-growing savings, from his lethargy and from his self-hatred about what he'd done.

'I was dithering,' he concluded. 'I knew I had to come clean, but I didn't want to hurt you. Rachel wanted me to break it off with you and go travelling with her. You wanted to buy a house and move to the country. Part of me wanted to run off with Rachel because I was sure we'd be over anyway when I told you what I'd done. But a bigger part wanted to stay with you. I thought that maybe... well, I hoped to God that you'd forgive me. But then you walked in and caught us together. I could've died of shame. And it felt like the decision had been made for me.

'So I went, and I was torn the whole time. But I threw myself into it because I thought, if I'd broken us, it had to be for something, right? It somehow made it not so bad if I loved her, if she and I were meant to be. But I was kidding myself. By the time I realised it, I'd spent all the money I'd been saving for us. I came back to London two months ago and it's dismal there without you, Kits, dismal. When I was flat-hunting, I thought of you. When I moved into the temporary place I'm in now, I thought of you. And I haven't *stopped* thinking of you. I've made a big mess of everything, and I'll do whatever it takes – genuinely, anything – to win you back if there's even the slightest chance.'

He takes a big shuddering breath. I pass him his tea and sit down heavily opposite him. He looks so wretched I'm tempted to pour him a glass of wine after all, but then I remember the way his dear familiar body had been wrapped around Rachel's that evening, like two curling stems on a vine. He peeps up at me hopefully and I'm reminded of a thousand treasured moments when he looked at me like that. Our life together. It was the most precious thing in the world to me then.

'This is a lot to take in, Mitch,' I tell him. 'I wasn't prepared for it, and I've got a lot going on just now. I can't pluck all the perfect words out of thin air for you.'

'But you'll think about all I've said, about maybe... getting back together.'

'I don't know about that. The thing is, I've moved on. Not in terms of meeting someone new, but I have a life here now. I'm staying here.'

'Wow! But you don't have to, right? I mean, there's nothing really keeping you here, if you had the chance to make the life you always wanted in Surrey? I've been thinking about it, Kits. I know I wasn't always as enthusiastic about it as you were. I should've been, but I think I just wasn't ready, and again, I didn't have the balls to talk to you about it. Now I am. If nothing else, my mad detour with Rachel showed me that. Now I genuinely can't think of anything better than house-hunting with you, finding a place near Cooper, playing footie with her boys on weekends, keeping chickens. Even white ones, if you really insist.'

I give a tiny smile. We always disagreed on the colour of our imaginary chickens. I wanted white, Mitch wanted copper-coloured. All the same... *Nothing keeping me here*? I think of Cherry's infectious smile and array of colourful 1940s head-scarves. I think of Roly, serenely gazing into the middle distance, his impressive bulk a monument at the front of the office. I think of Nerys in her magenta lipstick and Derrick with his silky purple ties and natty hair, giggling into their pints in Driftwood. I think of Lisa and Meredith gulping gin in that huge and wonderful kitchen – *my aunts*. I think of Doris and Agatha, undaunted by their advancing years, accepting change, accepting limitation, but *never* admitting defeat. I think of Seafoam Cottage and all the life I haven't lived there yet. And I think of Cory. How would I even begin to explain all that to Mitch?

'There is actually quite a lot keeping me here,' I begin. 'For one thing, I'm buying a house. I exchange next week.'

'But you haven't exchanged yet,' he jumps in eagerly.

I give him a look. 'Hardly the point. The point is, this is where I belong. That much I'm clear on. As for us... if I'm honest, I don't see it anymore. I can forgive you, Mitch. I can see that you're genuinely regretful, and I really don't want to punish you. I know life is complicated. I know people make mistakes. But mistakes have consequences, and I don't think I could ever trust you again.'

'But you *could*!' he assures me earnestly. 'You must know, Kitty, some guys are serial cheaters. And then there are guys that just... mess up one time. Lose their way and learn from it. That's me. I swear that's me.'

'I'm sure it is. I never thought you were a bad guy. But it hurt me *so* badly, Mitch.' I'm visited by a memory of those long weeks after he left, when I lay in bed, curtains drawn, crying, stuffing my face with Maltesers, unable to summon enthusiasm for anything at all. I can't bear to think of it, and I certainly don't need to share the grisly details with him. 'This place, and the people here, have brought me back to life. I've made myself happy again, and I did it all without you.'

He sits quietly for a long time, and if there's any more to say, I can't think of it. I get up and open the back door, let in the air, stare into my little courtyard garden with its leafy invaders. *Could* I get back with Mitch? If he said he'd move here to be with me? Do I owe it to him, or to my former self, to consider it at least?

I stare into the leaves and a blackbird pops its head out, eyes bright, then flurries back into the cool depths of the tree. I smile. The simplest things are the best, the most comforting. Emotional vortices and complicated feelings are stifling and stop any joy from filtering through.

I turn back to Mitch.

'How are you doing?' I ask, going to sit opposite him again.

He shrugs. 'Are you really buying a house here?'

'Yes.'

'On your own?'

'Yes.'

'Is it pretty and quaint and everything you ever wanted?'

'Yes. It's perfect. And there's so much more, Mitch. The house is just the tip of the iceberg.'

'I could stay the night? We could talk all evening, catch each other up on the last few months. I could... think about moving here if you're really set on staying.'

'No, you can't stay the night. It would make things more complicated. I'm sorry, Mitch, I just don't see a way forward for us now.'

'You sound as if you've made up your mind.'

'As far as I can, in the space of about half an hour. Before that I thought you were still in Honduras or somewhere with Rachel. It's a bit of a turnabout.'

He sniffs. 'I don't know, I guess I hoped that you'd take one look at me and realise how much you'd missed me. I thought you might be angry – I was prepared for that, but you don't seem angry.'

'I don't think I am. As I said, I can see that you're sorry, and I care about you. But a lot of water's gone under the bridge since then.'

I take a deep breath. If I say goodbye to him now, to all those years we shared, will I regret it? But then I realise we already said goodbye, months ago. *He* said it, when he had an affair. And I said it, when I said no to heartbreak and yes to trying something new.

'You'll always have a special place in my heart,' I say gently, 'but when our road ended, I washed up on a completely different one. There's nothing to be done about that.'

'So I'd better go.'

'I think that's best. I'm sorry, Mitch. Do you need something to eat before you go?'

'No, I'm alright.'

He gets to his feet and slouches to the door. We give each other a sad little hug, and the tension is horrible.

On the doorstep he turns back to me. 'Actually, you haven't got any crisps going begging have you?'

I root in the cupboard and find two packets of Skips, his favourite. Crisps, at least, I can do.

CHAPTER 48

'So... no regrets?' asks Cherry.

I shake my head, barely able to restrain my soppy smile because I just can't believe where we are. We're sitting in Seafoam Cottage. Ty Dihiryn. My house.

Roly called me this morning. As it was my day off, I wondered if someone was sick and he needed me to cover. But he was phoning to say that we'd exchanged on the cottage, a week early, and that the solicitors had said Shelley was willing to complete the same day, if I wanted. *If I wanted?* I bolted to the office and signed the deed.

'Yaaaay!' sang Nerys, nipping into the back when I appeared. I assumed she was going to make a celebratory cup of tea, but a moment later I heard a champagne cork pop and she came back with three cold mugs each containing a generous glug of sparkling gold.

'It's a shame Derrick and Bella aren't here,' I said.

'We'll arrange something,' said Roly. 'A team night out.'

I was on edge all day, so close to owning my dream home but still not actually, technically, *finally* owning it. I went to Time and Tide for hot chocolate. I texted Cherry. I texted

Cooper. I texted Mum. I texted Dad. I wandered down to the beach where I'd seen the woman swimming in the dark all those months ago, her partner patiently shining a path of light over the sand. I reflected that it doesn't have to be a partner who holds the lantern for you in your life. If you're lucky, your friends and family will do the job perfectly. I thought of Cory, half a world away, sending me the details of the house I'd always wanted.

I wandered about all day, restless, getting cold and damp in the intermittent showers. A storm was forecast but hadn't arrived. Finally, at five o'clock, when I felt sure the completion would lapse into the next day, Roly called again and said the words I'd heard him utter to dozens of clients over the months, words I'd said myself many times: 'Congratulations, Kitty. You're now the proud owner of Seafoam Cottage. Would you like to come and collect your keys?'

I was on the seafront at the time, eating an ice cream, too jittery to tell whether doing so in the cold was a daft idea or not. I legged it up the hill, licking my sticky fingers, tossing my tub into a bin, and burst into the office at 5.05 p.m. Roly put the keys into my hands, and for a moment I just *held* them, the keys to my new life. Then I reached into my bag for the special key ring I'd bought weeks ago – a silver frog on a lily pad – and transferred them over. The frog has green eyes (that remind me of Cory a tiny bit, but that's not why I bought it), and I gave a huge, satisfied sigh as I tucked the keys into my bag, where they belong.

'Regrets?' I say to Cherry now as we sit side by side in an almost completely bare Seafoam Cottage. 'About buying this place?'

'No.' She bumps her shoulder against mine gently. 'About saying no to Mitch yesterday.'

In all the excitement of today, it's easy to forget that just yesterday, if I'd wanted, I could have gone back to my old life –

Mitch and London and dreams of keeping chickens near Cooper. It feels unreal.

'No. No regrets. It came too late, and it felt all wrong. The thought of restarting something with him didn't make me feel all wild with hope and longing. It made me feel troubled, and that's not the way you're supposed to feel, is it?'

'No, my friend, it's not.' Cherry picks up the bottle of Shiraz off the floor and tops up our glasses.

There's a knock on the door. My door!

'Pizza! I'll go!' Cherry leaps to her feet and I hear her shuffle to the front door in her slippers, the sound of voices on my doorstep. I give up on trying to corral the smile and let it spread right over my face like sunshine.

I'm not going to sleep here tonight for the simple reason that there's no bed and I haven't sorted out the gas and electricity yet. Roly's call today took me completely by surprise, and the surroundings are spartan to say the least. But Cherry understood why I wanted to spend the evening here. She drove round to meet me, bringing wine, two beanbags, matches, a poker, her slippers and numerous other things I was simply too stunned to think of. (I have, however, brought one cushion I couldn't resist buying in Lisa's shop, even though I've nothing to put it on, three books, which I've propped on the windowsill and, inexplicably, a grapefruit.)

Shelley left the log basket full, so we got a blaze going in no time. It was clear that even though the snug back rooms make ideal 'winter quarters' and the larger front space is harder to heat, we *have* to spend this first, celebratory evening facing the sea. We can't *see* the sea – it's dark now and the rain's bashing the French windows with abandon, but it's out there. We can hear it sighing. Wind whips the garden so that all we can see in the darkness is the tortured writhing of the marram grass and other plants, ghostly shapes outside the window.

I have a moment of trepidation, remembering all the people

who told me how bleak the winter can be here. But Cherry, returning with the pizza, is having none of it.

'You can't get squeamish about rain, not if you're going to live here,' she tells me, seeing my face. 'It's fun. Dramatic! The wilder it is outside, the cosier you have to make it inside – it's a simple equation. When you move in, you can have thick curtains and lovely rugs and books and candles and paintings and throws... but just for tonight, at the start of your adventure, you don't need much.' She pulls a kitchen roll for greasy fingers out of her capacious bag of tricks.

'Fire, pizza, wine and a friend,' I recite. 'You're right. What else does a girl need?' And the house is indeed filled with a golden glow that seems to come from more than just the fire.

'So we're happy about Mitch – Mitch is sorted,' resumes Cherry, plopping back down on her beanbag and lifting the lid of the pizza box. 'What about Cory? Have you heard from him?'

'It's my turn to write,' I garble through a mouthful of hot, loaded pizza. *Gah! Too fast, Kitty!* 'We've exchanged a couple of emails since you last asked, not many. Just chat, you know. He sent me a couple of photos of Mexico – all beach and sunshine and cocktails – so I sent him a couple of Pennystrand in the rain to make him jealous – not.'

'Nice,' says Cherry, a long string of cheese dangling over her chin.

I try to sound casual, but the truth is, the sight of his name in my inbox makes my heart skip, and although his emails aren't long, they're thoughtful and full of details that I want to savour, as I would lines in a poem, or a dish made with unusual spices. 'I was going to email him last night, but then Mitch showed up and it threw me for a loop. In fact...' I pick up my phone and take a photograph of the room, totally bare, apart from the pizza box, wine bottle and fire. It's the perfect first-night shot. Then I take a cheesy (in more way than one) selfie of me and Cherry. She has her thumb up and a glass of wine in her other hand; our heads are together and we look ecstatic. 'I'll send them to him tomorrow.'

'Good. So that's proceeding nicely.'

'No, Cherry, nothing's proceeding – we're just keeping in touch a little bit, that's all. You can't possibly hope something will happen – he's thousands of miles away!'

She shrugs and sips her wine, her eyes glowing. 'I know some things, that's all I'm saying. Your Angelique in Covent Garden's got nothing on me.'

I snort. 'Right. Read my palm, why don't you?'

'Don't need to. I know what I know. And how about finding out you're a Parnell? Have you seen much of the wicked aunts? Does it mean you're filthy rich? Do you have to become a bitch now?'

'I don't think so,' I say, adopting a serious expression. 'Definitely I'm not rich – I wouldn't take a penny from them if they offered it. And the bitch thing... well, I thought about it, but I'm not sure I could pull it off.'

She grins at me. 'You're right. It wouldn't suit you. And they're leaving you alone? Behaving themselves?'

'Remarkably. They haven't interfered in anything – no unwanted advice or opinions, and Lisa's only asked me up for gin twice. I've gone both times, largely because Agatha's there now and I love spending time with her.'

'That's huge that they're keeping the house. And it's your mum's childhood home too of course.'

'Yes, but she hasn't been back there in so long I'm not sure she has any nostalgia for it. She's going to come and stay once I have furniture, and she did say she'd go and see her sisters then. There might be some sort of reconciliation, but I guess we'll have to see. Depends on what's said.'

'Honestly, Kitty, this is amazing! You've saved the family home, found Mrs Vincent's necklace, brought a little harmony to the miserable Parnells and made Lydia Hudson's son happy by, y'know, sleeping with him. You're some estate agent!' She raises her glass, and I chink mine against it, laughing.

'All part of the job description.'

'*And...*' she says, warming to her theme, 'when a certain vendor made the terrible error of listing her house with the evil estate agents across the road, you simply bought the house yourself, to save her the hassle!'

'You're a nutter.'

'No, no, you go the extra mile. I dub thee Agent Kitty.' She taps me on the shoulders with the poker. A little soot flutters onto my pizza.

'Thank you for being here with me tonight, Cherry. Can you believe I actually *own* this place? I hope we'll have loads more happy evenings talking nonsense in here.'

'I know we will. And plenty more adventures in store for Agent Kitty.'

Just then my phone buzzes and I glance down reflexively. I'd never normally stop to read a message in the middle of a heart to heart. But it's an email. From Cory.

'Do you mind if I just... for one second...?'

Since Cherry's sipping wine with her eyes blissfully closed, I pick up the phone and read.

Hey Kitty,

How's buying the cottage coming on? I hope it's not too long till you can move in now. Can't tell you how much it makes me smile to think of you staying on in Pennystrand. Not that it makes much difference with me here in Mexico (South Africa from next week), but hey, it's nice to think of you there. Thanks for the pics. Those brooding skies and the rain on the lens – yeah, that's home. Anyway, just wanted to let you know a bit of news. I've been talking to my agent and my sponsor and we've agreed that I can make it home for a month over Christmas.

It'll be the longest break I've had there in years so I'm pretty stoked. So's Mum, I guess you can imagine. I know you'll be visiting your family over Christmas, but hopefully we'll overlap at some point. It would be great to see you and catch up in person. Here's hoping xx

There's a photo attached of a hand holding up a huge glass of beer, as if in a toast. I can tell the hand is Cory's from the leather thongs tied around the wrist and the glinting golden skin. I smile. And smile wider.

'What?' asks Cherry, who's opened her eyes, with uncanny instinct.

I can't be bothered trying to hide my happiness and pass her the phone. 'Go on then – you'd better read this.'

A LETTER FROM TRACY

I wanted to say a huge thank you for choosing to read *The Little House by the Sea*. If you enjoyed it and want to keep up to date with my latest releases, just sign up at the following link. Your email address will never be shared, and you can unsubscribe at any time.

www.bookouture.com/tracy-rees

I have so enjoyed writing this story. When I was in my thirties, I worked in an estate agent's office and it was one of the most fun jobs I ever had! While I was doing it, I thought, as Kitty does, how wonderful it was to help facilitate this massive life change for so many people. None of the houses or characters in this book are based on real properties or people, but the variety and beauty of the different types of houses was certainly inspired by my time in the job. I found that each house held a story, and some of those I encountered were even more remarkable than the stories I've made up in this book. Others were more ordinary, everyday situations but were no less touching and important for all that. It really was a privilege, and I always thought what wonderful potential there was for a book in a job like that, so I'm delighted I finally got to write one!

Pennystrand is an imaginary place – unfortunately, since I've grown rather fond of it! Maybe I'll have to revisit it in fiction soon. But I did work in a seaside town in Wales. Like Kitty, I used to walk to lots of viewings, spent ages wandering around looking for cars because I'd forgotten where I'd parked them and I loved meeting people. When I came to making up my own tales, all these years later, I knew it had to be a summer read. It was blissful creating Pennystrand's crescent of beaches and writing about swimming in the sea, ice cream, sunshine, bees and butterflies, and I really hope you've enjoyed reading it as much as I enjoyed writing it.

If you did enjoy reading *The Little House by the Sea*, I would be very grateful if you could write a review. I'd love to hear what you think, and it makes such a difference to new readers discovering my books for the first time.

If you have any questions or comments, please do get in touch with me via Twitter, as I love chatting to my readers.

All best wishes,

Tracy

 twitter.com/AuthorTracyRees

ACKNOWLEDGEMENTS

I wrote this book at the end of a very long, very busy spell of work, and I was flagging! Only two things saw me through: my love for the idea and the story as it developed, and the people in my life who were so very understanding and supportive.

A huge thank you to my wonderful agent, Hayley, who has had the patience of a saint as I've worked my way through various commitments I took on before we joined forces. Hayley, you've been unswervingly understanding and helpful, and I'm so looking forward to the road ahead.

About Team Bookouture... there are no words! Nevertheless, I shall try. First of all, thank you to my wonderful editor, Kathryn Taussig, who has been a friend and champion from the very beginning of my writing career, whose support means the world to me and whose editorial comments without fail make me laugh out loud. Thank you too to Natasha Harding, for all your enthusiasm and support and for staying in the picture! That's just wonderful. In fact, the whole team (too many to name, but you know who you are) is unbeatable for professionalism, communication, enthusiasm and skill. There are some serious smarts in that company! It's a joy to work with such talented people.

Thank you to my friends – you really do put the sparkle in my life with your support and love. Again, there are too many of you to list by name, but this time a special shout-out to Lucy Davies and Patsy Rogers, whom I met when I worked as an estate agent and who remain the most wonderful friends to this day.

Thank you, Mum and Dad for hauling me over the finish line and for always loving me and cheering me on. I am so very blessed. You are the absolute bestest!

And thank you to *you*, the person reading this book, for choosing my story. It makes me very happy!

Finally, thank you to all the bloggers and reviewers who work so hard and so generously in the industry and help spread the word about books they've enjoyed – what a wonderful and valued thing you do.